Zombies
for
A Cure

# Zombies for A Cure

Edited by

Angela Charmaine Craig

Elektrik Milk Bath Press

Zombies for a Cure
© 2012 by Elektrik Milk Bath Press.

Cover art © by Dani

Cover design by Dani

Interior layout and design by Seraph B.

Published by Elektrik Milk Bath Press. For Information please contact Elektrik Milk Bath Press, P.O. Box 833223, Richardson TX 75083.

www.elektrikmilkbathpress.com

Copyright © Angela Charmaine Craig, 2012

"The Return of Gunnar Kettilson" copyright © Vonnie Winslow Crist. First appeared in *Cemetery Moon #6*, 2010. "Seven Eight Five One Four" copyright © Alyn Day. First appeared in *So Long and Thanks for all the Brains*, March 2012.. "Zombie Psychology" copyright © Sarina Dorie. First appeared in *Untied Shoelaces of the Mind, Issue, #5*, 2011. "A Mind is a Terrible Thing to Taste" copyright © Nick Kimbro. First published by E-Volve Books, January 2012. "The Song of Absent Birds" copyright © Mark Onspaugh. First appeared in *The World is Dead*, September 2009. "Dancing Blue Zombie" copyright © Marge Simon, art copyright © Sandy DeLuca. First appeared in *Vampires, Zombies & Wanton Souls*, March 2012 "Hot August Night" copyright © Marge Simon, art copyright © Sandy DeLuca. First appeared in *Vampires, Zombies & Wanton Souls*, March 2012. "Painting of a Zombie" copyright © Marge Simon, art copyright © Sandy DeLuca. First appeared in *Vampires, Zombies & Wanton Souls*, March 2012. "Zombie Love" copyright © Gene Stewart. First appeared in the *Cold Flesh* anthology, 2003. All other material is original to this anthology and is individually copyrighted by the authors.

All rights reserved.

No part of this book may be used or reproduced in any manner whatsoever without written permission, except in the case of brief quotations embodied in critical articles or reviews.

This is a work of fiction and all names, characters, places, or incidents are products of the authors' imaginations or are used fictitiously. Any resemblance to actual persons, living or dead is entirely coincidental.

ISBN 978-0-9828554-7-8

# For Noodles

(And all those who love her)

# Contents

| | |
|---|---|
| Introduction | 13 |
| Zombie Mommy | 16 |
|     Jennifer Clark | |
| Run for the Roses | 17 |
|     Gerri Leen | |
| The Song of Absent Birds | 21 |
|     Mark Onspaugh | |
| Yesterday's Dead | 37 |
|     Carolyn E. Bentley and Daniel M. Pipe | |
| Should Zombies Really Crawl from their Graves | 44 |
|     James S. Dorr | |
| Deadly Jobs | 45 |
|     Gregory L. Norris | |
| Stream of Dead Conscious | 55 |
|     John McCarthy | |
| At the bar near the cemetery | 56 |
|     Brian Rosenberger | |
| Conrad | 57 |
|     Joshua Clark Orkin | |
| Hot Zombie Chicks and Cocktails at Gore's | 61 |
|     Jamie Brindle | |
| Dancing Blue Zombie | 72 |
|     Marge Simon w/Art by Sandy DeLuca | |
| The Zombie Solution (A Shakespearean Sonnet) | 74 |
|     Terrie Leigh Relf | |
| The Return of Gunnar Kettilson | 75 |
|     Vonnie Winslow Crist | |
| The Ferry | 83 |
|     Kathleen Crow | |

| | |
|---|---|
| necessary items for surviving the zombie apocalypse | 87 |
|     Brian E. Langston | |
| Painting of a Zombie | 88 |
|     Marge Simon w/ Art by Sandy DeLuca | |
| Beyond the Shed | 90 |
|     John McCarthy | |
| Zombie Love | 91 |
|     Gene Stewart | |
| Hot August Night | 102 |
|     Marge Simon w/ Art by Sandy DeLuca | |
| Remnants of the Insensitive | 104 |
|     Colin James | |
| Night of Passions | 105 |
|     M. Alan Ford | |
| Quality of Death | 119 |
|     Clifford Royal Johns | |
| Zombielocks | 121 |
|     N. E. Chenier | |
| You Can't Live Forever | 127 |
|     Heather Henry | |
| The Sitting Dead | 143 |
|     Patrick MacAdoo | |
| Isthmus | 154 |
|     Gerardo Mena | |
| Guesswork | 155 |
|     Richard Farren Barber | |
| Southern Hospitality | 163 |
|     Ryan Dennison | |
| Seven Eight One Five Four | 167 |
|     Alyn Day | |
| Zombie Psychology | 175 |
|     Sarina Dorie | |
| The Zombie Orchestra | 178 |
|     dan smith | |

| | |
|---|---|
| at the zombie dance club | 178 |
|     dan smith | |
| zombies can't text | 178 |
|     dan smith | |
| Parade | 178 |
|     Brian Rosenberger | |
| Love Bites | 179 |
|     Robert Neilson | |
| Zombies at Casino Buffet | 189 |
|     William Van Wurm | |
| Anglo Saxon Zombie Conquest | 192 |
|     Stewart S. Warren | |
| A Mind is a Terrible Thing to Taste | 193 |
|     Nick Kimbro | |
| Zombie A Go-Go | 201 |
|     Brian Behr Valentine | |
| Cloud Gazing | 204 |
|     John McCarthy | |
| Dead Song | 205 |
|     Jay Wilburn | |
| Skin Eulogy | 216 |
|     Colin Gilbert | |
| Wings | 217 |
|     Megan Dorei | |
| Contributors | 235 |
| | |
| The Contributors Would Like to Honor.... | 243 |

# List of Illustrations

*ShroomZombie*     *36*
    Daniel M. Pipe

*Dancing Blue Zombie*     *73*
    Sandy DeLuca

*Painting of a Zombie*     *89*
    Sandy DeLuca

*Hot August Night*     *103*
    Sandy DeLuca

*Untitled #29*     *233*
    Frenchi

# Acknowledgements

This was a hard book to put together for so many reasons, and I owe a great amount of thanks to many people who were there along the way.

First, I want to thank all the wonderful authors and poets and artists who showed an interest in this project, with an especially huge thank you and infinite good wishes to those who were willing to donate their work for this worthy cause. You are as generous as you are talented, and it has been a huge pleasure working with all of you.

Next, I should say thank you (and I'm sorry) to both Frenchi and Boo because you both know how I love to freak out, and just for being who you are.

Thanks, also, to Marge Simon and Sandy DeLuca for their constant e-mails, and for their extreme kindness and caring during what turned out to be a most unfabulous year.

And finally.... Thank you, Richard, for always making me laugh—even when things are no longer funny.

# Introduction

Even as a very small child, my sister always loved zombies. As the older sister, I tried to be supportive but, to be perfectly honest, zombies were never really my thing. I liked the pretty monsters—but my sister… well, she always had a thing for the ugly boys.

When we set up the call for our *Dia de los Muertos* anthology, we received a chunk of stories about zombies and, while the stories were not bad, they were not what we were looking for. Still, we thought that would be a good project for the future and we put it on our list but promptly got busy doing other things.

Then, in 2010, after 18 months of remission, my sister's cancer returned. She had hybridized tumors, but her primary cancer was Adenoid Cystic Carcinoma (ACC), a rare and aggressive cancer which is infamous for, among other things, not responding to chemo. She had already had surgery to remove the new tumor and was getting ready to undergo a few rounds of experimental chemo. Our small group decided that it was about time to do that zombie book and my sister, who was always charity minded, wanted to donate the proceeds to a cancer-related charity. The first contributors we spoke to were excited by the idea of a zombie-themed charity anthology, and they offered to donate their time and talent, as well as helping to spread the word.

As we started putting the book together, my sister was becoming increasingly ill. The chemo was making her extremely weak and she would often joke that it was worse than the cancer, which, despite the aggressive treatments, was continuing to spread. In addition to being exhausted, she was having terrible headaches and trouble with her vision and was no longer able to help with the book.

Still, even at the worst, her constant wit and wicked sense of humor carried us through. She would joke with us, saying the saddest thing was knowing that now her beloved zombies wouldn't want her—"After all," she said, "nobody likes tainted meat." We told her not to worry, it wasn't like the cancer was in her brain… there was still hope. But it was, and there wasn't.

She died on March 1st 2012. She was only 29.

When we knew we were nearing the end, I asked her if there was anything she wanted me to include and she said she wanted everyone to know that the worst part of cancer was not so much what it did to you, the patient, but what it did to the people you love. She had a young son, and a husband, and a mother and sister, and a nephew who worshipped her, and she couldn't stand the pain her impending death was causing in those around her. To her, cancer was not a solitary thing. "It isn't just about you," she said, "it is also about everyone who loves you and how it affects their lives, too."

This was more and more evident as the stories continued to come in, with many of the authors and artists who submitted offering to donate their work and sharing stories of their own family members and friends who had battled cancer. In the spirit of inclusion, we wanted to offer our contributors a place to honor those brave fighters. You will find their names listed at the back of the book.

Most of the pieces you find here have been donated by their creators, which allows us the opportunity to donate a larger amount of funds to our chosen charity. We offer our unending thanks and appreciation to them for their generosity. And we thank you, the reader, for purchasing this book, for supporting both this project and our commitment to what we feel is an extremely worthy cause.

## Zombie Mommy

He has been watching her disappear
for weeks now.

A fading bruise, she staggers
into the kitchen mumbling something,

then pours Life into a bowl
for the last time.

He thinks of how his father
used to praise her cooking.

Tearing meat from the bone
with his greasy teeth, he'd say,

*how tender you make everything, hon*
and she would smile a small smile.

He is too young to know that
these memories are decaying inside her,

shredding apart even her finest thought:
that she is his mother.

She spills the milk,
doesn't bother to clean it up.

He notices the left tip of her nose is gone,
has splashed into the tiny world sloshing below

his chin. He pushes away her offering.
As the fin of a grey shark circles the last grains of hope

he drowns in one inch of thought—
that even though past the point of healing
                                        he loves her still.

    —Jennifer Clark

# Run for the Roses

## Gerri Leen

Zombie Horses can't be beat, doo dah, doo dah
Just be careful what they eat, all in the doo dah day.
  — *21st Century Folk Song*

"They just got so fragile, those oldtime race horses. One, two, maybe three races and boom, a condylar fracture, or a sesamoid break. Out for months, maybe for good. Retired to stud, to breed more of the same. It's why we don't use them anymore." Ramon patted Zero Tolerance on the neck carefully as the reporter watched. The horse bared his teeth and eyed the hand that fed him with something very different than affection. "You just do not want to fall off these horses."

"I saw the footage from Gulfstream."

"Maybe they shouldn't have called that filly Maneater?" Ramon laughed. "These babies will run for days if you have the right bait."

Squalling infants would have been the best lure, but the public would never have gone for that. Instead, thrillseekers signed up to ride the pace truck. They got to skip bathing for three days so the "still alive" smell was ever so clear to the horses. Horses who were run with muzzles but no whips. Whips were useless on them, didn't make them go—no pain, no gain. But brains… oh yeah, horses would run all day and into the night for some brains.

Fresh, though. Cadavers were of no appeal. Dummies rubbed with raw meat didn't fool them, either. Horses weren't the brightest of animals, but they were bright enough.

"What do you have to say to the public outcry that racing should be stopped?"

"Because one jockey got eaten?"

"With a lot of people watching between the simulcast and ESPN coverage."

Ramon shrugged. "Real Thoroughbreds can't cut it. And people don't like to watch Quarter Horses the way they do Thoroughbreds. Personally, I'd rather watch a mule race but they make these babies look like pushovers when it comes to being trainable." He patted Zero Tolerance on the cheek and nearly lost his fingers.

The reporter was studying the horse. "Why do you work with him?"

"Why do lion tamers do what they do? Why do fighter pilots?" He laughed and eased out of the stall. "It's fun."

"It's idiotic. That horse would eat you in a minute if he got loose."

"Yep, he sure would." Ramon sighed. "Lady, you have no idea what it was like before the zombie horses. I was a rider before I became a trainer. I nearly was killed when Cyber Warfare broke his leg in the stretch of the Belmont. There's never been a zombie horse broke down that way. Never."

"I accept that. But the old time horses didn't eat people. Did you hear that this morning at Zia Park, a zombie horse veered off the track during morning works and ran into the group of clockers."

"Seriously?"

She nodded. "He bit three of them."

"Yikes." He shook his head. "They're off to Zombie Nirvana then. Damn shame. People willing to rise in the dark just to clock horses are few and far between."

"Your empathy is touching."

"The owners don't pay me for empathy. They pay me to get their horses to the finish line first."

"And you're the most successful trainer to do that. I mean look at Zero Tolerance—the favorite for today's race, right?"

Ramon tried not to preen.

"What's your secret?"

He smiled. "Creative feeding."

She took a step back.

"Not humans. You think I could get away with that in this day and age? Everyone is tracked." He smiled. "But there are other warm blooded creatures."

"I don't want to know." She seemed to shudder. "You realize I'm going to use this in the story."

He shrugged.

"You want me to use it, don't you?"

He laughed. "People think my horse here has recent experience with live meat, they may get a little spooked on the track. And this race is big. We both know that."

She nodded. "The biggest." She turned to the cameraman. "We've got what we need. Go get this filed."

The cameraman packed up and left, seemed to be happy to get clear of Zero Tolerance.

"You're not going to edit it?"

"Why bother? You orchestrated this from the beginning to say exactly what you want." She moved closer to Zero Tolerance. "I don't think you feed him live meat."

"No?" He touched her hair. "I could feed you to him."

"You could. If you want to spend the rest of your life in prison." She turned to look at him. "Or Zombie Nirvana if they decide to make the punishment fit the crime."

He dropped his hand. "Just joking around."

"I'm not." She smiled in a way that was distinctly creepy, then moved to the stall door, closing it—closing them in with Zero Tolerance.

"What are you doing?"

"The job I was hired to do."

He realized Zero Tolerance was making no move for her.

"Eau de Corpse. It's what David Marsh uses when he works with Captivate."

"Marsh?" Marsh had gone on record saying he was going to win today. That Captivate would beat Zero Tolerance.

"He may have paid me to do this." Again the creepy smile. "There'll be an inquiry. The horse will be quarantined until the issue is resolved. The race"—she reached over and unhooked Zero Tolerance's tie-down—"will be long over by the time this boy races again—do you think his owners will send him to Marsh once you're dead?"

The horse sniffed her briefly, then turned to Ramon, blocking his way to the exit.

"Why?"

"I get five percent of the winnings. That's not chump change. Also—just like you said. It's... fun." She laughed softly as she leaned against the wall and crossed her arms across her chest. "Bon Appetit, horse."

Zero Tolerance's big white blaze was the last thing Ramon saw before the pain began.

# The Song of Absent Birds

## Mark Onspaugh

Dylan Walsh dried his breakfast dishes and put them away. He wiped down the counter and made sure the burners were turned off on the stove.

He was dressed in a blue and white plaid flannel shirt his grandchildren had sent him. He wore this with a tee shirt, jeans, and heavy work boots. He pulled a jacket off a hook by the front door and slipped it on. Although the temperature in the Underground never varied, it always felt cold to him in the winter. He supposed it was age creeping into his bones rather than a winter chill from topside.

He checked himself in the mirror before he left. It was a big day and he wanted to look his best. He had gotten his hair cut and his mustache trimmed. His hair had receded quite a bit in the last ten years, and the lines on his face were much deeper, but he figured he didn't look too bad. He had managed to get old without getting fat, and tried to keep up with contemporary styles without looking ridiculous. He had gotten a manicure, too. Marie might have laughed at that. He smiled, then grabbed the bouquet of margarites and walked out the front door.

A little sign on the door read, "Doctor Dylan Walsh, MD, OB-GYN." Maintenance would be removing it tomorrow, but the brass had said he could keep the apartment. A perk for forty-five years of loyal service.

## 22　Mark Onspaugh

In the corridor, left would take him to the public tubes and transportation throughout the Tri-Sector area.

Doctor Walsh turned right.

He walked to an exit marked "Authorized Personnel Only." He punched in his code and the door opened for him with a faint click.

He stepped into the service corridor just as Mac pulled up. He was driving one those little electric carts they all used. The front of the cart read "ZDC—Official Use Only" and a series of numbers and letters. It seemed like a lot of fanfare for a glorified golf cart.

"Morning, Doc," Mac said, his bulk dwarfing the little vehicle.

Kyle "Mac" McCready offered him a beefy hand and hauled him up onto the passenger seat. Once the doctor was situated, Mac stepped on the accelerator and they sped off.

Mac talked the entire way to the access shaft. Non-stop.

Nothing important or compelling, just stats on the inter-sector magball playoffs and the coming election. Walsh could tell Mac was trying to distract him. He'd known the young man most of his life. There was almost no one under thirty in his sector that he hadn't delivered and treated.

At an intersection Mac yielded to a flatbed vehicle carrying several figures wrapped in heavy white canvas and bound with bright yellow nylon ropes. The bundles were secured with colorfully striped bungee cords. One wrapped bundle thrashed spastically.

"B'n'G," Mac said, grinning, "Binding and grinding." As he passed the flatbed he and the other driver, a fellow "zed-head," gave each other the waggle-finger "hang loose" greeting.

Mac had grown from a skinny little kid with freckles to a big, beefy block of a man with a head the size and color of a canned ham. The freckles were still there, though, and Walsh knew the other zed-heads razzed Mac about them, calling him "Opie" and "Howdy Doody." Jesus. Those TV characters were ancient when Walsh was a kid. He guessed that was the blessing (or curse) of a crystalline memtrix. Nothing of pop culture got lost, just preserved, recycled, reused.

Like people.

They scooted along the corridor, which smelled vaguely like machine oil and cloves. Unlike the public ways which were a riot of colors, sounds and smells and lined with shops, food and service kiosks, and ad-info screens, the service corridor was gray and unremarkable, its smooth contours sometimes erupting in a profusion of pipes and conduits, then becoming featureless again. The cart was smooth and quiet, its efficient little hum no match for Mac's chattering.

If Mac was worried about what they were about to do, he didn't admit it. Of course, nothing illegal would occur until the hatch had been breached.

They passed an access port for the grinders, and Walsh could hear the hollow thrumming as the big drums started up, waiting for the cargo now some one hundred yards behind them. He tried not to think of what happened beyond those walls. As a doctor he knew human corpses were just a collection of bone, blood and muscle. Rendering them down to their essential components before they reanimated was logical and efficient.

But as a husband and a father he wondered what might survive once life was over, what ephemeral and splendid energy might now be irrevocably linked to dead matter. Surely something had changed since The Incident. Dead was no longer dead, so what remained? What essence of a person was retained inside a zed? It was a question that had been argued since The Incident.

People still called them "zombies" in the early days, before activists claimed the term too pejorative and judgmental, ill-befitting a group that contained so many friends, relatives, civil servants and sports heroes. The more politically and emotionally neutral "zed" took its place. Thus, members of the former Zombie Retaliation Force were now members of the Zed Defense Corps. Walsh had never liked the term zombie, either, but for different reasons. He still remembered a time when a zombie was a term for a supernatural creature, someone raised from a grave to act as a servant. And "zed"? Colorless and without any poetry, which is just what the brass wanted. He himself preferred "shamblers" or "lurchers." Some called them "wanderers," but Walsh felt that was a little too romantic for a creature that wanted to feed on you.

About a year after the evacuation a new Christian sect surfaced, calling themselves the Saint Lazarus Church of the Resurrection and the Life, the Undeath and the Unlife. They were trying to resolve questions like whether shamblers had souls. Having never been one for organized religion, Walsh always felt questions of sacred versus profane were intensely private, more so now that the two seemed fused. Besides, the tenets of the Lazarus sect had never seemed particularly inspired or well thought-out to him. They seemed more of a "cut and paste" approach, borrowing from all the major religions and several science fiction novels of the 1960's. He politely refused membership and they had finally stopped leaving leaflets and donation envelopes in his office mail drop.

Two workmen were repairing a water pipe as they passed, and neither gave them a second glance. It was as Mac had said: if you seem to be on official or authorized business (he used the slang term "righteous"), then people left you alone.

Walsh's hands were cramped and he realized he was gripping the bouquet too tightly. Mac had balked at the flowers at first, saying Walsh might as well mount a big neon sign on the cart proclaiming "I AM GOING OUTSIDE!" Walsh told him he was being paranoid, that he had often taken flowers with him on his rounds.

He loosened his grip, holding the bouquet with one hand as he flexed the other. His hands had been so nimble, once. Clever little creatures that could stitch a wound or bring a child into the world. Now arthritis was making them strangers to him, twisting them into wicked shapes for cruel shadow puppets. Unpredictable and unreliable, manageable only through more and more frequent doses of various pain relievers.

Old age sucked.

There was a sudden lull in Mac's monolog and Walsh realized he had never asked Mac about their destination.

"Have you seen it, Mac?"

Mac looked at him, puzzled for a moment. "The Forest of Anubis?" he asked.

"Yes."

"Yeah," he said, nodding, "Every zed-head takes a tour of the woods. Course, it changes every year, that's what makes it even creepier. You never know how it's going to end up."

"A colleague of mine was trying to chart migration patterns of the sham—uh, zeds."

"Shit, Doc, I don't care what you call them. You should hear some of the terms we use when we're not around civs. Maggot-bags, pus-buckets, meat-puppets..."

"I guess you're right."

"Migration patterns, huh? Brass has talked about that kind of stuff. Thing is, they always thought they'd reach some point of diminishing returns. Old zeds falling apart, new ones being ground up and burned or recycled. 'Asses to ashes' as my old man used to say. Some point where the attrition rate of maggot-bags would outstrip the supply."

"But that's not happening."

"Fuck no. Part of it's that the damn things don't seem to fall apart. Oh, they rot plenty fast, but they seem to stop decaying with just enough musculature left to move around. Techs are going nuts trying to figure that out."

"And some sectors don't believe in recycling."

"Yeah, bunch of unlife fanatics. No burning, no grinding. They just turn their zeds loose on the surface as some kind of bullshit living memorial." Mac looked at him guiltily. "No offense, Doc."

Walsh waved him off. "I've heard there's also been smuggling, even in here."

Mac nodded, his mouth drawing in a thin line. "Top brass is really pissed about that. Here they hope to reclaim the surface and our own people are smuggling friends and relatives to the surface before the B & G Wagon arrives. T.B. says that any zed-head involved in or aiding such practices gets a one-way ticket to the Big Blender."

"I appreciate the risk you three are taking for me, Mac."

He patted him on the shoulder. "My pleasure, Doc. Besides, all you're smuggling is flowers."

They rode the rest of the way in silence, passing several access shafts until they came to one he needed.

Mac parked the little cart near a weapons locker and they were met by the guard on duty, Dana Chang. Dana had been one of Walsh's patients, as had her husband Andy and daughter Delia. She smiled when she saw him.

Dana helped him out of the cart and gave him a quick hug. Her husband had suffered a burst appendix fifteen years ago and they had nearly lost him. His hands had been faithful and true in those days and worked their magic. Five years later his good hands delivered the

## ★ 26 Mark Onspaugh

Chang's baby, Delia.

Dana led Mac and him to the hatch, which was being guarded by a fresh-faced young corporal named Oganesyan. It didn't matter what his first name was, all newbie zed-heads were called "Chuck," as in "ground chuck." Some found the appellation distasteful, but Walsh knew it was to remind the newbs that that's all they were to shamblers topside: fresh meat.

Chuck wasn't happy about breaking the rules, but wasn't about to argue with vets like Mac and Dana. The hazing of zed-head newbs was the stuff of nightmares, with some losing a finger (or worse) or becoming infected with Zed-17 and ending up in the grinders. The brass tried to curtail it, but they knew that living underground created a lot of lethal pressures that had to be vented.

Dana had shut down the west perimeter cameras "for maintenance." She had also overridden the sensors so that the hatch could be opened without setting off alarms. Such procedures were not unheard of; several times a year outer cameras and perimeter fences had to be repaired. And security was a bit more lax this time of year, everyone thinking of the big holiday festival in the central quad. People feasted and prayed, exchanged gifts and decorated homes, sang and danced and lit candles, all to show gratitude for another year of survival.

Both Dana and Mac were armed with the latest n-guns, what the zed-heads called "poppers." Each popper could deliver exploding "jiffy-pop" or freezing "popsicle" rounds at a rate of fifty per second. Walsh had treated a Chuck or two in his time who had taken a popsicle round to the foot or thigh. The limb always had to go. Those who were unfortunate enough to take a jiffy-pop round usually bled out before the medics could do anything. Newbs killed topside were given three additional pop shots: one to the chest and two to the head. They were then left to rot, harsh examples for the newbs that followed. Those killed below in the training centers went straight to the grinders, eventually becoming fertilizer for the agri-combine or food for the Tri-Sector Zoo predators.

Dana nodded to Chuck and he punched in the code to open the access hatch. It opened with a sharp hiss and then silently slid into its recess. Dana and Mac had their weapons trained on the opening and Walsh held his breath, but nothing was there.

Dana held Walsh's flowers as he pulled on the gloves and wool hat he had stuffed in his jacket. He took the bouquet back, and then Doctor Dylan Walsh walked out of the hatch, his heart beating fiercely.

He walked out into the snow, breathing topside air for the first time in forty-five years. He took in great draughts of it, delighting in the sensation of air actually cold enough to chill your insides. His eyes teared up and he coughed, doubling over for a moment. Mac moved toward him, but Walsh waved him off, laughing.

"The air is so sweet," he gasped.

Mac nodded and grinned.

The sun shone sulkily through the haze, just enough to provide a pearlescent light. His breath puffed out in little clouds and his boots crunched through the snow as Mac and Dana led him to the perimeter fence, a sturdy affair of steel plates welded in a large circle. It was ten feet high, fifty feet in diameter and surmounted with cameras and razor wire. No shambler could surmount that barrier. They reached the gate, which was secured with a heavy sliding bolt.

Dana had her tru-vu and checked the outside. She did a complete sweep and nodded. Mac unlocked the gate and they opened it far enough for him to slip through.

"You know where you're going?" Dana asked.

He knew she was actually giving him a chance to back out, to change his mind. He held up the little GPS monitor and it peeped once, as if answering her.

Walsh squeezed through the gate, and then stopped in stunned silence.

He had seen photos and film of "The Forest of Anubis" before, but it was something else to be in it.

Instead of trees there were hundreds of shamblers, perhaps thousands, frozen in place. Many stood, silent and still, their arms at their sides, temporarily suspended from their ceaseless wanderings, their insatiable appetites. The sun sparkled off their agonized and ruined faces, now crystallized and dusted with snow, terrible spun sugar confections for an unending Dia de los Muertos.

Each shambler had a clearance of about three or four feet around it, as if they did not want to be crowded during their period of suspended animation. Walsh wove his way carefully through the figures, forcing himself to remain calm in this Land of the Dead. He listened for the customary growl of a shambler, for their mournful, awful wailing, but there was only his own breathing.

Walsh chuckled. Seventy-five and he was still able to get the heebie-jeebies. He consulted the monitor and moved forward, hearing only his own breathing and the crunch of ice under his boots.

Then there was another sound, a strange low whistle. Walsh thought there might be a bird singing, but then he remembered that a strain of the zed virus had killed most of the birds topside.

This sound had a mournful quality to it, like blowing into a bottle or jug, and he realized many of the frozen dead had ragged wounds that went entirely through a limb or torso. The same wind which was chilling him and sending up little frost devils was also whistling through this frozen charnel house, making the corpses into a sort of hellish pan pipes, an instrument worthy of the god Hades. What madness and despair would be found in such music?

Walsh shook his head, chiding himself for being seduced by the strange and perverse amusements of this place. He had to hurry, so he walked a bit faster, trying to ignore the eerie sound and concentrate on his goal.

Come the spring, the sun would thaw them out. Their chaotic neurons would begin firing again and they would lurch, shamble, crawl and worm their way in search of food.

Mac and Dana caught up to him, leaving Chuck to guard the gate and contact them if there were any unwarranted movements on the perimeter sensors.

"Welcome to the Forest of Anubis," Mac said, gesturing in an expansive manner. "Also known as 'The Valley of the Corpsicles' and 'Maggot-Bags on Ice'."

"What do you think brings them here in such number?" Walsh asked.

"Prof of mine said it's the smell of the grinders," Dana said, "they smell the tang of flesh and blood that isn't quite turned. Guess it'd be like good barbecue to us."

"I heard it was sound," Mac said, "the maggot-bags are like dogs, they can hear all kinds of shit we can't. Somebody else said they can see emanations from power sources, some kind of adaptation to find living people."

"It's a marvel that people just… let them be," he said.

"Believe me, Doc, if they could get the funding, they'd have us out here every year with some porta-grinders making pus-burgers."

"Or at least expending a few thousand rounds for head shots," Dana added.

"The newbs do come out here for target practice," Mac said. On seeing the alarm on Walsh's face he quickly added, "No one goes as far as we're going, Doc. It's okay."

Walsh nodded, relieved.

The three of them hiked about a quarter of a mile, watching the ground for crawlers who had frozen low to the ground. There was no danger of attack, of course, each was frozen solid, about as dangerous as a leg of lamb just out of the freezer. However, tripping over such an obstacle might mean a serious injury for an old man like him. He did not want Dana and Mac to have to carry him back to the hatch.

Most of the undead they passed were dressed in rags that had long ago faded to colorless tatters or were soiled beyond recognition. Still others were completely naked, their clothes no match for the punishment of endless wandering.

And there were those whose role in life was still recognizable from their costumes or uniforms. People released or smuggled into the open by grieving families or well-meaning friends.

They passed soldiers and cops, joggers and toddlers, business types and the elderly.

Here was a contingent of Scots, dressed in the proud kilts and tartans of some clan, their visages something out of Macbeth.

Here a nanny with a stroller, its occupant like some grotesque doll, its lips a clown smear of crimson.

Here a naked young man, frozen in an attitude of lithe grace, a latter-day David save for a missing hand and ribbons of flesh hanging from a ravaged abdomen.

Here a group of little girls, still in their school uniforms, their pigtails and pixie cuts belying faces of demons and ghouls, carved now in ice and frost like Norse trolls.

Here was a zed-head pinned under a sno-mobile who had been set upon by others as the temperature had dropped. Come the thaw he would join them, all previous hurts forgotten as they searched the countryside for living flesh.

The forest was a good square mile, packed with nightmare growths that would move on in spring, Shakespeare's Birnam Wood made flesh.

Every race, every variant of humanity was represented in a great sculpture garden of flesh and ice. A spectrum of hues dialed down to varying shades of blue-gray.

Dana checked her tru-vu and pointed, but Walsh had already spotted her.

Marie.

His heart quickened because, unlike the others, Marie had a hand out, as if beckoning to him. Walsh hurried to her and Dana and Mac hung back a respectful distance.

Even under the patina of ice and snow he could see she had not changed in forty-five years. He had become old, but his Marie was still twenty-five, her flawless skin now rendered like a work of fine crystal. Her hair was still as fine and blonde as when it had smelled of flowers and cinnamon.

She had been so beautiful, so young.

It had been seven years since The Incident. Their first and only son Taylor was a healthy little boy five months of age. They had been scheduled to evacuate to the Sector 25 complex, and Marie had fallen in the tub. She had died instantly. To this day he had cursed the irony of surviving an apocalypse only to be killed in such a banal way. People with shamblers or potential shamblers in their homes were legally bound to destroy them by decapitation and burning before evacuating.

He couldn't do it.

Apparently a lot of people couldn't. The size of the forest attested to that.

He had taken their baby and left Marie dressed in her favorite sundress, one that had been a gift from him early in their courtship. Knowing she would soon wake to a strange world, he had secured a GPS cuff to her ankle. He had then kissed her goodbye, his eyes blurring as he got onto the bus, their baby wailing in his arms.

Every night he would check the tracker's monitor for some sign of her. When Taylor grew older he joined his father. They placed the monitor between them on the kitchen table like some oracle, and waited for a pronouncement on the fate of Marie. As they waited for a signal, they wondered where she might be, wondered where her travels might take her.

They had dreamed of exploring the world as husband and wife, and Walsh thought that desire might be in her, still. Of course, the fact that she might be looking for him, some steadfast memory driving her too-cool flesh in restless search had caused him many a sleepless night. Had he doomed her to a futile, meandering existence?

Walsh had never remarried. As long as he knew Marie was out there somewhere he had worn his ring and stayed true.

Taylor had grown into a fine man and left to raise his own family in a nearby sector. He was a supervisor in hydroponics and had long ago stopped wondering about his mother. To Taylor, the important part of her was in heaven, the rest an empty shell of which he had no real memory. If his children had ever wondered about their grandmother, they had never asked Walsh.

Walsh stopped checking the monitor about fifteen years ago. He had first put it in a drawer, then in a box that contained their wedding album and a light blue sweater Marie used to wear, the scent of her long faded, except in his memory.

Three months ago, the peeping of the monitor brought him out of a deep sleep. He had awakened thinking he was hearing a clock radio alarm he had owned as a boy. He stumbled to the closet and gazed at the monitor in wonder and guilt.

He had given up. She had not.

Now they were together again, meeting in this impossible place where the dead waited for the sun to free them.

"I brought you some flowers," he whispered, "Margarites, your favorite." He tried to place them in her hand but they fell to the ground. He chided himself. She was not some doll to pose and make pretty. "I'm sorry," he said.

He took off his gloves and stuffed them in his coat. He ran quivering fingers over the sweet curve of her cheek, the pads of those fingers freezing slightly on her generous mouth and stinging as he pulled them free. Would she taste him come the spring thaw? Would it spark some atavistic memory, some inchoate longing?

He ran his fingertips lightly over her left breast, its size and shape halted by viral alchemy and freezing temperatures in the youthful contours of their courtship. He worried now at her being so scantily dressed, the sundress sheer and lightly patterned with light yellow margarites over a field of pale blue. A blue now faded to match her pale flesh. He tried to ignore the blood stains down the front, daisies turned to macabre roses, and the fact that much of the dress was torn and tattered. His Marie would have been appalled by her own appearance, and for a moment he feared she might be embarrassed.

In life, she had worn the dress on a picnic in Griffith Park. They had found a little knoll under a huge oak. The park had been full of sound, the music of a carousel, the distant laughter of playing children and birdsong in the trees. So many birds in those days! Finches, wrentits, mocking birds, jays, thrashers and quail. Even the hummingbirds and crows had added to that marvelous cacophony of life. He and Marie had eaten fine old cheeses and artisanal breads, crisp red apples and luscious, juicy plums. They shared a bottle of wine he had been saving, and he toasted her beauty and the sheer joy of being with her. Then Marie had slyly revealed that she was wearing nothing underneath her pale blue sundress. Out from under the shade of the old oak the sun had shown through the light fabric, illuminating her soft curves, the cleft of her sex, the rosy pink of her nipples. They had made love near the site of the old zoo, a place no longer frequented by visitors and echoing with the ghosts of creatures long extinct. Her eyes had widened slightly as he had entered her, and then a knowing smile touched her as their rhythms matched, their breathing becoming that of a single creature.

Though he had dressed her in that same sheer and ephemeral confection, he had also modestly clothed her in a simple white bra and cotton panties. She might be lost to him, but he could not shake such ingrained feelings of propriety. Those feelings resurfaced when he saw that she still wore the lingerie. It was silly, but he was glad his sweet wife had not roamed the Earth naked and bloody, some perverse Venus bringing nothing but wailing and terrible teeth.

Marie had often gone without makeup, and he had not applied any to her before leaving. He wouldn't have known where to begin. He had brushed her shining hair and pulled it through a scrunchy into a ponytail. She lay there, looking much like she had on that picnic. He held his tears until he and Taylor were on the transport, and then could stay them no longer. He thought he might never stop weeping.

Now there was an ugly gash on her left bicep, and he wondered if it caused her pain. The wound was bloodless, and the physician in him surmised that she must have caught her arm on a projecting bit of rebar or a shattered door jamb.

Wandering was not without consequence for his Marie.

"I'm sorry," he whispered, old tears reappearing with surprising swiftness, "I'm sorry I have been away from you all these years."

She stood there, her face neither forgiving nor reproachful, no tears of happy reunion or festering resentment. If he stared long enough into her frozen face, he was sure some trick of the light would lend her the appearance of animation like those old wax figures, but he knew better.

She was dead.

And yet...

In such a time where death brings no rest, might not the mind itself be active? Might old pathways fire, however sporadically? Might not old memories bloom like temporary fireworks across the scarred and barren mindscape?

Couldn't there be something beyond hunger, beyond the drive for hot blood spilling over mouths that should be forever closed?

Might not the girl he had first seen under a tree orgasmic with cherry blossoms be there still?

It was a question that might never be answered, and his time was short.

He told her of their son and his family. That their eldest granddaughter had a child of her own, one named Marie in her honor. He told her of his work, his patients, of the trials of living underground and how much he missed her.

He told her how he loved her, and that he had decided—

"Doctor Walsh?"

He turned, the sound of a human voice and his own name like foreign things, syllables of a long-dead language.

Mac regretfully pointed to his watch. "We gotta get back... changing of the guard."

He nodded, thinking of what waited back in the Underground.

## ★ 34 Mark Onspaugh

Years of retirement spent with other seniors. Perhaps some teaching or lectures, he might even write a book.

And then, the grinders. No bells tolling in the Underground, just the massive drums studded with metal teeth, their hollow booming the mechanical equivalent of the wailing topside. There was no one who would smuggle the corpse of Doctor Dylan Walsh to the surface. His children were too pragmatic, products of living in confinement with chaotic and ravening storms outside the gates. Storms that might literally consume them if they did not live practically.

What happened next had only been a vague contingency when he had gotten up that morning. A silly pipe dream that his logical side had nearly forgotten, for it was foolish and selfish and risky, particularly to his young friends.

But sometimes an old heart can be surprisingly strong against a mind grown weary with too many years of memory, too many years ahead of emptiness.

He turned and pretended to kiss Marie's cheek, placing the gel capsule in his mouth and crunching down on it. He then motioned to Mac and Dana. Something in his face caused them to hurry to him.

"I thank you both for bringing me out here," he began.

"We owe you a lot, Doc," Mac said, Dana nodding.

"I have just ingested a lethal amount of Harrowcept," he told them, and watched their faces move from incomprehension to horror.

Mac moved to pick him up and Walsh waved him off.

"Mac, you know this is where I want to be. Where I should be."

"They'll look for you, Doc."

He shook his head. "I'll be frozen before reanimating. No one is going to expend the resources to bring one old man down to the grinders."

They looked doubtful, and he could see the guilty looks as they considered the ramifications to their careers.

"I'm sorry, I know this will complicate things for you," he admitted.

"No worries," Dana said, "we… we don't know anything."

"Yeah," Mac agreed, "your disappearance will be a mystery to us, should anybody ask."

"And Corporal Oganesyan?"

"We'll take care of Chuck," Mac promised.

Dana kissed his cheek. He couldn't feel it. The Harrowcept was weaving a net of numbness over him.

Mac gave him a rough hug, wiping a tear from his eye. The two made their way back to the gate, looking back at him several times. It was difficult to wave, so he saved his energy.

As the gate closed, he placed his arms around Marie's waist, her extended arm providing just enough support to hold him up. He placed the flowers between them, hoping some of their brightness might attract her eyes when sight returned.

"Please know me," he whispered into her ear, "please know me and take me back. I'm sorry I left you. Please don't leave me alone in the dark."

He rested his cheek against her shoulder, tears freezing his eyelids shut.

"Come the spring," he whispered hoarsely, "we'll go on a picnic."

Walsh thought he could hear her sigh, though it may have been an errant breeze. Still, he smiled and let the cold take him.

# Yesterday's Dead

Carolyn E. Bentley and Daniel M. Pipe

Waiting for change always seemed to take longer than it should. Annie had never liked to wait. Waiting for the rain to stop. Waiting for her breasts to grow. Waiting for Billy Marshal to kiss her. Waiting for a reply to her college application. Annie was not good at waiting. She'd developed a myriad of ways to fill time spent waiting but none of them seemed appropriate at the moment. Making out a grocery list while someone died was a bit more callous than she really wanted to be. The orderly had already strapped on the mask that covered the lower half of his face, but she recognised the blue, blue eyes that watched her over it. Mike Shephard. He stared at her in mute appeal. She knew he saw the containment suit and thought she was here to save him. She wasn't, but figured it would be cruel to tell him that.

He'd volunteered to go over the river on a rescue mission. Survivors were still trickling in from the other side. They would call up on emergency lines, walkie talkies, waving flags from rooftops. There was a story going around that one guy had even used smoked signals. Some of the time the rescue vehicles just drove back through the gates erected on the bridge. There were always a queue of people waiting outside the quarantine station to see if their loved ones were among the refugees, but it didn't matter anymore if the faces were familiar or not. They were always greeted with embraces and tears. That anyone continued to escape, to survive, was miracle enough some days. Other times, the rescue teams came back trailing bullets and flames with a mob of the infected undead raving at their heels. It was such a mess. They kept bulldozers close by to shove the detritus into the river, leaving the bridge blackened and scraped like some cutting board from Hell.

Annie had been holding her own vigil outside the quarantine zone when the rescue convoy had left with three trucks that morning. They returned when the sun was high in the sky with just one truck and a single refugee; a little girl whose family hadn't made it. Six men, two women irrevocably lost and Mike, who was getting ready to switch sides. Now here he was on her patient roster.

According to the driver, it had been six hours since Mike was infected. The longest hold-out was nine hours, but she didn't think Mike had that long. He'd beaten records in high-school football. Maybe that's why he thought he could outrun them. But he wouldn't be beating any records tonight. Not tonight, and not ever again. Mike's skin was already starting to turn that powdery shade of blue that meant his blood was pulling away from the surface areas, concentrating in the deep tissues. His eyes hadn't started to go yet. But they would, soon enough.

She checked his vitals. It seemed pointless, but the study required it, of course. And the routine helped her to stay focused on things she could control. She'd gone into medicine to help people. To cure disease. Now she felt like the little Dutch boy, plugging holes while the dike crumbled at her touch. And the individuals, the people, that seemed so important once upon a time, became nothing more than bit players in a grotesque comedy. Every person a parody of themselves. Every person transformed by a landscape that trembled with the footsteps of the doomed.

Once upon a time she would have paid to see him like this. The petty cruelties imposed on geeks like her had seemed inhuman back when she was sixteen, but Annie had been well-tutored since. Inhumanity was watching a newly infected mother eat her own child. After that? Having a guy draw attention to the fact that you'd started your period in the lunch room and calling you 'Bleeder' for the rest of the year just didn't seem that bad.

Bleeder, she thought. How cruel. He would be the bleeder now. She couldn't imagine his wife and kids watching him turn. Or even the little girl he'd saved. Still, she was glad someone would be with him. So many people waited for loved ones they might never see again. Mike Shephard's wife and children would know when and where Mike died. She could give them that much, at least.

It was the girl that got her. That child meant she couldn't keep him in the jock box. He hadn't stayed static and unchanging after high school any more than she had. He'd grown into a husband, a father, and judging by his actions, a good man. The fact that in a very short time, Mike was going to turn into something altogether different because some bright boy working in biotech hadn't quit while he was ahead struck her as the height of unfairness. Annie bit her lip and did the unthinkable. She stepped closer to his bed and laid her gloved hand on his. He twisted it in his cuff till their fingers meshed, then clamped down tight. A tear left a silver track from the corner of his eye down to the edge of the mask. She looked in his eyes again and realised, he didn't want her to save him. He just needed not to be alone.

Something garbled came from his throat. Oh god. He was trying to speak. "yr...name?"

Of course he wouldn't remember her. Hell, she'd stared at his records for a good ten minutes before she'd put it together. Twenty years can change even friends into strangers, and they'd never been that.

"Call me Annie."

"Little girl...K?"

She nodded. "Yes Mike, she's doing just fine." The girl was physically unharmed, but Annie seriously wondered what sort of world they were saving her for. The very idea of people afflicted with this disease had wormed it's way into the consciousness of people who'd never seen them and was setting fire to the human mind. The walking dead. Zombies. No amount of doctors giving news conferences were going to change what they were in the popular imagination. A prayer group had marched right into a hot zone carrying crosses with arms outstretched. No one even considered a rescue attempt.

"Tell Lucy... sorry..." Mike blurted out, struggling to keep it together. His records listed Lucinda Shephard as his spouse. He had two children at home too. Girls, five and eight. Little wonder he couldn't leave the little girl behind.

"I will. I'll tell her you love her. Your kids too."

He nodded, eyes swimming. Thank you, they said. Thank you. Thank you. Thank you. His grip was getting tighter.

"Let go Mike. Please." He shook his head, and the tracks darkened as the capillaries let go. Shit, shit, shit. "Think about it, Mike. Why hold on to me when you went to all that trouble to save the girl?" She wasn't sure she was getting through to him. He closed his eyes tight, till the thin flesh of the lids crimped like those paper umbrellas that came with the girly mixed drinks. She heard him suck in one painfully deep breath and then he loosened one finger at a time, as if it took every ounce of determination he had to just let go. She pulled away gently, patted his wrist. "Thank you, Mike. You're not alone, ok? I'm right here."

How desperately she wanted to help him. When she looked at Mike, she saw all the thousands who didn't make it over the Allegheny river. All the people taken in the confusion and fear that followed the first outbreak. If she could help Mike, she could help them all somehow. She could have a piece of them back. And maybe, just maybe, she could save some of them from the darkness. There was no saving Mike. He was the subject of a medical study and she was just there to administer a test, but at least he wouldn't be alone.

He opened his eyes and she met his gaze without flinching. Those lovely blue irises were surrounded by blood-drenched sclera.

She glanced at her watch and noted the time in his chart. Six hours and thirteen minutes. She had to wait to inject him at seven hours. The timing seemed cruel. But it had to be seven hours according to the parameters of the study. The reagent was supposed to destroy the genetic material in the bacteria and viruses. It wasn't enough to kill the zombie. Rats, dogs and other mammals that ate carrion could transmit the disease. Soldiers on the front lines needed a neutralising serum they could use if they were infected, and the military wanted to know how many hours they had to use it. Seven was the number Mike drew. Lucky number seven. She hoped he was lucky. She hoped with everything in her that he just melted into oblivion.

The fact was, not all zombies lost their minds completely. Some knew enough to remember a little of who they were. To lament what they'd become. Their screams and howls were as heartbreaking as they were terrifying. She patted his wrist again and saw the veins on the undersides of his arms were standing out like strands of thick purple yarn. His breathing became hoarse as his lungs labored and rattled. She covered his body with sheets and a rubber cover. She left only his face exposed, covered with that mask, his eyes still trained on her. She hated being the last thing he saw before he died. People deserved to see beauty at a time like this, or someone they cherished.

Too many people met their ends with nothing but ugliness around them. That's what had happened in Baltimore. The hospital was the spearhead of the failed treatment effort, and the next in a series of epicentres for the plague of walking dead. She remembered hearing recordings of people making phone calls from the hospital rooftop. Shock came first, but it soon gave way to screaming pleas. As horrifying as those calls were, Annie was still a little jealous because her phone never rang. At first, she held out hope that meant there were survivors or that some people had escaped. The handful of traumatised refugees from across the river were all strangers. Now she waited only for the hope in her chest to die and leave her in peace.

She looked back at Mike, and repressed a shiver. He had a Chinese puzzle box of microbial horrors, enhanced viruses and bacteria lurking under his skin. They were consuming his body, but remaking it, too. She knew the next stage was close when he began to moan. Annie remembered hearing labouring women sound like that when she'd done a pedes rotation. It had seemed an incongruous way to herald the arrival of a new life, but Mike wasn't giving birth to any living thing. He was being reborn into some blood-thirsty parody of himself. The moan strengthened into a full blown shriek, but he hadn't taken his eyes off her. They fluttered madly, irregular, yet never lost their focus.

God, why was this taking so long? Waiting for the hands of the clock to move was driving her mad. The claw tips of minute and hour seemed poised only to mock her.

Annie looked at her watch again. Six hours and twenty-one minutes. He was on the tightrope now, teetering on the edge of being Mike and not Mike. The pain had to make it that much easier to lose himself. He choked behind the mask, and his tears ran red. Each gasp of air was punctuated by a gargling wail. He didn't sound human any more. He sounded like the biggest, meanest dog ever. Annie turned away to get the injector ready.

"Annie!" She froze, mid-reach. Mike's voice was full of phlegm, blood, and anger. Guilt welled up in her. She'd turned away from him before he was really gone; he was using her to ground himself. She didn't need to get the injector yet. There was still time. She swallowed hard, took a breath, and turned back to him.

"Anniieeee," Mike's head rose against the strap. His voice was guttural. Desperate, like a lover calling her name in the heat of passion. And then he started to laugh.

Annie grasped her right elbow with her left hand, hugging herself. She'd done that since she was fourteen. Whenever she was unsure of herself. Waiting for the rain to stop. Waiting for her breasts to grow. Waiting for Billy Marshal to kiss her. But she didn't have to wait for Mike to turn into a zombie any more. He'd slipped out behind her back. Her heart felt too big in her chest. Her breasts felt too big. Everything felt too big.

"Anniiee, Anniiee, Anniiee," Mike turned her name into a savage mantra, straining against the restraints with each repetition. He wasn't blinking any more, just boring into her with those terrible, bloody eyes. No one ever said her name any more. Not her first name, her personal name. She was Dr. Marshal, or Doc, or Ma'am. She'd gone numb for want of hearing that name in a familiar tone of voice. A longing that haunted her now. "Anniiee, Anniiee, Anniiee…" like a frat house of sociopaths waiting for a stripper, all huddled in his head. Waiting to get out. But Annie still couldn't turn away. The new Mike held her just as effectively with horror as the old one had with compassion.

Annie realised she was trembling and her nose had started to run. She lifted her hand to wipe her face and hit her faceplate. It was a bitch to cry in hazmat. The plastic sheet at the doorway rustled and she turned around to hide her face from Sgt. Ruiz, the guard for her section. "Dr. Marshal? Is everything all right, ma'am?"

"Yes, it's fine. The restraints are holding. I…" she had to take a deep breath.

"Ma'am?" He had to raise his voice to be heard. The zombie jerked at the noise and turned the growl on him, but he was unmoved. Only veterans were given guard assignments in research stations, men inured to horror.

"He was trying to tell me something, before he turned. A message for his wife. Could you get me something to write with, before I forget it?"

"Sure thing Ma'am." It wasn't his job. But he was smart enough to see that the e-board on the desk wasn't what she needed. He glanced at the zombie, slid back through the plastic, and gave her the mercy of privacy. Annie contorted enough to swipe her nose on her shoulder from inside the suit. She let her mind settle into the cool mud of routine, and loaded the injector. There would be a reckoning for these days. *But not today*, she thought.

Sgt. Ruiz returned a few minutes later, hands empty. "Are you OK now Ma'am?" he asked patiently.

"Yes, thank you." She smiled at him, grateful for his tact.

She undocked the stylus and began to write.

> *Dear Mrs. Shephard,*
>
> *Before your husband passed away, he wanted me to tell you and your children that he loved you all very much. He wanted to say that he was sorry. He couldn't leave the little girl behind. He hoped you would understand. His last thoughts were of you.*
>
> *I cannot say enough how great a man your husband was. He was brave to the very end.*
>
> *My heartfelt condolences to you and your children,*
>
> *Dr. Annmarie Marshal, CDC quarantine station 26.*

Annie picked up the injector and walked toward the gurney with the struggling monster under the sheet. She looked at her watch again. Six hours and fifty-seven minutes, but she couldn't wait any more. She flipped up the edge of the sheet and stabbed the injector into his leg.

## Should Zombies Really Crawl From Their Graves

Should zombies really crawl from their graves
one should take extra care walking past cemeteries
since, flesh-eating proclivities aside,
being trampled in cross traffic is not fun.
Consider. Graves can be dirty and cramped,
and if you were a zombie you'd be in a rush
to put distance behind you—
to leave the graveyard scene quickly as possible.
Nevertheless, zombeism has drawbacks,
and should you be one, you'd be smelly and unkempt,
you'd shamble and stagger, have trouble getting dates,
and, once again, that flesh-eating thing
would make it especially hard to blend in
and be re-accepted as (more or less) human.

    —James S. Dorr

# Deadly Jobs

Gregory L. Norris

*Deadly Jobs Episode 3.11 – "Zombie Heat"*

FADE IN:

HOST IKE ROME strides across the main courtyard, the MOANS of the dead audible from somewhere nearby.

                    IKE
Hear that? That's the sound of cold, dead cash, folks. The good people of La Moraca—those who survived the recent plague of the dead, that is—have come up with a brilliant solution to not one but *two* problems.

CAMERA SHIFTS to the left, off Ike to the enclosure, where DOZENS OF LIVING DEAD are penned. The bodies claw at the chain link fence. Voices HOWL. Back to Ike.

                  IKE (CONT'D)
Like a lot of communities faced with a surplus of animated corpses and a lack of burial space, the La Moraca Marshal Law Council are killing two situations with one bullet.

Back to the DEAD, who MOAN. Ike leans into view, flashes his trademark grin.

> IKE (CONT'D)
> Sounds like a *Deadly Job* to me…

CUT TO OPENING CREDITS.

 

Ike Rome pulled a red pen from his back pocket and ran a line through the sentence.

"Mark, instead of saying, 'turning ice-cold flesh into home-heating-Heaven,' I'm just going to ad-lib it. Seems more natural in that instance."

The show's producer folded his arms and nodded. "Whatever you think works best, Ike. We can always go back in Post if we need to."

Ike thumbed the dirty bill of his baseball cap and flashed the opposite of the dimpled smile that had propelled his lower-tier cable network TV show to the top of the ratings following the plague.

"Damn, they stink," he sighed, shaking his head. "Smells to me like the center of Stinkville. Stinkier than a skunk that died up another skunk's ass."

"You getting all of this, Jimmy?"

The cameraman flashed a thumbs-up.

"Good," said Mark. Ike was clearly *on* and playing for the camera, which would make this one easy in the editing booth.

"And it's *Jeremy*, not Jimmy."

"Light check," Ike said.

Folding his arms, he assumed the classic macho pose that had endeared him to so many shell-shocked viewers following the eleven-month pandemic that had claimed almost a quarter of the world's population before vomiting them out of their body bags and back to their shuffling feet in the first ugly wave. With his All-American good looks, bedroom blue eyes, unshaved face and dark hair in an athlete's cut, Rome more than defined the part of blue collar buddy in his jeans and muddy boots. An everyman ready to help lift the world up—at least for one hour a week.

"Couldn't be cuter," Mark said. "Jimmy?"

"*Jeremy.*" The cameraman offered another thumbs-up.

"Let's do this," said Ike.

**Ike introduces CHARLIE BARROCKS of the La Moraca Town Council. The two men casually approach the pen.**

> **IKE**
> It's my pleasure to introduce to you the brains behind the solution, Doctor Charlie Barrocks. Doc Charlie—

**The men shake hands.**

> **BARROCKS**
> A pleasure to welcome you to the La Moraca flesh-to-fuel plant, Ike.

> **IKE**
> 'Flesh-to-fuel.' So tell me, how does this whole dirty process work, Doc?

> **BARROCKS**
> Quite easily, actually...

Barrocks adjusted the holster at his hip and checked his handgun—a Glock Safe Action semi-automatic, Ike saw. "First things first, it never hurts to be prepared."

Ike waved a hand in front of his nose. "I hear you, man. *Deadly Jobs* are dirty business. We did a show last month up in Maine where the lack of Atlantic Ocean traffic is resulting in a surge in seafood stocks... only it's become *deadlier* because they're never sure what's down there, crawling around and getting snagged in the fishermen's nets."

"Exactly," the man said, "like a lot of towns, we found ourselves with an overabundance of the living dead and not much else we could do with them. But we're on the cutting edge here in La Moraca, doing what much of the rest of the planet is too afraid to."

Jeremy trained the camera on the pens. Bodies dozens-deep clawed at the fence and moaned. A policeman with a destroyed face scrambled for a handful of Rome's shoulder, filthy claws missing by a good few feet.

"Because?" Ike pressed.

"For a start, there's the danger involved with wrangling the deceased. Centuries of religious dogma and the very nature of a dead person's appearance leave the living at a distinct tactical disadvantage—most of us see a loved one die and then rise up again, not truly alive or even that person we adored—and our first instinct as a society is to run right up to one of those disgusting bags of rancid meat and lay a kiss on their cheek. Right near the mouth, which is a recipe to be bitten and turned. Can you honestly imagine planting your smoocher on something like *that*?"

Barrocks waved a hand at the crowd of corpses. A ballerina had joined the cop in attempting to latch onto a piece of Ike.

Ike covered his mouth. "Are you trying to intentionally make me hurl, Charlie?"

"One of those things will happily rip off your lips. They've got no more compassion for or memory of any of us than, say, the worms wiggling through a pine box after it's planted in the earth."

"Seriously, dude?" Ike said.

Then he turned and vomited.

"You get that?" Mark the Producer asked.

Jeremy the Cameraman flashed a thumbs-up.

"Great!"

**WE SEE images of the reanimated dead as Ike speaks in VOICE OVER.**

### IKE (V.O.)
So first, there's the danger of going in and manually taking out the living dead, one at a time. A recent study conducted by the Post-Pandemic Militia reported that in almost one

hundred percent of cases, living humans suffered bites, scratches, and subsequent infection when attempting to rid an area, even the smallest township, of reanimated corpses.

Charlie Barrocks takes point.

**BARROCKS**
**And then there are the dangers that come *after* the dead are killed for the second time…**

"Danger?" asked Ike.

"Sure. You can't just leave the bodies lying around to rot," Barrocks said. "We know it isn't safe to handle these things, even after you cap them in the skull. You can't compost them—we still don't know the results of eating food grown in soil polluted with the remains of these foul things."

Ike's curdled stomach lurched again. A sour burp shuddered up his throat. "Sure, we know we shouldn't bury them because of the risk to the water *tab*…"

A sour taste like lemons broke on Ike's tongue.

"…*ble*."

"Fire's the only safe option. And with coal, oil, and natural gas shipments interrupted by the global crisis, we arrived at this idea to not only solve the one problem, but that other, bigger thorn in present day humanity's ass…"

**IKE (V.O.)**
**La Moraca was already going green before the Pandemic struck. The good people who call this fine community home were recycling an estimated sixty tons of trash in their garbage-to-heat program, using it to generate warmth in municipal buildings, the schools…**

even the town's library.

Shot of Barrocks, arms folded, standing in front of the pen.

                    **BARROCKS**
Oh yeah, we've been leading the way in green innovations.

INSERT FAST-MOTION spool of Ike vomiting in the grass.

                    **IKE (V.O.)**
Green?
    (beat)
Coming up, I show you why they call this a deadly job…

PREVIEW of Ike armed with cattle prod, shuffling a LIVING DEAD down the killing chute, toward the 'burn box.'

                                  **FADE OUT.**

"So, you want to do it like this," Barrocks said, hefting the cattle prod from one hand to the other. "We start off giving them several hard jabs, enough to break them out of their overconfidence."

He ran the top of the prod into the cop, a woman in flannel with a big butt and unflattering flattop, and the whisper-thin Bohemian corpse with the Van Dyke goatee, each instant of contact creating noxious puffs of smoke. At first, the three individuals universally snarled and lunged at Doc Barrocks, but a few more repetitions stole their bravado and had them falling back toward a corner of the pen where a trap door waited to be sprung.

"Simple enough," Ike said.

"Don't get cocky," Barrocks warned.

Ike shrugged then speared an elderly man missing his nose and a teen punk with a shaved head wearing a filthy T-shirt that bore the name of a band Ike had never heard of.

"This is it?" asked Ike.

"No, this is the first step: getting some fuel into the firebox. Like bugs, you'll see the living dead have a tendency to swarm," Barrocks said.

True to his claim, another half-dozen individuals wandered away from the fence they'd thrown themselves against throughout the taping of the episode and cloistered at the back of the pen, near the trap door.

"And now for the easy part. Roderick, lift up the gate."

From somewhere off screen, the man Ike assumed was Roderick flipped a switch and the trap door swung open. The dead spilled through in a tangle of limbs and surprised hisses. Most quickly recovered. The remaining corpses in the pen followed through the door willingly. In short time, the pen emptied.

"Now, for the real beauty of the situation," Barrocks said, waving for Ike, Jeremy the Cameraman, and Mark the Producer to follow. "These seventeen sticks of stinking stove-lengths will warm our town for at least the next two days, just like any other ton of organic trash."

The corpses shuffled forward through the killing chute, unaware of gates closing in sequence behind them. At the third junction, all the players passed into the main building, living and dead separated by brick walls.

"We call that the 'burn box.'"

Ike grinned. "And why is that, Charlie?"

On cue, sharp tongues of orange flame blasted through the incinerator, visible through observation windows set into the brick. The rush of energy was followed by a roar of angry voices—voices, like bodies, sounding as though they'd at long last arrived in the searing depths of Hell.

The shouts soon cut out. Barrocks spread his arms akimbo and smiled. "*Ta-da...*"

**FADE IN:**

**EXT. THE PENS – DAY**

**Black smoke belches in the background. Ike and Doc Barrocks**

again meet in front of the pens, which now sit empty.

                IKE
That was fairly straightforward—and disgusting.

             BARROCKS
It's all in a day's operations. We were really lucky in La Moraca. After putting down our own casualties last winter, we've enjoyed a continuous stream of fresh product coming at us from all sides.

                IKE
*Fresh?* Lucky for you that you have a use for them.

             BARROCKS
True, which leads us to the next part of the job—the really deadly part…

    They appeared in the wide-open space between the town's dump and recycling center and the grasslands beyond: more than a dozen, all moaning, all dead and hungry.

    "And this is a daily affair in La Moraca?" Ike asked.

    "That's right, Ike," Barrocks answered. "They keep streaming up from the San Fernando Valley or down from San Fran… we'll keep toasting the suckers like marshmallows. Corpse-wrangling has wiped out our unemployment rate—any La Moracan willing to contribute to the cause gets free heat and electricity. Now, pay attention and stay frosty."

    The garbage-wranglers each carried a gun in one hand, a cattle prod in the other.

    "And we—?"

    "We bring back the burning beauties. Focus, Ike."

    A thing that had once been a man, mulleted and dressed in cowboy boots and blue jeans, half its face missing, fixated on Ike. Ike brought up the cattle prod and capped the dead man right against the cheek, singing hair in the process. The corpse roared, lunged. Ike stung him again.

"That's the spirit, Ike," Barrocks hooted. "You've made a friend. Now, walk him back to the dump, to the pens. He's taken a liking to you. That's right…"

Ike backed away. The dead man pursued. Jeremy the Cameraman recorded every second of the encounter.

"You getting this, Jimmy?" Ike asked. "Are you seeing how amazingly deadly this job is, Post-Pandemic America?"

Jeremy flashed a thumb's-up. "Name's Jeremy, Ike. And yeah, I'm getting it all!"

Mullet's dead eyes locked onto Jeremy's voice and then his thumb. The dead man turned away from Ike and toward the cameraman.

Ike jabbed Mullet in the side. "No, wait, *you!*—over here!"

"Hey now, control that walking stove-length," Barrocks said.

"Whoa, dude," Jeremy said right as the dead thing in his lens lunged forward. "Help!"

Mullet jumped Jeremy. Two bullets blasted into the dead man's head, but not before he'd taken a decent chunk out of the cameraman's throat.

**WE SEE Ike standing in front of the pens, which are again filled with the dead.**

**IKE**

And that, folks, is why they call it a deadly job. The people in La Moraca have taken life's lemons and made, well… a wienie roast.

Ike crumpled up the last page of the script. There was no further use in following what had been written, because the episode had changed. Drastically.

"You ready?" Ike asked.

Mark nodded and lifted the camera. "Let's go make some incredible reality television."

Ike poured himself into his on-screen persona, again becoming that guy, that *dude*. The everyman all of post-plague America had fallen in love with.

"Just to show you how seriously we take our *Deadly Jobs*, in La Moraca, one of our own made the ultimate sacrifice. My faithful new cameraman Jimmy Womack—"

"*Jeremy*," Mark whispered.

"Jeremy Womack was bitten during the taping of the episode's riskiest segment. Jeremy has graciously agreed to allow us to include his inevitable descent from one of the living to the living dead to show just how dangerous what we do really is…"

Ike stabs at DEAD JEREMY with the cattle prod. Dead-Jeremy backs toward the trapdoor.

IKE
It's a deadly job.

Dead-Jeremy and the rest of the deceased charge through the trapdoor and on to the burn box. APPROPRIATE MUSIC PLAYS, soft, sad. A DIRGE.

A DEDICATION runs, with date of birth, date of death, date of rebirth, and date of re-death honoring the late Jimmy Womack.

**FADE OUT**.

# Stream of Dead Conscious

amaranthine moan of swelled tongue
like I know what I want to say
but just end up moaning
locked-in syndrome of rage
I wish I was really locked-in with no
movement but I can and that is why
I kill everyone and that is why I sag
my head to the right like gravity
was pulling my ear toward some office
of some leader who is going to punish
me for offenses I committed because
of peer pressure I don't want to commit
cannibalism everyone else does
and then I just find myself making excuses
later after the blood is in my teeth
and the shirt that I haven't taken off in months
is stuck to my gouged belly like grape juice
on white carpet and I keep spilling
myself discipline is hard I have none
I see someone running and I limp
I run I walk until my feet bleed
until I see a gun and then I can feel
myself smile inside my mind
I close my eyes and lunge headlong
into the path of that living man's
barrel and fear and I don't care
because I'm either going to eat or die
and I am fine with both outcomes

—John McCarthy

## At the bar near the cemetery

They stumble over the words
due to stage fright
or lack of saliva.
A jaw; unhinges
drops to the stage.
The crowd dead
to be expected.
The regulars never leave.
Zombie karaoke
tonight, every night.

—Brian Rosenberger

# Conrad

## Joshua Clark Orkin

Conrad watched his mother as she toiled over the sink. In her hands was a large glass pan that had held the night's casserole. She scrubbed determinedly at a stubborn grease stain, her face scrunched with frustration. Suddenly she turned, throwing the soapy sponge across the kitchen and releasing a terrifying shriek. The sponge struck the refrigerator and slid down its face before coming to rest on the black and white tile. She sat down heavily on the floor, her back against the cupboard, and wept. Conrad grabbed his backpack off the kitchen table and stormed out the back door.

The wind was wet against his face as he rode his bike down the deserted road. A light drizzle was falling and thin wisps of fog hung low in the air. He slowed before an old farm house with peeling white paint. On the porch sat an old man in a rocking chair, smoking a pipe while wind chimes clanged gently in the wind. The embers glowed as he sucked at the end of the polished wood, then dimmed as he released a small cloud of his own into the foggy night. The man stroked his long white beard and contemplated the boy on the bike before him.

Conrad emitted a sharp whistle through his teeth and the sounds of movement came from the house behind the man. An old golden retriever came bounding out the front door and ran to the bike. Conrad leaned down and rubbed the dog's head affectionately. He looked at the old man and reached back to lightly pat the backpack he wore. The old man shook his head slowly and drew on his pipe. Conrad put his

## 58 Joshua Clark Orkin

feet to the pedals once more and rode on. The dog kept pace by his side.

He rode for a long time until he came to a dirt road that turned off into the forest. There he leaned his bike against a tree and unzipped his backpack. He took out a large flashlight and turned it on before zipping up the bag and slinging it over his shoulder. He called the dog to him and the two walked side by side into the woods.

The light illuminated the path before them as the soft patter of rain fell on the leaves over their heads. The drizzle was light and had not yet reached the forest floor. Dry leaves crackled beneath their feet. Conrad's breathing began to quicken, but his eyes remained fixed on the path. Soon they came to a clearing and Conrad shone the light on the ground until he found the remains of an old fire with some logs stacked neatly beside it. Here he squatted and unzipped the backpack once more.

He took out a small cloth bag, tied at the top with a ribbon, and placed it on the ground beside him. Then he started a fire. Once the tinder caught he added a few of the larger logs and soon had a small, steady blaze going. He turned off the flashlight and sat cross-legged before the flame as it rose and danced with the wind, splaying light across the clearing and casting the forest beyond into darkness.

The old dog lay down at his side, and he absently scratched the top of its head as he stared into the flame. A long while passed. Very slowly, he reached into the backpack and removed a small leather-bound book. Opening to a dog-eared page, he began to read aloud. The words were in an archaic language, full of harsh, guttural sounds. When he finished, he picked up the cloth bag and undid the ribbon. Then he leaned forward and poured the contents into the flame.

There was a slight hiss as the fire accepted the offering, and the flame grew larger and burned a fluorescent green. An unnatural wind blew through the clearing and the flames twisted cruelly. By his side, the dog began to whimper. The two sat together in silence, waiting.

Suddenly the dog perked up its head. It looked off into the darkness beyond the light. Rising to its feet, it began barking madly. Conrad helplessly tried to calm the old animal to no avail. Without warning it turned and bolted off into the night. Conrad scooped up the book and threw the empty cloth sack in his backpack. He stood and listened. From far in the distance he heard growling, followed by a sharp yelp. Then silence. He whistled through his teeth and waited, but there was nothing.

A number of minutes passed. Conrad, unsure of what to do, sat down again by the fire. He looked around uneasily, gripping the little book tightly in his hands.

Then he saw them: two red eyes, staring unblinking from beyond the line of trees. He scrambled to his feet then stopped. Completely still, he stared back as rain drummed on the leaves above. Slowly he tried to open the book, but his hands shook and it fell. He leaned halfway down to retrieve it then froze again. The eyes had moved. Just a fraction. He took one halting step backwards. Then another. Then he turned and fled into the woods. Trees flashed by and branches stung his face as he ran blindly through the underbrush. The path forgotten and the light of the fire fading behind him, he ran until he couldn't breathe.

His ears filled with the strange grunting coming from behind him as tears streamed from the corners of his eyes. Then he stumbled and went down. He felt hot air on the back of his neck as he lay face first in the leaves. Something sniffed the back of his head. A foul, rotting odor filled his nostrils. Then, through the haze of madness he noticed a black lump in front of him. His eyes widened as he recognized the remains of the old dog. The eyes and tongue were missing and the hairless body was horribly defiled. With an odd detachment he noticed there was no blood. All the blood was gone. He began to shake uncontrollably as his mouth gaped in a rigid, soundless scream.

Then a voice rang out and the sniffing paused. The guttural language of the book filled the forest. The creature moaned and pulled back. The words continued, harsh and relentless. Conrad heard the wretched thing backing slowly away. Then it was gone.

Slowly he looked up. Before him stood the bearded old man. Still violently shaking, he picked himself up before the man's sad eyes. The two of them walked back to Conrad's bike in silence. Neither mentioned the dog.

Conrad rode back to his house alone. He locked the door behind him and stood leaning against it. The house was dark and his breathing began to slow.

## ★ 60  Joshua Clark Orkin

He set his backpack on the kitchen table and slumped into a chair, putting his head in his hands. He noticed the sponge, by the base of the refrigerator. He walked over and picked it up. Then he walked slowly to the sink and found the dirty pan. Turning on the water, he began to scrub furiously at the stubborn grease stain. He scrubbed until there was nothing left.

# Hot Zombie Chicks and Cocktails at Gore's

Jamie Brindle

I'm not like the other schmucks. That's the first thing you should know about me.

I mean, sure, I don't smell so good, and I like a delicious, fresh brain just as much as Joe Zombie down the road, but I'm different.

What you've got to understand is that I'm an original, true-blue 2012 edition. Year Zero. Retro, baby. I didn't jump on the bandwagon like so many other zlobs.

That's what I tell the ladies, but frankly, I sometimes wonder why I bother. They hardly ever listen to me anyway. And isn't that just a sign of the times?

I haven't met a smoking hot zombie chick since the spring of '13. Things were different back then.

Let me tell you.

I first met Melaena at some mall deal. It was April 12th 2013, and things were still fresh back then. It felt like we had direction. Like we were *going* somewhere.

Anyhow, we had the humans penned in pretty tight, they weren't leaving anytime soon. They had some sharpshooter up on the roof, but hell, how many bullets did they have? We could wait.

"Hey sugar, how would you like to taste *my* grey matter?"

That was the first thing I said to her. Pretty basic, I know, but those were heady days. The basic stuff worked more often than you might think.

She smiled at me. There was something I couldn't place at first about her smile. It was *special*. Then her lip moved, and I realised it was a maggot. It was kind of cute.

Just then there was a crash as a group of humans decided to make a break for it out of some back door they didn't think we had covered. I was so into this chick, though, I didn't even look up.

"I'm Melaena," she told me.

"Pretty name," I replied. "What's it mean?"

The trend was to re-christen yourself with a zombie name back then. Shit, we were such idealists.

"Blood in the stool," she explained, and flashed me a sheepish grin. "I used to be a pre-med before…" she let the words hang, and gestured around at everything.

"That's beautiful," I told her. "I'm Rot."

I had to shout because one of the humans had just fallen over and they were screaming pretty loud. If I had wanted my share of the brains, I could have gone forward and tucked in. But suddenly I wasn't so hungry anymore. Melaena was enough for me.

"Listen," I said. "I know this great little bar. It's real special, kind of invite-only. You wanna blow this joint?"

She shrugged, and one of her shoulders flopped slickly in the joint. Jesus, this chick was driving me wild!

"Sure," she told me, and that was that.

Gore's is a pretty special place, like I said. Or rather, it *was* pretty special. Some chain's taken it over now, and there's nothing so much to write home about anymore. But back in the Spring of '13, Gore's was the place to be.

It used to be some top-secret research facility, back in the day. Matter of fact, the rumour at the time was that it was where the whole zombie thing started. I mean, everyone knows who did it now, of course, and why. But back then, the whole thing seemed magical, and everyone had a theory.

Anyhow, Gore's was on the bottom floor of this humongous research building. It was about ten stories underground, and it was *big*. Difficult to bust open, but Gore managed it, and man, it was just like opening up a gourmet box of extra special chocolates.

That place was just chock-full of the nerdiest, smartest science geeks you can imagine. The *brains* on those researchers! Gore used to have them chained up behind the bar, thirty or forty of them. He had a selection of hammers and whisks, and he made cocktails to order, real classy.

"So, you come here often?" Melaena asked me, lurching seductively into a seat next to me.

I shrugged, trying to play it nonchalant.

"Now and again," I told her. "What would you like?"

Gore showed up just then. He was a class act himself, skin as grey as gutter snow, and real sharp teeth.

"If I can recommend," he said smoothly. "We have a very fine visiting languages professor freshly harvested from our, ah, vineyards. The frontal cortex is, unfortunately, nearly all gone, but he does have a rather splendidly developed left tempero-parietal region, not to mention an especially juicy basal ganglia."

"Sounds good," said Melaena firmly. "And don't stint on the CSF, huh?"

"I wouldn't even dream of it," said Gore smoothly. "And for sir?"

"The usual," I told him.

Gore raised an eyebrow. Half of it fell off.

"Sir intends to settle his bill soon, I presume?" his voice was polite, but I knew better than to underestimate him.

"What? I'm not still good from those teachers I brought in last week?" I asked, not that I needed him to tell me. You got credit in Gore's by bringing in a supply of the finer brains. A zlob could get by on estate agents and bureaucrats, but shit, that wasn't real living. People came to Gore's for that little something extra. And that meant Gore was always on the lookout for dealers who could keep his cellars stocked.

"Sir, please," Gore's voice was like honey being poured over an iron rod. "There were only three of them. And they taught at the community college." I sighed. This zlob was going to ruin my play if I wasn't careful. I waved a hand at him airily.

"Sure, sure, I'll bring you something good. Just get us our drinks and get out of our hair, huh?"

Gore bustled off to get the drinks. In the background there was the sound of a buzz-saw starting up.

When I turned back to Melaena, she was staring at me with those beautiful green eyes of hers. Not that they were that far along, but decomposition comes to us all in time.

"You go hunting for this place?" she asked breathlessly. "Wow, what a cool job!"

I spread my arms, trying to look humble.

"What can I say?" I moved closer. "I like to make a difference to society. I want to do something that matters with my death."

From behind the bar there was a deep crunching sound, and what was left of the languages professor suddenly started singing something urgent in Armenian.

She nodded, looking serious.

"I don't suppose…" she started hesitantly, then stopped, shy.

"What?"

"Well, I don't want to be forward," she went on, "but I'd love to come with you one time."

I couldn't believe it! The day was just getting better and better!

I shrugged, trying to play it cool.

"Word is, there's a wild pack of computer programmers that have a camp just North of the city," I told her. "I was thinking of making a trip out there later this evening as it happens. If you'd care to accompany me, you'd be most welcome."

Just then, Gore turned up with our drinks.

Melaena took a slurp of hers and looked at me with delight.

"That's incredible!" she exclaimed. "Man, I can't believe I've been chowing down on car salesmen when there's good shit like this in the world!'

Gore looked happy.

"We aim to please," he said.

"Որ ճանապարհը դեպի ոսկե գուզարանից իմ ընկերը," said the visiting languages professor, but only very softly.

By the time Melaena and I got out of the city, there was a lot of sexual tension between us. It was in all the little things, like the way she laughed and tossed her hair back, or the way she swayed her hips so hard they dislocated with sexy little popping noises. To tell you the truth, I was tempted to ask her back to my place right then and there, and to hell with Gore and this hunt. But then, I had a feeling that half the reason she was hot for me was this mission of ours, and I didn't want to ruin that. I decided I would just have to wait.

The sun was starting to go down and we were well out of the city when we started to see signs of our prey. It was subtle, but I knew what to look for.

"See that?" I pointed at a flash of grey half-hidden under a bush. Melaena nodded.

"What is it?" she asked.

"The outer covering to a 1982 Commodore 64, complete with attached tape deck and dot matrix printer," I told her. "They're so close, I can almost smell them."

We didn't have much further to go. Before long, a little string of smoke was visible, rising up against the muddy red of sunset. If only the other zlobs had a tenth of my imagination, then these nerds with their juicy brains would have been history by now. As it was, the country was rich for the pickings if you only knew where to look.

"Remember, we need them alive," I told Melaena. "So here's how we're gonna do this. You wait here in this bottleneck, and I'll circle 'round and flush them down to you."

"Then what do I do?"

"You lay hidden in the bushes and bite their ankles off as they come past."

The plan was simple enough, and it should have worked like a dream.

I climbed up through the bushes, then came in close. They were lit up by their fire, and they couldn't see me at all. Jesus, they were chumps. I mean, they might have had big brains, but they were not wired up for practical thinking. They hadn't even posted sentries.

There were five of them, four guys with bad hair and skin, and one chick who must have weighed two hundred pounds and was clearly their leader.

"Argh!" I shouted, and came stumbling at them out of the darkness. That was when things began to go wrong. I'd played this routine a dozen times before—usually I had a net or a pit or something waiting instead of Melaena, but still, basically it was the same plan—and it had never failed before.

Every other time, I only had to give a groan and a lurch, and those puny little critters would be high tailing it out of there as fast as their delicious little legs could carry them.

This time, things were different.

"Oh dear, not another one," said one of the men, sounding bored. "Come on Glen, it's your turn."

"Mine?" said the one evidently called Glen. "But it was my turn last week! It must be Ralph's turn today."

"Fine, it's Ralph's turn," said the first man, not even looking up from the fire.

This left me feeling rather shaken, I can tell you.

"Um…Urgh?" I tried again, feeling as if I'd lost my momentum.

"Yes, yes, we heard," said Glen absently. "We're all very terrifed. Oh dear, a zombie. Gosh. And so on."

This really wasn't going according to plan. I decided that I would just have to take a bite out of one of them, show them who was boss. I lurched forward as fast as I could, and heard something snap in my back. It felt lovely.

*The woman*, I decided. Get the leader out of the way, and surely the rest would fold.

I rushed towards her, and she rose in front of me like a great delicious fleshy snack.

Then something strange happened. I was just reaching out for her, just about to grab her and reel her in towards my sharp teeth… and suddenly I was stopping. My nose was twitching. My hand was frozen in mid-snatch.

Something smelt delicious. I mean really delicious. I mean it was so amazingly, stomach rumblingly, mouth wateringly delicious that the smell just bypassed my thought processes and latched straight onto my muscles. That's the only way I can explain it. I just couldn't help myself.

My head swung round to the right, towards where the man known as Ralph was holding something up. It was difficult to see in the darkness, but it looked like it was a bowl filled with dog food. It glistened in the flickering light of the fire. It was the source of the delicious smell.

"Here good zombiezombie," crooned Ralph. "Does zombie want some delicious fresh brains?"

I had to admit, zombie did.

*Oh well*, I thought as the last threads of my self-control disintegrated, *I'll just have a taste, then get on with the business of capturing these puny humans.*

I fell on the bowl like I hadn't eaten in a year. It made all the other trash I'd shoved down my throat since the Big Change seem like offal. Even Gore's shit seemed like cheap rubbish by comparison.

"Aw, he's sweet," said Ralph, patting me absently on the head. "Can we keep him?"

"No," said the woman firmly. "You always want to keep them. Why do you always want to keep them?"

I finished the last of whatever had been in the bowl and licked my lips. It had been delicious, but now things had gone quite far enough. They seemed like decent sorts for humans, and I felt kind of bad about it, but we had to face facts. I was simply further up the food ladder than them.

"Thanks for the food," I told them, standing up. "And look, this is nothing personal. But I'm afraid I'm going to have to bite off your ankles and drag you back to the city now. It's kind of my job," I added, feeling like a bit of a Judas.

"You see?" exclaimed Ralph, completely ignoring me, and turning to the woman. "He's just adorable! Doesn't he make you laugh?"

To my horror, I realised that Ralph was right. All the humans standing around the fire were either smiling at me or outright laughing. That made my blood boil. Enough was enough.

"Fine," I said. "Have it your way."

I lunged forward and bit Ralph's nose off.

Except I didn't.

That's what I meant to do. I sent the message to my muscles, I began to move forward…

"Stay," commanded Ralph.

I stayed.

"Bad zombie," said the woman. "Don't you know it's nasty to bite people's noses off?"

As soon as she said it, it seemed… true to me, somehow. I mean, deep down I knew it was the most natural thing in the world to bite a guy's nose off. But on the surface, what she said sounded absolutely right. I couldn't escape the feeling. It was like her words were crushing me.

"It's sad, actually," said Ralph. "He doesn't have any idea, does he?"

"Have any idea of what?" I asked. "I'm sorry about your nose, by the way."

"About what happened to you," said the woman. "About what happened to the world. About what made you the way you are."

I managed to draw myself up at that. Back then, we were such idealists, like I said.

"Sure I do," I said, trying to sound scornful. "There's been an uprising. Your day is over. All the little wars, all the little petty corruptions, all the human mistakes… they're all gone, they've all been washed away. It's time for your species to move over. You can call it revolution or evolution, but that doesn't matter. The point is, things have changed, and your time is done."

"That's impressive, actually," said Ralph, one eyebrow raised. "It managed to justify the whole thing without resorting to God once. Usually, God's the first thing they cling to."

The woman shrugged.

"You think we should tell him the truth?" she asked.

I couldn't stand the way they were talking over me, so I decided to try and bite Ralph's nose off again. It still didn't work.

"How about it, zomb?" asked Ralph. "You want to be enlightened? You think you can handle the truth?"

"There's nothing you can tell me that'll convince me I'm not talking to an inferior species," I replied. "Now would you mind just leaning over and putting your nose into my mouth?"

I had to admit it, I was feeling kind of desperate by now.

The woman laughed.

"Nothing we can do to tell you?" she repeated. "Fair enough. How about something we can *feed* you? Or maybe something we've *already* fed you? That speaks for itself, really."

I licked my lips. An icy tingling feeling was beginning to form at the base of my spine. At first I thought it was just a fractured vertebra beginning to fill up with pus, but deep down I knew I was wrong. Deep down, I knew that feeling was dread.

"Go on then," I said brashly. "Do your worst."

And they did.

They just opened their mouths and explained everything to me.

And right then and there, on a hill a few miles outside the city, surrounded by computer nerds, right then and there was where I lost my illusions. That was when the world changed for me. After that, the heady days were over.

I sloped off back down the hill.

"You think we should have told him?" I heard Ralph asking the others as I left.

"It'll be for the best," the woman replied. "If I was him, I'd want to know."

Melaena wasn't impressed when I came back alone. She wanted to know what had happened, what had changed, but I didn't have the heart to tell her. I said I'd made a mistake, that those chumps were real stupid, not fit for Gore's at all. She listened, and I even managed to talk her into going to grab a few city hall employee's—I always ate trash when I was feeling down—and for a while I thought that things would be okay.

But afterwards, sitting next to each other by the bodies, we both knew something was wrong.

"What's the matter?" she wanted to know. "Was it me?"

"You were perfect," I told her quickly. "The way you cracked that skull, the little slurping noise... You're a real classy girl, it's just..."

"Just what?" she asked. "Was it too fast for you? I'm sorry, I was just so hungry. We can go slower next time."

"No, it's not that," I could hear the frustration in my voice. "It's just... well, I ate a lot at Gore's earlier. I must have been more full than I thought."

"You shouldn't feel bad about what happened, you know," she told me, putting a beautiful, slimy hand on my shoulder. "It's very common.

You'd be surprised how many zlobs can't finish a whole brain these days."

She smiled at me desperately, and I tried to smile back.

How could I tell her the truth? How could I tell her that after what the humans had fed me, after what they had told me, that I would never be satisfied with human brains again?

We went our separate ways soon after that. We told each other we'd meet up again, but we both knew that was a lie.

I never saw her again; a few months later, I heard she'd left for Paris. Good luck to her. I hear a zlob can do real good for herself in the Old World.

Not long after that, some big corporation took over Gore's. I'm sure you've heard of them. I guess we all have now. When that happened, the last thread of my doubt snapped, and I knew the heady, wild days were over.

So that was the story of the last smoking hot zombie chick I met, and how I completely failed to score with her. To tell you the truth, it took me a while to get my mojo back after I had that truth-bomb dropped on me by those computer nerds in the woods.

Like I say, things are different now. No-one's an idealist anymore. I mean, some zlobs pretend they still believe we're the result of a government experiment or an extraterrestrial plague. But we know the truth. Deep down we all know.

It all made such perfect sense. As soon as you heard it, you just knew it was true.

And when the big chain eateries started opening up again, was there really any doubt?

Turns out we were the result of a secret experiment, all right, but it wasn't the government that was running it. Turns out it was just the marketing department of a rather famous fast food chain.

You remember the rumours you used to hear about what went in to burgers back in the day? All the cheap cast off bits of meat, the bits that were no good for steaks, or even for sausages. The bones, the eyes, the little stringy bits of gristle.

And the brains.

All those cow brains, millions and millions and millions of them.

They would just have been thrown away, otherwise. That would have been no good. They have to squeeze the last ounce of profit out of the operation, don't they?

That was why they commissioned the virus.

It was top secret, of course, and it was supposed to be selective, very subtle.

It would just worm its way into the taste centres of the human brain, flip a little switch, and suddenly cow brain wouldn't taste so bad, after all.

Turns out genetic engineering is a bit more tricky than that.

Turns out that it's not so easy to do something quite that specific, and certainly not without side effects.

One aspect was completely successful, however. Once we had been infected with the virus, we became completely submissive to whoever it was that fed us the brains.

But hell, I don't mind.

After all, what have I got to complain about? I do alright. Got myself this nice little eatery where I serve old-style dishes for other old-style zombs, like me.

Even got myself a girl. She's not smoking hot like Melaena—actually, she's a vegetarian—but what can I say? She sneaks bean burgers into the Brain Jamboree when she thinks I'm not looking, but company's company.

I keep my own little collection of smart-looking humans right up there in cages above the counter, and a list of cocktails, just like Gore did. I even still have the visiting language professor, what's left of him. I'm saving him for a real special occasion.

Everyone looks the other way when the delivery van comes with the cow parts, but hell, what does it hurt to pretend?

I was there at the beginning, back when the movement seemed real, back when being a zombie meant something.

Does it matter if it turned out we were wrong?

# Dancing Blue Zombie

Tonight  the bar is redolent
with sandalwood perfume,
Boney James is smokin' hot,
his sax lights up the room

in blood bright swirls
while she sways on, eyelids
drooping, mouth a moue,
ignoring you until
the music ends and then

(glowing cobalt in the spotlight)

she moves across the floor
to sit beside you, takes a sip
of your champagne, lights up,
smacks her lips, and smiles
just once, before she bites.

—Marge Simon

# The Zombie Solution
(a Shakespearean sonnet)

Your face is covered with oozing sores
and your limbs are tangled and clumsy;
your breasts are a mass of mangled gore,
and your nether parts? Treated falsely.
I must save you from this human hoard
that's bent on your destruction!
We need to form a xeno rights board
create an amendment to the constitution!
Just imagine what the world could hold. . .
but I can see you have misgivings,
and may shy away from this rather bold
proposition, seeing as you have other leanings.
If you will but consider my honest plea,
we'll co-create a zombie-vampire dynasty!

—Terrie Leigh Relf

# The Return of Gunnar Kettilson

Vonnie Winslow Crist

Celia sat straight-backed on an oak bench in her moonlit kitchen with the long-handled ax stretched across her lap. She listened for the shambling footsteps of her husband, Gunnar Kettilson, comforted in small measure by the presence of her great aunt beside her on the bench.

"Do you think he will come?" Celia whispered as she rubbed the wooden ax handle with her thumb and wondered if there'd be maggots.

"We should light the welcome candle," said Rona.

The white-haired woman set the butcher knife she'd been holding in her right hand on the floor, stood, propped the fire poker from her left hand against the bench, and walked to the fireplace. She withdrew a blazing splinter of wood from the fire.

> *"This night, one night, by full moon's light,*
> *We call you, Gunnar Kettilson.*
> *Come Home, cruel Draugr,*
> *Come home, bitter revenant,"*

chanted Rona as she lit a solitary white candle balanced in a silver candlestick, and placed it on a windowsill.

The elderly woman extinguished the splinter, returned to the bench, and patted Celia's forearm before picking the butcher knife back up. "We should know before long if we sealed him in the grave or if he'll return."

"What more could we have done?"

Celia's aunt answered her with a tilt of her head and a flutter of her heavily-veined hands.

As they sat in silence listening to the seawind in the trees, Celia recalled the somber funeral procession that carried Gunnar up the hill to the cemetery. She'd followed closely behind the casket beside Rona and Gunnar's father, Lars. The whole village had marched after them. The whole village *had* to attend, because Lars owned the fish factory, cannery, and most of the fishing ships where the villagers worked. And Lars retaliated against anyone he suspected of not showing sufficient respect to the Kettilson family.

"Lift your chin up, woman," Lars had growled as they'd followed the casket. "Be proud you were married to a Kettilson." Then he'd grabbed her upper arm, squeezed it hard, glared at her with his cold blue eyes. "And unless you're carrying his child, I'll have you out on the street within a year. And if you carry a babe…" he'd scowled, and added, "he'll be mine at birth. You were never in love with my son, only interested in the Kettilson money."

Celia had opened her mouth to argue, but before she could utter a word in her defense, Aunt Rona had stared the hulking patriarch of the Kettilson family in his pale, mean eyes, and hissed, "Shame on you, Lars. She's lost a husband, and he's not yet beneath the ground. The spirits of the dead remember such slander."

Lars had pressed his thin lips together so tightly that they'd turned white, but he hadn't argued with Rona—for Rona was fae-blessed, the old woman was known for her rune-reading, healing herbs, and blessing spells. And Lars would naturally suspect she knew darker magics, too.

Celia watched the welcome candle's flame flicker. She wondered if Gunnar saw its light from the graveyard. Poor Gunnar. Celia's eyes filled when she thought about her husband. His mother was dead before he was three. It was whispered in the dark corners of the village that Dalla Kettilson had been beaten to death by her husband in front of their son. Though the official story given by Lars was that Dalla had slipped on a rain-slick stone and tumbled over a cliff to the sea rocks below, and no one dared challenge Lars, lest the same fate befall them.

Gunnar had grown up in a household without a mother's love

where the least infraction resulted in tongue-lashings and belt-beatings from Lars. She believed that's where her husband's temper had been honed. Kind to her when they first met, sweet to her while he courted her, Gunnar grew angrier after their wedding. His death at the cannery had almost been a blessing, for Celia had fully expected to die at his hand.

Though he'd tried to control his temper, Gunnar had flown into a blind rage twice during their brief marriage. The first time, he'd accused Celia of flirting after he'd seen her talking to the butcher on the street in front of his shop. In his anger, he'd flung her down the stairs. Luckily, she'd only broken her arm.

The second time had occurred after Lars told his son that Celia had worn a revealing dress to the fish market. Gunnar had slammed her against the wall, and then hit the wall beside her head with his fist five or six times. She'd shown him the dress she'd been wearing, and he'd realized his father was manipulating him again.

After both violent fits, he'd knelt before Celia crying, and begged her forgiveness. And, though she knew it would probably be the end of her, Celia had forgiven Gunnar.

Leave him, friends had whispered. But leaving Gunnar meant leaving the village and Aunt Rona. And Celia was sure that no matter how far away she fled, there was no escaping the revenge of Lars Kettilson.

Celia wiped her eyes with the back of her hand. Perhaps the saddest thing about the marriage was that Celia really did love Gunnar, and she knew that Gunnar loved her, too. He was just so damaged from his childhood, and every day at work, Lars poured even more nasty, ugly thoughts into his son's ears. And then there was the babe. Only she and Gunnar knew about her pregnancy, and he'd seemed so happy. Maybe a baby would have made a difference in. . . .

"Listen," said Aunt Rona as she leaned forward. "Someone is coming."

"Do you think it's him?"

"Who else? The villagers are locked tight in their homes tonight with no candles burning. This is the first full moon since the first new moon after Gunnar's death. This is the night he can return." The fae-blessed woman who was her great-aunt brushed a tear from Celia's cheek with her leathery fingertips. "We are alone, my dear. No one will even look out their windows until dawn."

"Lars keeps his candles burning. I can see the Kettilson keep lit bright as day through the window."

Aunt Rona snorted. "He's a fool. Always was."

"Perhaps Gunnar won't return." Celia bit her lip. "We did everything we could to keep him beneath the ground. We placed a pair of open scissors on his chest; we hid twigs from an Alder tree in his clothes; we even tied his big toes together to make it impossible for him to walk…"

"Yes, we did what we could." Her great-aunt patted Celia's forearm again. "Still, the undead have their ways of figuring out how to return."

"But he should be confused. We had nine men from the village lift and lower Gunnar's coffin three times. And each time they turned the coffin around. How can he find his way?"

Aunt Rona shrugged. "We didn't wall up the door he exited by the last time, so he can still enter this house."

"The door couldn't be walled up. Gunnar's father forbade it."

"And you, my dear, were too kindhearted to drive straight pins through his eyes. Both things might have helped." Her aunt lifted her hands up, let them drop to her lap. "But a determined draugr will always find a way to rise from the grave."

"But I did nothing to harm him. I only loved him. Why should he hurt me?"

"The undead return to finish the unfinished. The undead return for vengeance. The undead return for their own reasons."

A loose shutter slammed against the side of the house, and the broom they'd used to block the back porch clattered down the steps.

"Did you hear that?" gasped Celia.

"It is Gunnar," responded her aunt as she tossed a handful of salt into the air in front of them.

Both women tightened their grips on their weapons as the dragging, thumping sound of footsteps on the back porch grew louder, then stopped. The door handle jiggled.

"Do you think he'll be death black or corpse pale?" queried Celia in a quavering whisper.

"*Hel-Blár* or *nár fölr*? It matters not. Our actions must be the same," answered the fae-blessed old woman.

The two women stood and faced the draugr as the kitchen door swung open.

"Celia," the white-faced corpse slurred. "Celia."

And, as Celia had feared, there were maggots. Wads of squirming white fly-children oozed from the wounds on Gunnar's once handsome face where the canning machines had sliced into him. His longish blond hair was caked with dried blood and dirt. His feet were bare, and frayed red twine was still attached to the two big toes.

"Celia," the draugr who'd been Gunnar said again as he lifted something in his pallid hand.

"Lars," gasped Celia as she saw what dangled from her late husband's left fist by its thick white hair.

The moonlight bounced off of Lars Kettilson's exposed teeth. It appeared that the draugr had ripped his father's head from its body. Blood dripped from the ragged bit of neck attached to the head and from the sides of its mouth. Lars' blue eyes were wide open and glassy. His face had a surprised expression on it.

"It would seem Lars Kettilson should have extinguished his lights," noted Rona.

Though she couldn't tear her eyes away from the grisly trophy in the draugr's left hand to look at her aunt's face, the tone of the old woman's voice indicated she was happy with the way things had turned out for Lars. Slowly, Celia's gaze drifted over to what the draugr Gunnar clasped in his right hand. She gulped down a scream. It was a heart, not unlike the sheep hearts she'd seen in the village butcher shop. But Celia knew this heart didn't belong to a sheep.

The draugr nodded at them, turned around, shuffled through the kitchen door onto the porch. He paused, turned, and beckoned the women to follow him with the hand that held his father's heart.

"Do as he asks," urged Rona as she stepped beyond the ring of salt at their feet.

Celia followed her aunt's example, though she still gripped the ax tightly. "What does Gunnar want?"

"We shall find out," answered Rona the fae-blessed. "We shall find out, indeed."

The women followed the draugr to their backyard fire-pit where earlier they'd stacked wood soaked in oil in readiness for the ritual to send a soul back to the realm of the dead after zombification.

The draugr Gunnar surveyed the readied bonfire and grunted. He tossed his father's head and heart onto the wood, and then, knelt beside the fire-pit. He turned his mangled, maggoty face up to gaze at his wife and slurred, "Celia, save me."

"I can't," she responded. Her eyes burned. Her throat constricted. The ax in her hands felt heavy and awkward. "I can't."

"But I can," said Rona as she grabbed the ax handle, lifted the woodsman's tool, swung it horizontally, and lopped off the draugr's head.

The head bounced, then rolled to a stop three or four meters away. The draugr's body toppled over, spilling a stream of black blood and maggots at their feet.

"Gunnar," Celia screamed, then reached for his body. But the sight of the wriggling maggots kept her from touching him.

"Bring a lit splinter from the fireplace," ordered her aunt.

Celia's feet seemed frozen to the ground.

"Now," shouted Rona.

She ran into the house, pulled a piece of kindling that burned brightly from the fireplace, and hurried back to her aunt. While she was gone, Rona had used her knife to carve out Gunnar's heart. She tossed it onto the ready-to-be-lit bonfire beside Gunnar's head and Lars' head and heart as Celia handed her the kindling.

*"Gunnar Kettilson, rest now beneath the sod.*
*Your wife is safe and will bear you a child..."*

Celia gasped at the words. She'd told no one but Gunnar of her belief that she was pregnant.

Her uncannily wise aunt smiled at her, nodded, and then continued the chant:

*"Your last deed was a necessary act.*
*Depart in peace, and do not look back."*

In a harsher tone, Rona the fae-blessed continued.

> *"Lars Kettilson rot beneath the grass.*
> *You showed kindness to none.*
> *And none will mourn as you pass.*
> *Go to your new world,*
> *Cursed and despised.*
> *May you suffer and burn*
> *'Till the stars leave the skies."*

Celia's aunt drew a sign in the air with her forefinger, tossed the flaming kindling onto the well-laid, well-oiled bonfire. It flared into a roaring inferno.

"Help me," she instructed Celia.

The women loaded Gunnar's decapitated body onto a sledge and dragged it back to the cemetery. They pushed the headless corpse into its open grave. Rona withdrew a small vial of water from a nearby holy well and sprinkled it on Gunnar's remains.

> *"Blessed Mother,*
> *Purify this good man's flesh.*
> *Let him sleep in peace*
> *'Till the final awakening."*

Celia and Rona sang as they pushed soil on top of Gunnar's body. When the corpse was covered, they returned to their house. And though the sledge was easier to drag without the weight of Gunnar's body, Celia's feet felt leaden as she neared the bonfire.

"When all that is left are embers, we'll shovel them into buckets, place the buckets on the sledge, and drag the ashes and embers to the sea," explained her aunt. "There, we'll toss them into the waves."

> *"To be scrubbed and scattered*
> *to be pounded and purified,"*

chanted Celia.

"Yes, my dear, and then we'll find Lars' body. Have a quick service and burial. No open coffin. No questions."

"Won't people want to know what happened?"

"People will know what happened, though none will ever speak of it save on icy winter nights when sea winds wail, cold trees tap at the window, and children huddle around the hearth begging for stories of ghosts and trolls and draugar."

"It doesn't seem fair. Gunnar could have been a good man."

"Gunnar was a good man," Rona assured her. "He crawled from his grave to see to it that you and his child would be provided for, and I dare say that his spirit will hover close to you all the days of your life."

Celia watched the fire consume the wood, oil, and flesh of the Kettilson men. She shook her head. "I think you're overly romantic, Auntie."

"Perhaps Celia, Mistress of Kettilson keep."

"What?"

"You're the grieving daughter-in-law of Lars, widow of Gunnar, and soon-to-be-mother of Gunnar's child. You'd better get used to the title."

"I didn't consider…."

"No, but I think Gunnar did," replied Rona the fae-blessed as she nodded at Gunnar's shade standing guard, even now, beside his beloved Celia.

# The Ferry

Kathleen Crow

Zombies can't swim. They can float, what with all the gases being released from their rotting flesh, but they can't swim. And, saints be praised, fish like to eat them. So if they're in the water for any length of time, they quickly become a non-threat.

On land, they're still incredibly deadly. They're not overly fast or smart, but they are relentless. Worse yet, they rarely ramble alone. So if you run into one, chances are there are probably fifty more of its closest buddies stumbling somewhere around the next corner.

The radio has been advising survivors to find the closest island they can in order to regroup. The problem, however, is that with survivors moving toward large lakes and the coasts so are the zombies. Another dilemma is that most islands can only sustain a finite amount of people. Life has become rather problematic over the last few weeks.

Word is that Vancouver Island is still accepting survivors. According to news bulletins, a ferry docks in Vancouver for exactly five minutes once a week. They change the day and time each week because no one knows if zombies have memories or not, but there's no point in having a set time if all it's going to do is allow the zombies to graze at their leisure.

Once the ferry has picked up that week's survivors, it goes to one of the smaller islands where everyone is given a complete physical. Anyone found with a bite mark of any type is automatically shot.

## ★ 84 Kathleen Crow

Everyone else is allowed to go to the main island.

In the past I've always considered the northwest a little dreary for my tastes, but now I'm all about the cloudy skies and cool weather.

I look at my newly looted watch. I'm not proud of the fact I stole it, but after missing last week's ferry by fifteen minutes, I swallowed my pride and robbed an abandoned jewelry store.

Peering through my binoculars, I spy other survivors hiding like I am. There's a family of five hiding in a store almost directly across the street from me: parents, two teenagers and a toddler. About a hundred yards behind them, in the mouth of an alleyway, are four fairly scruffy looking boys, probably teenagers or early twenties. I can't help but wonder if there are any other survivors hiding, waiting, praying.

I turn the binoculars toward the ocean and find the ferry moving slowly toward us. I figure it'll dock in about three minutes.

Looking across the street, I wave my arms once and catch one of the teenager's attention. I raise three fingers. She grabs her father's arm and points in my direction. I hold my hand up so that he can see what I'm saying. Once he nods, I look further down the street and flash my fingers at the boys in the alleyway. They nod as one.

When the boat is five hundred yards from the dock, I stand. I know the others can wait a little longer, but my age is going to work against me. I need all the lead time I can get. I move as quickly as I can toward the pier.

As the ship gets closer, the motor grows louder and, despite it being noisy enough to wake the dead, I can hear moaning behind me. The undead know a dinner bell when they hear one.

I pick up the pace, ignoring my knees as they scream in protest. "Now!"

Seconds later, the family races past me. The teenage girl is sobbing as she runs, but she's not letting her emotions slow her down at all.

"Hurry!" the father shouts at me as he runs past.

I can hear the running footfalls of the group of young men coming quickly up behind me.

The ferry's engines are thrown into full reverse as the boat glides into place beside the cement dock.

I hear more moaning emanating from side streets, sounding almost like gleeful anticipation; but I refuse to look, keeping my gaze on my goal.

The mother makes the mistake of looking and trips over debris in the street. Somehow she manages to land on her back, keeping the screaming toddler safe.

"No! Keep running!" the father yells at his teenagers as they start to slow down.

One of the boys behind me races past me and scoops the toddler into his arms, never breaking stride. A second one grabs the mother's arms and yanks her to her feet, before he continues after his friend.

The mother's face is one of horror as she looks behind us. The third boy grabs her arm and forces her to turn and run. The fourth grabs my hand. "No one's dying today," he tells me. "Move your ass."

I can see men and women on the ferry, aiming their rifles over our heads. The sound of bullets hitting flesh behind me is much closer than I'd hoped.

"Come on!" people are yelling.

The father and the teenagers are already on the boat.

"Full reverse!" I hear one of the men on the upper deck bellow.

"Mom!" the teenage girl screams, while her father and brother restrain her.

The boy with the toddler dashes onto the boat, with his friend at his side. The mother and third boy have enough momentum that they simply jump the distance as the boat slowly retreats.

"Go on!" I tell the young man beside me. "No point in both of us dying."

He looks like he wants to argue, but I give him a shove. Being a gentleman is only going to get him dead. He puts his head down and runs with all his might. His leap is one of beauty, something that would've been a great dramatic moment in a movie.

I keep jogging, knowing there's only certain death if I stop.

The ferry is almost to the end of the pier as I step foot onto it, but I grit my teeth and keep moving. When I focus on the boat, I see a dozen people on the back end with life preservers in their hands.

God love them. When I reach the end of the pier, I dive into the frigid ocean and swim almost twenty feet underwater before I surface. My backpack tries to pull me down, but life preservers swarm around me. I grab two and am practically yanked from the water.

★ 86 Kathleen Crow

The boy who ran beside me earlier kneels by me. "That was cutting it a bit close."

I grin. "Close only counts with horseshoes and nuclear bombs. Not zombie apocalypses."

# necessary items for surviving the zombie apocalypse

fishhooks
needle & thread
chlorine tablets
blankets
underwear (two pair)
extra newspaper
cake (cut into six parts)
rubber tire
lightning rod
mason jar
handle of bourbon
matches
rags & old t-shirts
hatchet
gas mask
flairs (x2)
headphones
walkman
old Guns & Roses CD ("Appetite for Destruction")
windup flashlight
shortwave radio
Goji berries
box of hope
clear vision
book of Hopi wisdom
guitar strings
collected works of Adrienne Rich
compass
unwavering compassion
star chart
maps (topographic)
map of the human heart
belief (in anything)
whispers, joy
seeds, sparks, candlelight

—Brian E. Langston

## Painting of a Zombie

You weren't at the bloody crossing
when the song of rails announced
the thunderous entry of passing souls,
you can't hear the roaring in my ears,
the sound that rolls through time,
so many centuries of pain.

I was there, I heard it all quite well
without opening my eyes, without a breath.
We are the victims, sorry that you won't
live long enough to see past our faces,
our pale eyes rolling east to west,
our endless moans, but that's our way.

My hair has lost it's color, as have I.
We are one in the same, framed
by an unknown artist's brush strokes
against the canopy of endless night.

—Marge Simon

# Beyond the Shed

Beyond the shed:
the vacant world.

Once there was a moral man
who taught his sons respect,
saying, "that is someone's child."

Now, someone's father
is in my shed, confined
by chains around his raging
neck. His fingernails
like rotting bark, clawing
at the flap of dog door I slip
raw meat through. Respect
the appetites; even at the end
of the world, they are still
the most truthful of things.

After dinner, groaning toward
the vacant world, a zombie dreams
of hunting with uninhibited
and unrepentant instincts.

—John McCarthy

# Zombie Love

## Gene Stewart

Rain slashed at the windshield wipers as Byron Craid's 18-wheeler splashed through yet another hubcap-deep puddle. He kept expecting to skid into the swamp on either side of the road, so violent were the gusts of wind. And the macadam was crumbling on either side, he could see that much every time the lightning ignited the sky.

He drove slowly, but visibility was down to almost nothing now and his stomach was growling and he could use a couple beers, too, and maybe some shuteye back in the sleeper. It had been ten hours since he'd last pulled off the road, but this stretch of Louisiana wasn't likely to offer up much in the way of rest stops. He sighed and drove on, hoping to keep the rig on the narrow two-lane, hoping no deer or possum scuttled out in front of him, and hoping no teenagers out for a joyride came around a blind curve into his lights. So far, he'd been lucky and had seen no other traffic at all.

No surprise there, he thought. Swamp folks drive boats.

A few minutes and a few miles later, as he yawned, he spotted the neon glow of a sign through a blur of rain. A bar, looked like, and at once his mouth itched for a beer. He slowed even more, squinting, trying to spot a parking lot. He figured the muddy pond in front of the place was probably the lot. Either that or several pick-'em ups and an old tail-fin Caddy had all decided to go for a stormy night's swim.

He swung the rig into the lot and found the far right side big enough to let him park. He let the engine idle for a moment, considering letting it run while he went in for a beer and maybe a burger, or what ever gumbo a dive like this might serve. Then he figured he might be sitting inside a long time, and shut off the rig. That way he could take his time, rest up.

Didn't pay to push your luck on a night like this, he figured.

As soon as he popped open the cab door he was soaked, and his right heel slipped off the chrome step as he swung himself out. Good thing he was holding onto the chrome handle. He dangled for a second, then regained his footing and clambered down, slamming the door shut as his boots splattered water and mud.

He patted his keys, a comfortable lump in his front jeans pocket, as he dashed toward the ramshackle building. It was unpainted and, as Craid got close, smelled of old fish, stale cigars, and tarred rope. There was also a whiff of something sweeter that made him want to gag, but he couldn't place it.

It was a bit more than a shack, but only because official shacks have only one room. This had two, with a half-wall separating them. As Craid entered he was on the rightward side of the place, where the bar stood. Some tables and chairs were scattered on the bare wood floor, people at them sipping beers and talking quietly to the strains of Randy Travis singing about lost love and other eternal truths.

Craid got a few looks but none lingered. He was a trucker, beer belly under a white tee shirt, an open light-blue denim work shirt over that, sleeves rolled to the elbow, jeans, square-toed boots, and a trucker's wallet with a chrome dog-choker chain.

His hair was Elvis long, but out of his face, and black. Hadn't been combed since his last motel room, which was about three nights back, somewhere in Tennessee he thought.

The floor creaked and some of the boards wobbled as he strode to the bar and slid an ass-cheek onto a cracked red leatherette swivel stool. "Beer."

The barkeep, a younger man, slender and blond, with pale gray eyes and a scar across the bridge of his nose from some knife-fight he'd probably won, served up a bottle of Bud without hesitation. "Passin' through?"

No, I'm homesteading, gonna live right here in your bar. "Yep. Got a load of old furniture." Craid sipped the beer from the bottle, having been offered no glass. He looked around, noticed several more men in the room to the left, where a pool table listed steeply to one side. He heard the crack of pool balls as someone broke. "You're doing pretty good business, considering the weather."

The barkeep smirked, the left side of his mouth jiggling upward as if itchy. "We do all right most nights."

"You got anything to eat?"

"Might can grill you up a burger, if that'd do."

"Do me fine, I'd appreciate it. Make it two."

The barkeep walked to a door, pushed it open, and yelled something. He came back. "Like an order of shrimp with them burgers?"

"Sounds fine."

The barkeep stayed where he was, having apparently already ordered the shrimp to be deep fried. Craid figured maybe they'd get eaten one way or the other anyway, with this crowd.

As he sipped the beer, Craid noticed two younger men, looking nervous, coming toward him from the pool room. Each carried a bottle of beer and the way they walked, it wasn't the first they'd had that evening. Craid kept himself relaxed, outwardly, but braced for trouble. Sometimes the local boys got bored, he knew, and used passers-through for entertainment.

Instead of hassling him, though, the two didn't even acknowledge Craid. Instead, they each dug in their pockets, then set their bottles of beer on the bar with money under them.

Craid noticed that each guy had put down more than a hundred dollars. Had they drunk that much beer? Lost a bet?

"Uh, Harley, we decided t'try it."

"You boys sure, now?" The barkeep didn't move to pick up the money, but had his hands near it.

Craid glanced at the younger men. Their eyes were big, and they breathed fast and shallow. They were excited. Maybe aroused, he thought, not glancing down to confirm the suspicion.

The taller, darker one said, "We're sure. Set us up, huh?"

"Okay, guess it's a free country." He reached under the bar and came up with an unlabeled bottle. It was clear glass and held a clear liquid.

Moonshine, Craid bet.

The barkeep poured two shots, and the younger men, who wore

jeans and plaid shirts, slammed them down. Each shuddered and one gagged but held on when his pal slapped him on the back.

"Okay, now what? We gotta wait?"

The barkeep said, "Nope. Just go on down, take your pick, and have your fun. But you damage the goods, you replace 'em. Remember that and you'll do fine."

The younger men laughed and traded looks. They slapped each other on the back and punched each other's shoulders. They moved past Craid to a narrow door set to one side of the bar. The door had no handle, but popped open as they stood before it. Pulling it all the way open, they entered a dark space and the door, as if on springs, slammed shut after them.

Above the door a crude sign, made with a wood-burning kit, read:

ZOMBIE LOVE

Craid's lower belly stirred. Whores?

He instantly wondered if he could even remember the last time he'd gotten laid. Since the divorce and Sally's remarrying, he hadn't exactly been Mr. Bachelor About Town.

He watched the barkeep count up the money. Looked like two hundred each. A bit steep for whores who'd work in a dive like this, but then again, maybe it was something special. You found some interesting variants in out-of-the-way places sometimes, he knew. Most truckers knew that much after their first trip across country.

His burgers arrived, with a mess of deep-fried shrimp in a basket and plenty of hot sauce. Slices of fresh onion and crisp lettuce leaves livened the burgers, along with a nice barbecue seasoning with cajun bite to it. He ate in something akin to bliss for awhile, and managed to swallow another beer, too.

But the notion of getting his ashes hauled, as the old saying went, kept niggling at him. He felt that old breathless eagerness deep down, and knew damned well he could afford it, too; his wallet was fat from cashing a check just a few days ago at that motel. Although he used plastic for most of his expenses, he always carried plenty of cash, just in case.

As he sat deciding, the two young men came back out through the narrow ZOMBIE LOVE door. Each looked stunned, and somewhat humbled. In subdued voices, they asked the barkeep for beers.

The barkeep grinned his one-sided smile and set two beers down. He glanced under the bar, nodded when a faint green light glowed, then pulled up another bottle, this one dark brown glass. From it he poured two dark brown shots. "Here, boys, on the house. Celebrate a little."

They thanked him and slammed down the shots.

Craid couldn't get over how amazed and gentled they looked. He'd seen that expression and demeanor on young guys coming out of good bordellos before, and knew it usually meant one of two things. Either the boys had just then become men, or there was something truly special in their recent past.

This thought got him revved up. He decided to go for it, figuring he needed the release and the rest after. As the two younger guys took their beers to the pool area, where a slow, quiet game continued, Craid dug out his wallet and found two hundred-dollar bills. He folded them and placed them under his empty beer bottle.

The barkeep, who'd been at the far end serving more beers to a pig farmer and his son who'd just come in, their bib overalls stained with more than mud to judge by the pig farm smell, ambled back to Craid, then froze as he noticed the money under the beer bottles. He looked up into Craid's eyes, saying nothing. Then, leaning in, he touched the money with his fingertips and said, "You sure, mister?"

"I'm sure I'd like to find out."

The barkeep held Craid's gaze for a few instants longer, then gave a slight nod. "House rules are, you damage the goods, you replace 'em."

He'd heard this before. "Seems fair enough." He winked. "No other rules?"

The barkeep's grin quivered. "Nope. Do whatcha want, them zombies don't care."

"Zombies."

The barkeep made the money vanish, set the empties under the bar, and pulled up the clear bottle. He poured a shot and slid it toward Craid. "On the house."

"Moonshine?"

Another flip of the grin's tail. "You could say."

What the hell, even that little bit of rubbing alcohol would do no harm, he figured. Bottoms up. It tasted like straight grain alcohol strained through the farmers' stained overalls, then seasoned with something sweet, like allspice or cinnamon. About took off the top of his head, but he held it down. "Wow, got a kick."

"It do that, yes sir." The barkeep pointed to the door.

"Zombies, huh? Is that the gimmick?"

"No gimmick. They's zombies, all right. Pure an' simple. Feelin' no pain, but don't be markin' 'em up. Remember the house rules."

Did the girls take ice baths and use body make-up? Did they play dead for you? Was that the draw? He started fantasizing about trying to get a reaction out of a pro who was paid to play dead, and some of his ideas got a hold of him. He got off the stool and headed for the narrow door, thinking that this could be exciting, if a bit strange.

The door popped open. He figured the barkeep had a foot pedal that released the latch. He pulled it open and at once felt a draft of cooler air. It smelled dank, too, like a closed-up cellar. There was just a hint of tainted meat to the slate and moss smell, and Craid mentally saluted the clever bastards for having thought to leave a burger lying around to add ambiance.

He stepped through the narrow door labeled ZOMBIE LOVE and found himself in darkness. He paused, and his eyes adjusted to a faint green and blue glow on the walls. Looked like mold of some kind, maybe lichen.

It gave just enough light to show him the stairs leading down, at the bottom of which he came to a rightward corridor. A faint light, a forty watt bulb painted dark blue, glowed at the far end of the short corridor, which was made of cheap fiberboard paneling of the kind found in doublewide living rooms all across the great United States.

The scents intensified, but he breathed through his mouth and it didn't bother him. He reached the blue light, which was mounted above a closed door. He turned the brass knob, which felt slightly sticky.

Inside he found a room full of naked people, mostly women but some men. All stood expressionless and motionless, their backs to the four walls, their hands at their sides.

For some reason Craid was greatly aroused by this, and went about choosing his partner carefully, examining each woman. Some were older, some barely of legal age. Some sagged, others were pert, and one was quite heavy, but with a serene face, as if happy to be so fat. None wore makeup, and none reacted to him as Craid stood before them and boldly looked them up and down.

He reached out and touched a girl's breast.

Ice cold, it held his finger marks for a few seconds. In the dim blue light, it looked like bruises slowly fading.

He leaned down and kissed the nipple.

It was so cold he recoiled, but the girl did not react.

"Is that your choice, sir?"

Craid started and turned to find a woman in a long silk gown, her black hair flowing over her shoulders, her eyes aglow. She was not a zombie, and at once Craid pegged her for the barkeep's wife. Made sense. Every bordello needs a madame to keep things running smoothly.

"Uh, yeah. This one." She looked maybe twenty, with dark brown hair to her shoulders, deep brown eyes that never seemed to blink, a tilted back nose, full lower lip, and knockout knockers just the handful he enjoyed. Her belly was flat, her legs long. Her skin tone, although sallow, was firm.

"Please take her by the hand, and lead her through here." The madame gestured to a beaded curtain in one corner. "You may use any unoccupied room for as long as you wish, and please remember the house rules."

There was only one that he knew of, but he nodded. He took the icy hand and led the girl, who walked smoothly enough, through the beaded curtain. With a shudder he noticed that she didn't blink or wince when a string of beads touched her left eye; amazing control, he thought. Yoga, must be something like that.

He entered another hallway with doors on either side. Some stood ajar, others were tightly shut. He took the first one to the left that was ajar, and found in it a rickety old mahogany bed, not unlike the antique junk he was hauling just then, and a lamp on a plain wooden bedside table. Beside the lamp was a wash basin with water in it, a pitcher with more water, and a folded white towel. A container of hand lotion stood by the lamp.

"All the comforts of home, huh?" He had let go of the girl's hand as they'd entered the room. She now stood, expressionless, just inside.

He had to move her to get the door shut.

He guided her to the bed, then had to push her to make her sit. She nearly tumbled off the edge, but he lay her back, copping a quick feel along the length of her body. Damn, she is cold, he thought. Must be the cellar air, which was, in truth, quite cool.

"So what's your name? It's okay, you can drop the act now, we're okay in here."

The girl lay exactly as he'd positioned her, gazing up past his shoulder. She said nothing.

He frowned, then leaned down, placing an ear to her lips. She was breathing, he found, but very slowly and deeply. Yoga, he decided. Had to be. Maybe self-hypnosis thrown in.

His eagerness was confused now with puzzlement and, yes, a touch of concern. He wanted to make out with her, she was so beautiful, but this dead act was creeping him out a bit. Could he go with it, and experience it as a kind of fake necrophilia?

In his home town in Virginia when he was growing up a local undertaker had been caught with a body, and the rumors had been both lurid and somehow obscene. He'd never felt such an urge, himself, but this tempted him, it surely did. He found he was hard, and wanted to give it a try.

He started undressing; then, as an experiment, placed the girl's arm up, as if she were reaching for the rough stucco ceiling.

The arm stayed up.

He got undressed and began fondling her, and discovered he was breathless. Felt like a young buck, and his heart hammered now, even as a deep languor came into his muscles, relaxing him. The moonshine and beers, he figured, were helping.

He lubed up, then found he had to adjust her, moving her legs and even hefting her rump and rearranging her shoulders. It was during these clumsy maneuvers that he spilled her onto the floor.

"Oh shit, no." He jumped up, leaned down. "You okay?"

But she had not reacted to this, either.

He grabbed her arm. "Come on, up, honey." He tugged on her and she came with the tug, and got awkwardly to her feet.

That's when he saw the gouge.

The blood rushed out of his head and, dizzy, he sat down. "Oh hell, no." She'd apparently hit the side of her face on the corner of the bedside table on the way down. Her cheekbone had shattered, her skin had ripped, and her eye partly dangled.

Craid's belly churned and he nearly threw up. "Oh, hon, I'm so sorry." He did not know what to do; call the madame? He stood, stepped toward the door, and as he touched the crystal doorknob he remembered the house rules.

This was going to cost him. If a girl earned two hundred a throw, and he'd made her unable to do that, then they'd want restitution for lost earnings. Over how long a period? he wondered. How long would a person work in such an odd job?

Maybe a month's earnings? A year's?

He forced himself to calm down. To think it through. It wasn't as if they could sue him for it. Hell, this couldn't be legal, could it? Not even in Louisiana.

That meant thugs.

He wondered if he could get out, and get to his truck, before anyone found out what he'd done. Would they come after him if he boogied down the road? Maybe, but maybe they wouldn't bother.

Craid decided to give it a try, forgetting all about why he'd come down here now. He was done, and knew it. So what if he hadn't gotten anything out of it? Cut losses and book, he told himself, dressing. He almost bolted when he realized it would look strange if he were done so soon.

He forced himself to sit there a good hour, beside the girl's body, every few minutes wondering if maybe he should just go ahead and have his way, get his jollies, might as well salvage something good out of this, but unable to bring himself even to look at her now. He'd noticed how the gouge wasn't bleeding much, just sort of seeping. Almost as if her blood were frozen.

That notion gave him chills.

Finally he could stand it no longer.

He eased open the door. Peering out into the hall, he saw a guy leading a zombie into another room. That door shut. He saw no one else, so he stepped into the hall. He walked quickly to the far end, hoping for an exit. There was only a blank wall.

He retraced, and decided to brazen it out.

Walking into the selection room, he smiled at the madame, pretending to be sheepish and a bit contrite. "Must've been too pent up, sort of jumped the gun."

"It happens all the time, think nothing of it."

"Thank you, ma'am. Kind of you." And he walked down the other hall, and climbed the narrow stairs, and as he reached for the narrow door it popped open.

He walked through the bar to the door without even glancing at the barkeep, who called, "Sir? Sir, can you wait a moment sir?"

He paused at the door. Glanced back, as if casual. He saw the barkeep grinning big-time now, the guy's creepy gray eyes almost glowing with a kind of feral amusement. "Enjoy yourself?" the barkeep asked.

"Sure did. Worth every penny."

"Another satisfied customer." The barkeep glanced down, and his grin quivered as a faint red light glowed, and then he looked back up. He was holding the brown bottle, but set it back under the bar. "You drive safely now, y'hear? And y'all come back soon."

"I surely will." Craid raised a hand in farewell and got the hell out of there.

He nearly ran to his truck, but he was so damned tired. His legs felt heavy, his head muzzy. Driving seemed like the last thing he should do, what with being so exhausted from the hours on the road, and so full of alcohol.

Climbing up, he unlocked the cab, kicked off as much mud as possible, and sat down. He considered just locking up and crawling into the sleeper compartment for a snooze.

They'll find her.

They'll be angry, and want paid, maybe even some revenge.

Why did you run, you idiot?

It's just money, hell, you earn enough to pay these swamp zombies off. Bunch of sick weirdoes anyhow…

The last thing he remembered about being in the truck was watching the rain, which was slowing considerably, make drops that mated, merged, and slid downward on the windshield.

Then his awareness merged with the night and slid downward.

He smelled the cellar again, the faint taint of rot, and the dank molds. He smelled, too, the spicy smell, like black pepper and cinnamon, like allspice and a wicked cayenne. He opened his eyes and found that they stayed open.

He'd expected to see the interior of his truck. Instead he saw the zombie selection room. And he was standing in it. He felt cold, but couldn't shiver.

And the house rules crossed his mind: You damage the goods, you replace 'em.

Not replacing by buying a new one or making good on lost earnings, no. Replacing by taking the place of the damaged goods.

He was now a zombie.

The madame, her long black hair and sharp hawk's eyes contrasting to the barkeep's blonde hair and dead gray eyes, came into his line of sight. "Oh, you're with us. Good. Naughty boy, trying to run out on us like that."

The barkeep appeared behind her, grinning. "Sold your truck for parts to m'cousin Ray. Oh, and that load of furniture? Some of it fit right in here." And he laughed.

The madame came closer. "In case you wonder? That clear drink is what makes you this way. The brown one? Antidote. If you were a good boy and didn't damage the goods, you would've gotten that, too. But you tried to run off after what you did to poor Cindy-Lou. And we cain't have that, now can we?"

At least he knew her name, now.

He wished he could cry but found that his metabolism was just too damned slowed down.

In misery, he wondered what fate could possibly be worse, which was a kind of cosmic cue for the pig farmer to stomp down those narrow stairs, march across the selection room floor, and stand in front of Craid, saying, "Had m'eye on this pretty boy ever since I come in lass night."

Craid found himself wondering what happened to damaged zombies, and figured the gators in the swamp out back were fat and sassy enough to give him a solid answer.

Eventually.

# Hot August Night

Nobody knows I belong to Brother Love's Show.
It's a secret we've got, him and me—I'm singing
loud and sweet behind him in the choir,
'till intermission, when I change into a whore.

Then when he calls for souls to save, I come
waltzing in, red hot as an August night,
my hair teasy-pleasey down my breasts,
a dress with seams strained to bursting—

Certainly I'm never first, and never last, but
I'm the one they'll remember best, of course,
a sheep strayed from the fold, but quickly saved—
it's played that way, by Brother Love.

Very true he's crazy, but I love him just the same.
Love the way he tries to help the uninfected,
disconnected refugees from zombie land.
Nobody knows I'm part of Brother Love's Show,
and by the time we're all dead, none will care.

—Marge Simon

# Remnants of the Insensitive

Blue mangling green.
What else could be attributed
to her admirers who just stood there.
Her long lashes dripping blood.
And all takers underestimating.
I miss her flesh,
the cooking sounds she danced to.
Her arrhythmic lectures on stability
and her lovers who ate the food.

—Colin James

# Night of Passions

M. Alan Ford

I had never felt so strange. I could not move well, as if my limbs had frozen and were only now beginning to thaw, and a sensation at once painful and tingling crawled across my skin. It had started a moment before at my head, it seemed, and moved slowly in a flush down my body, taking with it the creakiness in my joints and the stiffness that moments before had afflicted the muscles of my arms and legs. I was not content where I lay. Rather I felt victim to an agitated turmoil, a longing to throw away prudence and leap to action despite the lassitude of my body and the cloud presently evaporating in steps from my brain. And I was certain I had heard voices not a moment before. One I was sure I recognized, though who it might have been escaped me, as most other memories seemed to have done. The other said, at least as I perceived it, "He is the puppet and this is the string."

The words, however, were thickly accented. On reflection I thought they might be more accurately portrayed as, "He da poppet an' dis da string," a dialect of those living more southerly than De Soto Parish, and a cause for alarm had I then realized I was in De Soto Parish and what was happening to me there. In any case, I eventually satisfied the troubled restlessness in my mind by sitting up and gazing about. It was night, and the darkness contributed to the dimness of my vision even as the veil fell from it. Trees above tangled their branches together and moved them about in a warm breeze, sounding to my ears like the tumble of water against a distant river's edge, though it came sharper and clearer even as the seconds passed. By the color of the turning leaves, I thought the season to be late summer, the warmth of it waning and tending toward cold autumn. I wore black boots and gray slacks, and my hands peeking out from the gray material of my sleeves appeared parched and darkened, as if I had recently spent far too much time in the open sunlight. This was all I cared to study, because at that moment I felt such a longing for home and bedside that I put all else from my mind and rose unsteadily to my feet.

Some yards away was an open iron gate fixed in a stone wall. This I made for with all the certitude of a priest in search of God. Beyond it I found a well-worn dirt road lined on either side with trees and hedgerows, and directly ahead a small store with doors locked and the only light a reflection of stars in its windows. At that moment I still had no concept of where I was, or even my own name, but I turned to the left and stumbled along as if I knew my direction. I moved with difficulty, the muscles in my legs still stubborn and the cloud in my head still throwing my thoughts into a forgetful void. I passed by houses here and there, spying through the windows the occasional family engaged in their evening meal, unaware of my progress in the darkness of the road, though one man leading a horse in the other direction paused in his steps as I passed, at first giving me a nod through the shadows, and then a startled gaze when I showed interest only in continuing my journey.

Bits of memories slowly came to me. First came my name, which was Mister Allen Griffen, late of the Third Infantry, and a gunnery lieutenant under a captain by the name of Johnson. I recalled more when I turned a familiar corner in the road and came upon a row of houses that had suffered under a devastating barrage. Most were completely destroyed, some only half so, and all burned and charred and marked by gunfire, as were the stone walls and fields surrounding them. I recalled at that moment not only my name and rank, but the march last year of General A. J. Smith and his army through the countryside and on to Mansfield. And only weeks ago, it seemed, came news of our surrender. This was truly as devastating to me as Smith's damage to the parish and the pillage of his army in their passing, and had I not by some mania been so determined to continue my journey through the dead night, I would have fallen to my knees and broken down in tears there in the road. All around me, the South lay in ruins, defeated and lifeless as if General Sherman's march had been a sword that had cut us in two.

I continued my own march for some time, past the carcass of my neighborhood, past fields denuded by fire and empty barns with their walls collapsed in on themselves, until I turned into a lane familiar to me in the dark. The gate was firmly locked, but I knew of a low point in the wall, hidden from the road by bushes, over which I easily climbed. As I came down the other side, a dog somewhere on the property set up a clamor, and I recognized the animal's voice. It was Jimbol, my own pet, barking at what he thought was an intruder. I must have been grinning from ear to ear as I made off for the house hoping to meet him. He came bounding through a stand of trees, but he did not greet me as friend and master. He paused, lowered his head at the sight of my outstretched arms, and bared his teeth with a growl. And in my head I heard what seemed to be a voice. It did not speak so much as enter my thoughts, and in that foreign accent it said, "Fight da dog! Keel da dog!"

Jimbol lunged at that moment. He had been trained to bring intruders down by the throat, and knowing this I took him about the neck to keep him from my own and held him high in the air. He sank his teeth firmly into my forearm. I suddenly felt searing pain, not only in that wound but somewhere across my abdomen, as if I was the body General Sherman's sword had thrust into and that injury had ripped open again, but I was too fully consumed by a sense of self-preservation to think much of it. Jimbol thrashed about in my grip, doing damage to my arm and threatening to struggle from my grasp. I had no wish to harm him, only to restrain his attack, but I nevertheless forced my thumbs deep into the flesh of his neck. I could not stop them. Jimbol's barks and growls turned to choking cries as I felt the structure of his throat crack beneath my fingers. After long moments of struggle, sheltered from sight by the stand of trees, he died in my grip, until finally I dropped the body of the loyal dog who had sat contented at my feet so many nights by the fire.

I was so overtaken by fear and surprise that I did not notice the lack of blood that should have stained the shredded cloth of my arm. I simply stood for a long time in stunned silence, until I felt the urgency to move once again, and did so, by stepping past the body and through the trees.

I came upon the house sidelong, among tall bushes before a window from which lamplight flickered. The pain of the wounds where Jimbol had bitten me, and of the unknown injury in my abdomen, fled from my mind as I approached the window, because in the parlor beyond I spied a woman sitting before a fire, her attention held so firmly by a book open in her lap she seemed oblivious to all else. She sat in a pool of light cast by a single oil lamp on the table beside her, like a painting in a frame, had the artist been a master of grace and loveliness. I recognized her, of course, as Suzanna, my recent bride, and with that recollection came another close on its heels, that of Zachary Overton Moore. The flood of memories triggered by those names almost overwhelmed me.

I recalled Mister Moore as one who had stayed absent from the War, it was rumored, through family influence, while his brothers fought and died. Moore, as I had learned upon our defeat, had proposed marriage to my Suzanna at a time when she thought I would never return. The toll of the War had thinned her prospects, as it were, and she had nearly acceded to his proposal, only to reverse herself on my return as a minor hero in the greater theater of battle.

My fists clinched at the thought of him, even as I recalled my betrothal in the weeks after the sad news of the War's end. It had been a bright spot in the darkness of defeat that gladdened us despite the misery all about. We had spent those weeks moving her belongings into my homestead. It was a small property compared to others in the neighborhood, but one from which we might start a family and build a life afresh. I'd had the foresight during the last months of the War to gather gold and Union notes, Confederate money being worthless, and she must have been living these few weeks on the treasure I had sequestered in the house.

Concern for her well-being and the rushing warmth of love overcame me in that moment. I had guessed by now what had happened to me, if not by what means, and I wondered what had happened to her. Before the start of the War, I had released what little chattel I'd owned in a conciliatory gesture taken by too few others in the South. The remaining house and land had surely passed into her hands, but did she live as a spinster now? Or had she turned to Moore's arms, once again driven by need? Or was she living here alone, unsure of her next step, and still grieving over the loss of me?

I realized that by the angle at which I stood, I could see myself partially in reflection from the glass. What I saw shocked me to the core. I still wore the gunnery lieutenant's uniform, down to insignia and hat, in which I had no doubt been buried. But the skin of my face had grown stretched and dry, its color darkened to resemble those I had released from servitude five years before, the hair bristling stiff and coarse from under the hat, the eyes sunken deep in their sockets, the lips peeled back tight across yellowed teeth. All the stories I had heard, assaulting me like demons from my childhood, had not prepared me for this. That such creatures were dull and stupid, sluggish in movement and void of thought, I now knew to be false. Everything was enhanced. The pain in my arm and gut, the surge of love for Suzanna, the inexplicable rage with which I had attacked my dear and loyal Jimbol, even the thoughts of defeat in our efforts at succession, all I felt as keenly now, even magnified, as the thrust and twist of a knife sent repeatedly into my body.

And why should they not? The brain as well as the body was of material constitution. If muscles should come alive to provide movement, and eyes sight and ears hearing, why then should the brain not come alive to provide thoughts and passions? I had the evidence before me. I felt love more strongly then ever. And passionate anger, and the crushing weight of defeat.

And, not least of all, the craving for revenge.

Despite their efforts, I retained some personal volition. With blackened fingers I raised the hem of my jacket and yanked the shirt from my belt. There I found the source of my pain, a deep slash from side to side just below the ribs, hastily stitched not in hopes of repair, but merely for superficial presentation. This as well seemed about to trigger recollections, but at that moment I happened to glance up through the window again, and there I saw Suzanna rising from her chair. The book now lay on the table as if she had just set it down, and she looked at me in hope and recognition, as if she could not believe I had returned. I wanted to speak, but did not know if I could. I wanted to tell her of my love for her, and that I would protect her against any threat, and all manner of things, but in that moment her expression changed to one of horror. She had not seen me clearly through the glass. Now, upon inspection, my countenance repelled her, and she stepped back until the cloth of her dress pressed against the chair.

In my mind I felt that alien voice again, and this time it seemed to say, "I tink he see her now." What that meant I did not know, but I succumbed to another episode of fury that surged up from my breast and out to each extremity. I had no explanation for it, but it compelled me to thrust my hands through the glass. It shattered and fell away, cutting my hands without blood, and despite my own will, I clambered over the sill and into the room. Suzanna, screaming, tried to back away once again and fell fully onto the chair. I do not recall it now, but I must have been screaming something incoherent through the anger that occluded my rationality, for she covered her ears as I approached. I most surely would have throttled her then and there, had she not come to her senses and sprang from the chair with an agility I could not match. She ducked under my arms and struggled through the open door into the hall, and I followed, despite willing all the while that my feet should remain still.

I remembered clearly that the nearest door to the outside was through the kitchen. And so I followed as she stumbled down the hall in fear. I lost sight of her briefly, as she had gained a few steps in her flight, but I knew I had guessed correctly when I turned into the kitchen. There I found her heaped on the floor, cast in dark shadows that flickered in the dance of a single, large lamp on the table, apparently a victim of the hem of her dress. She turned about as I entered, propped back on her elbows, and said, "Allen, what's took hold on you? Don't you know me?"

I wanted to call out that I did, but for answer, I reached down and grabbed her about the throat. I fancied I heard laughter as I pulled her into the air and pushed her against a cupboard where she choked beneath my fingers. As with Jimbol, my thumbs found her windpipe, and with all the vehemence that was foreign to me, I began to crush it.

At that moment the door opened and Charlie Mayes walked in. He was an older servant, the only one who had stayed at the house after I had set them free, and he did not at first see us struggling in the darkness beyond the lamplight. Suzanna could not speak and my attention was fully on her face. From the corner of my eye, I saw him close the door. He called out, as if he expected to find her elsewhere in the house, "I'm done with the shed, Miss Suzie," and he placed a ring of house keys on a peg beside the door.

All this passed beneath my notice, as my entire attention was consumed with the murder of my betrothed. Charlie turned about and gazed in shock at the tableau before him. Then he appeared confused, firstly as if his former master should not be killing that one's newlywed, and secondly that his former master should be there at all. He then strode the length of the kitchen and took hold of my arm, and only in that moment did I turn to acknowledge him.

The focus of my rage shifted in surprise to its new mark. I dropped Suzanna to the floor and engaged Charlie, the loyal domestic who had served my kin since my boyhood, who had taken the name of "Mayes" only because he had served in his childhood on the plantation of that family, and who had never gained the habit of calling Suzanna "Missus" as everyone else had after our marriage because it had sounded awkward to his ear. This was the man I grappled with as he called out, "Run, Miss Suzie!"

She did so, disappearing from the edges of my tunneled vision. Charlie was no shrinking violet, no frail flower of Southern womanhood, but a vital oak of a man who had spent his years at vigorous labor and could not so easily be brought down. He did, however, have a reluctance to harm his friend and former master, regardless of that person's situation. I suffered from a lack of such reluctance. We fought across the kitchen, toppling chairs and crockery and knocking the hat from my head, until I felled him with a blow and did him in by striking his head repeatedly against the floor. The sorrow of it would have overwhelmed me, had I been in my right mind. But I was not, and I gained my feet quickly, as if I had snuffed the life not from an old friend, but an insect I had stepped on without a thought. Instead of all due grief, I once again succumbed to a consuming rage that overtook me and compelled me to follow Suzanna out the door.

How long I searched for her, I do not know. Beyond our fields—dead now, pillaged as they were by northern soldiers—was a forest, and then a road lined with houses and barns half destroyed, and another forest farther on. Through this I wandered for a good part of the night, driven beyond my own will to find her, until I felt myself overcome by fatigue and sat down on a rock beside a small body of water. This I knew as a minor tributary of the Red River, a diminutive stream that fed a pool during the year and ceased its activity in the summer. The pool was drying now, trickling gradually into the larger river somewhere downstream, and would soon fade completely. For some time I sat listening to its whisper. Sounds were quieter now, ringing less sharply, and the stars above shone less brightly than they had hours earlier. Suddenly, without warning, I felt compelled to stand and did so quickly, then turned toward the road and made my way back through town by the same route I had come.

    I recognized the gate set in the stone wall as that through which I had originally ventured when first waking that night, and in the darkness and despite the gradual failing of my vision, I recognized as well the grounds toward which I now faced. It was the side entrance to a graveyard at the rear of a church, one I had passed many times on business and visited many times in my faith. This was unsurprising. The thing that brought me to pause was an open grave, the dirt piled inexpertly beside it and a coffin with the top pried off some feet away, and on the tombstone my own name with a date of expiration. I had no memory of how much time had passed since my entombment, though the weather was warmer and drier than I last recalled, and my house and fields dusty with neglect, and my own visage in the window not too far decayed. If pressed, I might therefore have guessed the period to be no more than a few weeks.

    I felt myself once again overcome with a peculiar, overpowering fatigue. The joints of my limbs felt stiff and inflexible, as if the muscles moving them were becoming stagnant. I attempted to kneel, but lost my balance and fell face down beside the grave. I should have been hurt, but curiously, I no longer seemed capable of feeling pain. Unable to right myself, I lay for some time with my nose in the cool grass, listening to my thoughts slow and dim as if, like the small body of water, they were gradually draining into some distant reservoir.

    I heard footsteps as if from a great distance. But then a strong hand grabbed my shoulder and turned me onto my back. The stars above appeared as dim as my thoughts, and fading. Vaguely, as through the veil, I saw two men, one tall and the other shorter, hanging above me.

"What all's happened heah?" one asked.

That voice I recognized. In a surge of final lucidity I recalled him. I remembered a beating at the hands of three hired cutthroats while he stood amusedly by, his clothes the cut of the country gentleman he had so often affected, and laughing as he said, "Don't y'all be breakin' bones, now. We'll need the body." The flash of a knife as one of them brought the ruckus to a halt with the threat of death. The other two holding me tight by the arms, and all of them looking to him for instruction. The slight smile beneath his tailored moustache, the firm nod of his head, and the cut of the knife across my abdomen. The chuckles of the whole party as they dragged me off, bleeding, from the road, in broad daylight, to cast me alone and mortally wounded into a ditch.

And I recalled his name. Zachary Overton Moore.

"I say, what's happened?" he called out again.

"Fo' why you ask me?" said the other. "I don see ever'ting gwan his head."

"Well law! I've a sight not to pay you 'till it's finished."

"Me, I finish, you wan give me time."

"More, yet?" I could not see him clearly, but in the darkness Zachary leaned down to peer at me closely. "She'll suffer and die, same as he done. You be sure of it!"

The shorter one laughed. His hands fiddled with something, then he said, as before, "He da poppet an' dis da string." He blew into my face a cloud of pale dust that scattered about. Moments later that peculiar tingling worked once again from my head to my extremities, and my muscles felt less stubborn and more vital, my thoughts came more abundantly, and the veil lifted slowly from my sight. In my renewed vigor I saw them a bit more clearly, Zachary's narrow figure and slim face still with the moustache, and his smaller companion, who stood with a stooped posture and wore the non-distinct clothes I associated with a beggar or street ruffian. He had with him a small leather bag, the drawstring of which he now pulled tight.

Still my eyes cleared and my limbs twitched. In the moments that my strength returned, so did my anger at Zachary. It came like fire into my mind, not an artificial rage from without, but truly from within, and I sat up straight and reached out for him. Zachary sprang back, frightened for the first time, and said, "Elijah!"

The stranger, known as Elijah, laughed all the louder. He said, "Stop it now!" I froze in response, my limbs becoming unbending steel, and Elijah said, "That man, he do carry on. I don' know what you done, but you got him riled like a rattlesnake what been stepped on."

I could not move. No matter how I strained for Zachary's neck, my arms went only so far and stopped. Zachary smiled, and putting hands on knees, he once again leaned over to look at me closely. "Allen, you're a pow'ful sight." He wrinkled his nose in disgust. "And a pow'ful smell, that's assured. You be a right nice gentleman and give my regards to Suzanna. Seein' as how y'all be travelling abroad on your nuptials, and I don't expect I'll be meetin' her again."

Elijah said to me, "You gwan 'ome, now," and I felt again that intractable compulsion. I rose and walked away from them, back out through the gate and up the road. All the while on my walk back through the night, I wondered if she had gone running off in terror from the house, possibly to find refuge at some neighbor's, or if out of loyalty to me she had returned, hoping to find conciliation with the form I had taken. In truth, I did not know how many of these thoughts were mine and how many were those of my adversaries. At the same moment in which one part of me wished her to be absent, another wished for her presence.

One thought, however, I knew to be my own. By no measure could they have planted in me such a thirst for revenge.

Upon reaching the house, I clambered once again over the wall and stalked once again past the body of Jimbol and through the trees. On this occasion, however, I made not for the window, but circled around the house and approached the kitchen door. The house still was lit with lamps, which told me nothing, but my excitement—or perhaps theirs—mounted when I found the kitchen door to be closed. It had been open on our flight from the house, which indicated she had indeed returned. Thinking my newlywed foolish beyond my recognition of her, I tested the doorknob and found it open, and entered the house a second time. I was relieved, however, to see the keys gone from the peg beside the door. I only glanced in that direction, not allowing my gaze to linger, for fear of their notice, and was rewarded when I continued across the kitchen without pause. My love had indeed returned to the house, but had removed herself quickly, or had done so after spying my second approach, for what need had she of the keys to the house while inside it? I felt satisfied I knew what they did not, which firstly protected her from my violence, and secondly afforded me the opportunity I needed to lead them astray.

In the light from the lamp on the table, I saw the body of Charlie Mayes laying quietly where I had left it, confirming that Suzanna had not yet sought assistance. Again without pause, but with an urgency I myself did not feel, I searched the house from top to bottom and found to my relief no sign of her. Their impatience must have been rising, because with each door I opened, with each stair I climbed and bedframe I peered under, the agitation grew within me, such that when the vital moment arrived I was so lost in frustration and anger that I nearly failed in my plans.

Just outside the kitchen was another door with a credenza standing beside it. Passing by this door, I turned my head to keep it in my gaze, hoping they would realize what lay behind had not yet been searched. I fretted as I continued on, knowing they would send me back out through the kitchen to prolong my search in the forest. But at the last moment, I suddenly felt an urgency to open the door. I stopped, turned about, and pulled it wide to reveal a wooden staircase descending into darkness.

They demanded light. I returned to the kitchen, took up the oil lamp and walked with it to the credenza, where I set it at such an angle that its rays lit the stairway. With my other hand, I reached out blindly for the knob of the open door, found the latch, and flipped it about so the door would remain locked should it close again. This I did quickly with two fingers, beneath notice, as I set the lamp down. Should they have gotten wind of it, or wondered why I relinquished the lamp rather than carry it down with me, all my plans would have come to naught. But there was light enough to see by, and they had no idea what the one hand had done while out of my sight, and so remained unawares as I descended the stairway.

Below was a basement and storeroom, neatly stacked with wooden chests, dusty furniture we'd had no use for, and the odd flotsam a house will collect. I searched the room and found nothing, but in the corner, behind an old couch and half covered with a blanket, lay a chest just large enough for a person to hide in. It would have gone unnoticed, had I not paused to glare at it for such a long moment that it gathered their attention. I was suddenly filled with victorious glee and an urge to thrust open the chest. I gripped it in both hands and with a great heave pulled it to the center of the room, for it was quite heavy and took all my strength to move. They should have seen it was secured with a padlock, but in the rush of my actions and their sense of victory, they had no time to coerce me otherwise as I grabbed up a heavy brass candlestick and went at the padlock with quick, powerful blows until it surrendered. I tossed its remnants away and threw open the lid, to reveal in the bare light coming from the doorway the crisp design of heaps of Union bills and the dull yellow gleam of gold bars. I gazed at it for some long moments, and knew Elijah saw it as well by the lack of his command and the feeling of stunned awe that overtook me. When finally I felt compelled by another overpowering compulsion, it was to stand away from the chest and sit squarely on the floor.

A long period of time then passed in which I remained silent and unmoving in the basement shadows despite my every effort to stand up and walk about. Eventually, I heard the sounds of footsteps on the floorboards above. At first I feared Suzanna's return to the house, but soon discerned that two people had entered, and moments later saw their shadows dancing about as they descended the stairway in a flurry of excitement. They ignored me entirely, passing by to let their rapt attention fall instead upon the open chest. They immediately set up a discussion as to the size and value of the treasure. Elijah lifted a gold bar into the light while Zachary fanned out a handful of notes, and the dialogue became heated as they turned to the subject of how equitably to split it.

In that moment I felt myself freed from Elijah's influence. He was distracted by Zachary's insistence that the smaller man had no claim at all on the cache, and with his attention turned away, I stood quietly and ascended the staircase behind their backs. At the top, I lifted the oil lamp from the credenza and flung it with all my strength down the stairs. It lit in a fireball as it burst open and tumbled, leaving behind it a trail of bright orange flames.

I could not see them through the conflagration, but they must have turned from the chest in surprise. Had he not been so startled,

Elijah would immediately have overwhelmed me once again. In the last moments before he did so, I managed to take the door in hand and slam it closed, hearing with satisfaction the solid click of the lock.

They screamed in fear and confusion, and seconds later I felt the need to open the door. I could not do so, as the keys were gone, so I threw my shoulder into it. I did so repeatedly and with all my strength, even as smoke billowed from underneath and the heated wood began to burn through the cloth of my coat, but like the rest of the house it was constructed of solid oak and would not give in the slightest. Elijah was loath to release me. He held a firm grip on my mind and made me continue to batter the door until with a final scream his influence over me ceased. Zachary remained for some few minutes after that. I stood by in any case, even though I could have departed, until his cries and wails tapered off and died with a final curse of my name.

Smoke now billowed thick and dark from beneath the door, and the raging fire called loudly with a consuming voice. I turned to the kitchen, and passing through it came once more upon the body of Charlie Mayes. He was heavy, but I managed to pull him out into the night and lay him on the grass where he would be safe from the growing blaze. After doing so, I felt flushed with a wave of fatigue. I made off across the fields and wandered for some time in confusion. Eventually I found myself once again beside the small, shrinking pond, and sitting their listening to it trickle away into the night had the effect of clearing my head and refreshing my vitality.

My hearing was fading once again, and my sight as well, but not yet so thoroughly that I could not see the flicker of lamplight across the trees when it appeared, and hear the sounds of light footsteps in the dry fallen leaves behind me. I turned to find Suzanna making her way among the trees. She had followed me, it seemed, and now in one hand held a lamp aloft, and in the other held the dangling ring of keys. She came to a halt and gasped in surprise at the sight of me, and from within came a true, honest urge to rise and embrace her. I dared not. It took all the restraint I had merely to stand and turn without sending her fleeing again into the night. But she was a strong woman, and brave, as I knew her to be, and when my visage fell fully into the light, she held ground against the fear and revulsion that must have been rising in her.

We gazed at each other for long moments. I feared to speak, still unsure of my voice or what it might sound like. When finally the silence between us broke, it was by her lovely tones, which said, as before, "Allen, don't you know me?"

Once again, I would have embraced her. But I took a deep breath that rasped thickly in my lungs, and said, "The house is burning down. For that, I'm truly sorry. The Union money's gone, but you'll find the gold if you go searching through it."

My own voice sounded harsh and dry, but clear enough to make myself understood. Unable to bear any longer her crestfallen gaze, I stepped past her and into the forest once again, hoping she would not follow. She did not, and with tiring steps I made my way back through town, keeping to the shadows as those alerted by the fire hurried about with shouts and calls. By the time I reached the churchyard, the veil had fallen once again so heavily over me that I could barely hear the rustle of the trees over my head and could see only as if down a dim, narrow tunnel.

But the words on my gravestone lay clear, and therefore easy to identify in the night. The only urge I felt now, honest and true, was to return to the genuine home in which I belonged. So stiff had my limbs become that climbing down into the hole was a chore I could not execute. I more properly fell into it, and landed askew, face down once more with one arm twisted under my body. I lay just like that and made no attempt to right myself. It was not uncomfortable, and I felt no pain now, and the earth beneath my cheek was cool and soft as a pillow on a warm summer night.

I wondered what they would think when they came here in the morning, to find my grave dug up and my body tossed just so, my house burned down and my widow with a horrifying story to tell.

But I did not wonder for long.

# Quality of Death

## Clifford Royal Johns

Elixir of life, my ass. Elixir of death is more like it. They put it in your veins when you die, then they tell you they've saved your life. "You'll never die now," they say, "because we can sustain your body forever. Isn't that great?"

But what they've really done is save their insurance payment. "You're not dead," they say, "so we don't have to pay out on the policy."

Four or five minutes later, when you've processed all the words—because everything takes longer when you're dead—when you've figured out what they've said, they're gone. You're sitting in your living room, your dead room, and wondering how to get anyone to listen to you long enough to have your say. From your view of the clock, it's taking you about a minute and a half to say a word. What must that sound like to them?

So you trudge over to your computer and turn it on. The screen goes to animated fish before you can type anything, and it takes you an hour and forty-five minutes to turn off the damn screen saver. Over the next three days, you carefully type out your description of the hell that is life after death, but the machine decides it's time to upgrade your computer's software. You release a mental sigh when you see the notice, "60 seconds to reboot." The system reboots before you can get the mouse pointer to the cancel button and click on it.

It takes you another day to get the letter back from the dead letter box, and the damn fish are back, swimming so fast they appear as blurs, and then you have to figure out who to send your missive to.

Your lawyer was no help when the insurance company first saved its payout. "There is no provision," she'd said. "You're still alive, so they don't have to pay."

Have to pay? That's not the point. They should pay, that's the point. Your grandson could use the money, he's a good, smart kid who should go to college. He could afford it if they'd let you die, but you're alive in perpetuity.

You haven't eaten in days, and yet you feel no hunger, you desire no food. You do not feel weak, just very, very…slow.

Eventually you decide to send the email to the newspapers. Finding addresses takes another four days, and your fingertips have worn off as has the end of your nose, but it feels good to send the email. That'll teach 'em. Maybe they'll get it now.

But they don't, of course. No one notices your letters to the editor. No one cares. You've been saved. "You're not dead," they say, but you are, because in between the moments of living that drop by like flashes of insight, are long, recurring fragments of your history oozing along at a painfully detailed pace showing you all the reasons you didn't use your life wisely.

And when your children's children ask the insurance company doctors why they won't certify you dead even though you obviously are, they just say it's not in the patient's best interest to be dead.

But of course it is.

So you decide to go for a walk. There's a very busy intersection at the corner. If you leave at 4 AM, you should be in the crosswalk in time for the evening rush.

# Zombielocks

## N.E. Chenier

Just lost my fourth tooth—and, yes, I'm still counting. I scowl down at the large tureen, its glistening jellyfish contents and my fourth tooth nestled there. Despite appearances and smell, what should have been gelatinous hit my mouth like a hockey puck.

Yep, these brains are too hard. What were they trying for, jerky?

Next platter, I test with my fingers first. No resistance, which should be a clue, but my brain doesn't do complex much anymore—which was why I let myself in to the mansion in the first place. It hasn't occurred to me that an unlocked mansion, a long table laid out with our favorite meal, may be a trap. All I'm worried about is food and preserving my teeth. Rex would chew a new hole in my ribcage for not having my priorities in order.

Before I can chew, the tissue dissolves on my tongue like an ebola-soured liver.

These brains are too soft.

With the smallest platter, I try to be smarter during the touch-test. Springy, not too mushy, not too firm. So, it's a go.

Whoa! This is the most delicious thing I've ever put in my mouth, living or dead. Gotta be baby brains. Wonder where the residents got their claws on baby bits these days? Must be farmed or cloned. Not that I'd know the difference. Totally worth a lost tooth, worth three.

I never get to eat this well. It's my size. See, I've always been puny for my age. The others don't let me go on group hunts unless my buddy Rex is around because I don't contribute enough. Borderline freaky-small in life; totally useless-small for what I am now. So I'm stuck doing salvage all the time.

Until now. Who in their right mind (or even half of one) would leave baby brains for any passing undead to gobble up?

With baby brains warming my belly, I get brave. Let's see what they got for entertainment.

Thankful for the tiles, easy to slide along. Hallways wide enough to navigate around the rugs. The house doorways yawn huge and splintery. Enlarged with sledgehammers or chain saws by somebody in a big hurry. Lots of rubble. There's been slaughter here. Gore graffiti all over the walls. Tinkertoy bone sculptures. Some of us can get pretty rowdy.

Screams come from down the hall. I shuffle toward the familiar sound. Too familiar. Home theater, about twenty seats, soupy with pus and mucous. Old meat funk. These cats know how to un-die in style. I take the seat front and center. Someone affixed a skull at each corner of the screen. Typical fare on play, but it's almost over. Hoping they have something more original queued up.

Ah, man, this seat's too gluey. I lean forward and the seat back sucks off my best tattoo, the one on my shoulder blade. It's still stuck to the seat back, my dragon—only in reverse. Cool, I didn't know the color went that deep. Guess I still got a wing and part of the tail back there around the new hole in my skin. Cool oozings wriggle down toward my belt—dislodged a few of my squirmy-wormy friends. I let them back in through the perforations on my arm. Tickles as they go in.

I try to peel the tattoo off the seat, but the skin shreds like wet toilet paper.

The next seat is matted with old, old blood, like asphalt on my butt. Nope, too rough.

The third try's a charm. Good one, blood still damp, smells preserved. Wonder what happened to the gang?

Ah, see? They got the darn film on repeat. If I see *Shaun of the Dead* one more time… Some of us just don't get the whole too-much-of-a-good-thing thing. It's all they got showing on any place hooked up to a generator. Zombies watching zombie movies—how original.

Can't find the controls. Can't sit through this one again. Time for a nap.

Bum leg makes it hard to navigate the stairs. Foot's about off at the ankle, so I've been poking along on the anklebone. Okay, enough of that. Detour out through the kitchen toward the garden.

Back door is in ruins, probably point of entry. Shed only shredded planks, broken tools bits. Rusted saw, axe and hammer heads. A shriveled arm, hanks of hair. They put up a struggle, both sides. I poke through the wreckage until I find it: pick axe.

Manage to keep the skin on my palms as I whittle down the handle to a barb spike, jam it up through my heel, behind the shin bone. Twist it till I got it screwed in under the knee. Black sluggish liquid oozes over the metal, but it holds. Lot bigger than the size-three original. Gives more balance than the foot flopping off the anklebone. Satisfying *ka-chunk!* sound with every step.

Bone-tired. I clunk to the first bathroom at the top of the stairs. The full tub is green-slimed thick. I slide in.

This tub's too viscous, like crouching in a barrel of old pig guts (been there, done that). I'd lose what's left of my skin were I to snooze-soak here. No, thanks.

Next one's on down at the end of the hall. Too dry. Saw dust. Like someone's emptied all his teddy bears into it.

Then, the one sandwiched between two small rooms. Doraemon toothbrush set perched on the basin. Mossy goodness, wet enough to comfortably saturate. The thick water gurgles as it fills my cavities. Ledge to prop up my pick-foot. Just right.

My squirmy friends get indignant, wriggle up to the surface. I watch them pop out one by one like buoys, and thrash on the algae, trying to wriggle to dry land. I suck them in through my nose. It only works with the right nostril these days. My hair fans out on the water. I still have some, in patches. The original growth, still flaxen.

Rex says my obsession with my pieces is another form of denial. Same way I haven't really bonded with the others means I haven't come to terms with being reanimated—See? There I go again. Reanimated? Like a cartoon or something? Now call it what it is: being undead. There. Maybe I'll hang out with the cats who live here. They have a pretty cushy set up. I can bond.

The water is thick in my ears. That's why I don't hear the beast enter.

A post slams into the water. The sloshing moss flops me over and the post scoops me out of the tub like I'm a wet rag. I'm suspended above the tub in the grip of a crane or something. Why would a tractor be in here?

"Somebody's been soaking in my bath."

The rumbling voice is so low-pitched, it's almost out of my hearing range. I'm upside-down looking into an eyeball bigger than my head. It's set in an enormous face that might have been patterned after a human's. Smells good, real good, like the tasties on the third platter. The memory of it has me drooling.

Yeah, might be in peril, here, but all I can think about is crawling through that eye socket and grazing my way in. Head like that, I could probably live (er, *exist*) in there for weeks before he even notices parts of his brain missing.

With one giant granite hand—the one not up-ending me—he reaches toward my face. I pinwheel my arms, as if I could swim away. Reflex kicks the bags of my lungs into action. All that does is push dirt and squirmies up my throat. His fingers are about to squeeze me like a bottle of rancid cheese-spread.

Then, instead of popping my skull between his thumb and forefinger, he tugs at my curls. They spring back into coils when he lets go. I spit my squirmies at him. They bounce off his eyeball like flies off a windshield.

"Easy on the hair, dude!" I say, or at least intend to say. It takes a couple attempts before my meat-tongue gets involved enough to make the right sounds. My voice is full of slimy marbles.

"You're still new," he observes.

Rex would punch me in the jaw for feeling flattered by that.

My captor is mostly head, with a stout trunk to hold it up. No neck. Long gorilla arms, long enough to hold me upside-down by one calf and still have us eye-to-eye. Stubby legs, thick as light posts. Nostrils like tunnels. "What are you?"

He grins. Has more teeth than I do, and each one is the size of my hand. "Gene-tant," he says, very proud.

Gene-tant. Mutant gene experiments, specifically designed to counter the plague of undead. "Thought you were urban legend," I say. "Why do you smell like baby?"

"Part of the lure," he says, totally savoring this. "Gotcha."

Actually it was the brain platters that lured me. Were they gene-tant too? What a feast there must be inside that skull.

He reads my ravenous expression clearly (or maybe it's the drool running hot rivers into my eyes). "You think you can get to it?" He knocks the top of his head with a fist, the sound of a concrete slab coming down on asphalt.

I nod. Oh, yeah, I think I can get in there.

He inclines his brow toward me, a ridged landscape with wire hairs poking up. "Give it your best shot."

Not dumb, not all the way. Still have some of my marbles rolling around in there and they know that that forehead would take out all the teeth I got left in one bite. Every instinct tingles to do it anyway, to chew through that barrier. *It'll crack*, the instincts insist; *that's what skulls do*.

I never had good instincts when I was alive, so never relied on them. And logic is worthless against a zombie plague. (Thus, I got plagued.) My sluggish logic could work for me here, though. Actually, I don't need much logic with the answer so plain: his Alice-rabbit-hole nose. Might as well have a welcome mat on his upper lip.

I dive up his left nostril.

"Hey! Hey!" His huge fingers grapple at my feet, but I pull them in. He catches hold of my pick-axe leg and yanks it. I'm in with hands and teeth, a good three-point hold on the gristly cartilage. Another wrench, a mighty twist, and he has the axe. My leg whips free with its dangle-foot. Too loose now at the hip. Fine. Won't need it where I'm going.

The Egyptians removed the brains of the dead and tossed them out with the trash, not because they thought of them as garbage, but because they knew our kind would screw up the embalmed corpses. What would be the point of mummifying if the undead just treated it like a gift-wrapped snack?

I crunch my way through the chasm of his sinus, a tight fit behind that swollen bone armor. Unable to reach me, he's throwing his head around like a pissed off bull. Chunky mucous swamps me. He's trying to blow me out. The phlegm sluices past me in a gust. He has to inhale, giving me just enough time to burrow in another inch.

Inch by inch, I reach the prize. I chew through one last membrane, and I'm in my new den. It's everything I ever dreamed it could be.

Done being a zombie. I'm a brain parasite now. I doubt even Rex would object. Cushioned on all sides by yumminess. It doesn't get any better than this.

My host is still ambulatory, has been for over a week. I'm guessing the group here are reject gene-tants. They gotta be, with cat-door-sized nostrils like that. Then again, they probably didn't hypothesize someone like me: new enough to override the instincts and, of course, puny. Gotta say it: I've never been so glad of my puniness.

Two more housemates. I'll take the shorter one next. I'll wait till they're all sleeping before I finish off this guy and make the switch. But I'm in no hurry. For now, I'm feeling just right.

# You Can't Live Forever

## Heather Henry

Mrs. Hazel McCormick felt the back of the pantry shelf for coffee filters. She had been about to give herself a sponge bath in the kitchen sink when the three flies that had annoyed her since the middle of the night, and which followed her into the kitchen, landed indelicately on her person. She was unclothed except for her underwear, with only her cotton housecoat wrapped around her thin frame.

The coffee filters were out of reach.

"Shit fire," she said, leaning on her favorite expression.

Teddy, her eleven-year-old Siamese cat, watched with interest from the nook table as Hazel retrieved the step stool from the laundry room, the end of his tail steadily curling and unfurling. Hazel stepped out of her slippers to negotiate the step. She noticed a mason jar on the top shelf and moved it within reach. Then she found the coffee filters and moved them next to the mason jar on the middle shelf. She surveyed her landing and took hold before stepping down.

"There," she said to Teddy. "A little something for our guests; then we'll have lunch." The mason jars held the remnants of a burned candle. With a butter knife, Hazel broke the wax and tipped the contents onto the kitchen counter. Pausing, she rubbed the knuckles of each hand. The cat adjusted himself slightly and trilled. "*Apple* cider vinegar," she noted, "not white."

She checked the expiration date and twisted the cap, wincing at the opening. A fly landed in the crook of her thumb and index finger. She watched it crawl over the soft tendon and the vein, her eyes narrowing. She poured a third of the vinegar into the mason jar, then tore the corner off a packet of Sweet-&-Low and emptied it into the jar. Now she had the attention of all three flies. "You see, Teddy. There's no need to parade around the house with a newspaper. I *told* him that." But the cat, seized by a sudden grooming spasm, had turned his long back to her. Hazel folded the triangular coffee filter in half and carefully tore a thumbnail's length off the tip. She positioned the cone into the mouth of the jar and set it on the corner of the counter. The flies delicately felt their way down the funnel toward the sweetly pungent liquid.

"Chrrrrrrip?" Teddy trilled. He dropped from the table with a soft thud and wandered over to his kibble bowl, which was empty. Hazel followed him and filled the bowl from a Tupperware container. He waited patiently for her to step away before eating. For herself, Hazel mixed cocoa, cinnamon, and dried milk with a little bottled water and spread the paste on two Saltines from a restaurant packet. She closed her eyes and wished for a little salted butter.

A thump from the backyard distracted her. She crossed over to the kitchen sink window. One of those *things* had impaled itself on the short fence that surrounded the back garden. It must have tripped over the rock wall, Hazel thought. She scanned the perimeter of the holly hedge for a sign of where it had entered.

Teddy, who had slipped between the mesh shade and the sliding glass doors, chittered as if tracking a bird. His tail, protruding under the shade, twitched. Outside, the thing hissed and thrashed. "God dammit," Hazel said, setting her top teeth flush. She looked around the kitchen for something to arm herself. Her eyes fell first to the block of knives, then to the marble rolling pin on the counter beneath it. She kept an eye on the thing from the sink window and secured the inside ties of her housecoat before tying the belt.

Hazel carefully pulled the cords to raise the screen, watching it fold evenly together, and looped the lines around the metal clasp at the doorframe. Teddy, an inside cat, crouched at the opening of the sliding glass door, his shoulder blades nearly touching. His long tail flicked with interest. Hazel paused in the doorway. In the patch of garden just in front of the skewered creature, tufts of purple petals sprung. "The crocuses are coming up!" Hazel remarked before stepping over the door track.

She surveyed the backyard before advancing. The thing had fallen forward, two prongs of wrought iron poked through the back of its shirt, bloodless. It kicked its legs weakly, as if it were trying to walk, but waved its arms in wild strokes, clawing at the garden soil and uprooting the tender purple clusters. As if it sensed Hazel's watching, it stopped, raised its head, and hissed.

She gripped the cool body of the rolling pin with both hands and stepped forward. She had never been a talented baker. Her pie crusts were greasy, not flaky. Her fillings never set. In fact, she had always considered the pin, a gift from her husband on their forty-fifth anniversary, a subtle barb. She thought about this now as she approached the dead thing, the rolling pin clutched to her breast.

The thing ceased its commotion and watched her, or seemed to watch. As she neared, Hazel saw that it was impaled on an angle, the fence spikes piercing under the ribs and exiting just beneath the shoulder blades. Its eyes reminded Hazel of cloudy marbles, the big ones, "Tom Bowlers" they called them as children. Milky, oozing mucus, they bulged in their sockets. The thing's jaw flesh had been chewed away and some of the teeth on one side were missing. It's mouth snapped and it's tongue lolled to the side of the missing teeth. Its arms, suddenly coordinated, reached for her.

Hazel thought she recognized the thing. It was difficult to say, of course, but she thought perhaps it was Mr. Bender, the orthodontist and early retiree. The one whose dogs menaced the neighborhood. The dogs were "intact" sexually, Mr. McCormick had explained. Hazel decided to approach the creature from behind. The thought of his dogs running loose infused her with urgency. She cut a looping berth across the lawn. The thing contorted itself to follow her movements. When she moved outside its scope, it sensed her, raising its head and stiffening. She reached within ten feet and stopped. For a moment, silence. Then came a low, guttural growl.

Cautiously, Hazel approached. She considered each step. The thing could reach her if it had sense enough to pull its arms over the fence. It twisted its head over one shoulder and then the other, baring its teeth. The closer Hazel came, the more it writhed, thrusting its elbows against the iron fence. The prongs in its back began to work loose.

Seeing this, Hazel acted quickly, adrenaline fueling her movements. She closed from the side and straddled its waist. The thing convulsed and the iron spikes wrenched through the dry meat and flesh, snagging its spine. Its legs slacked, but one flailing arm cleared the fence and grabbed hold of Hazel's housecoat. Hazel, who had raised the rolling pin over her head, clenched her thighs around its waist and pulled down with all her might. At the same time, the thing bucked, snapping its head back into the plummeting marble.

A dry crack and the thing went limp. Hazel's momentum carried her forward, her cheek landing between its shoulder blades. She gagged on the smell of stale death, jerking back and tumbling onto the grass. Her housecoat, still clenched in the thing's grasp, pulled open.

She felt the sun's gaze on her body. The sky was bright. A cloudless day. Wind stirred the chimes from the shepherd's hook outside the kitchen window. Shrugging her shoulder free of its sleeve, Hazel rolled out of her housecoat, onto her knees. Thinking she might vomit, she paused on all fours, but the nausea passed and she began to crawl toward the house, sliding her other arm out of its sleeve. The soft spring grass caressed her knees and legs. She stopped and sat back on her ankles, feeling the sun touch her shoulders and back.

After a while, Hazel pushed herself to her feet. She saw her reflection in the sliding glass door, naked except for her panties, her hair unraveled to her shoulders. She watched her reflected self walk back to the house. Teddy, who was cleaning himself in the doorway, looked up and squinted at her. Just before she entered, Hazel made a detour. She lifted the tinkling chimes from the shepherd's hook, setting them on the patio outside the door. At the doorway, Hazel paused, reaching down to stroke the Siamese. With a childlike cry, the cat arched his spine to meet her fingers, his tail raising like a flag. Hazel slid the glass door into place, turned the lock, then lowered the screen.

Beside the kitchen sink was a gallon milk jug three quarters filled with water. The last of the containers Hazel filled from the tap before the power went out. It was the water she used to clean herself, to brush her teeth, to wash her undergarments, and to occasionally rinse empty food cans. In the sink was the large ceramic mixing bowl. Hazel poured most of the water from the milk jug into the basin. A fresh washcloth and two towels lay on the counter where she had placed them earlier. She opened the washcloth and held it under the water with trembling hands. The cool water soothed her burning knuckles. Hazel closed her eyes and pictured herself going upstairs to retrieve the lotion from the master bathroom, sitting on the edge of the bath, and massaging it into her hands.

Her eyes still closed, she reached for the bar of soap and rubbed it between the washcloth till she felt the soft lather. She washed her face, her chest, her arms. Her loose hair clung to her neck. Scooping it to one shoulder, she washed her neck. Opening her eyes, she cupped water with one hand and remoistened the cloth. Lathering it again, she washed around and under each breast, around her stomach, under each arm. Then she soaked the cloth until the foam disappeared and rinsed herself in the same manner. She twisted the washcloth dry, shook it out, and hung it over the faucet

Taking the gallon jug, Hazel leaned over the sink and slowly poured the rest of the water over her neck and head. The water trickled down to her scalp, spreading in little streams to her forehead and temples. She felt for a towel and wrapped her hair, raising her head and squeezing the towel around the ends. She leaned into the counter, absently looking through the window.

That's when she saw *him*. Back against the hedge, watching her. A man, alive, like herself. A young, living man. As soon as their eyes made contact, he pulled himself through to the neighbor's side and disappeared.

Hazel blinked. She squinted to pull the hedge into focus. There was no trace of the man and now she tried to remember what she had seen. Suddenly aware of her nakedness, her whole body blushed. She pulled the second towel from the counter and covered herself.

"Puss puss," she called for Teddy.

No answer.

For a moment, Hazel didn't know what to do. Mentally, she checked each door and window. She could not remember locking the door to the garage. She went to check it.

"Puss puss," she called Teddy again.

Turning the deadbolt to the garage, she felt Teddy brush against her leg.

"Someone's here, Teddy," she said. "In the backyard. A man. An intruder." In reply, the cat flattened one ear. He hunched, then bolted to the laundry room. Hazel followed.

The kitchen was connected to the garage by a short hallway that opened, in the middle, to the laundry room. Atop the dryer, beneath a blue felt blanket speckled with Siamese hairs, Hazel's fresh clothes lay neatly folded in a laundry basket. She reached under the blanket and pulled out slacks and a long-sleeved knit shirt, setting them on the washing machine across from the dryer.

"What will we do, Teddy?" Hazel whispered, stepping into her slacks.

Teddy coiled and sprang to the top of the dryer, landing with a soft grunt. He climbed into the laundry basket, marching a few steps before settling down.

"This is no time to nap," Hazel said, pulling up her pants as she straightened. She unwrapped her hair, placing the wet towel on the washer, and pulled the blouse over her head. Then she combed the tangles from her hair with her fingers as best she could, sweeping any strays back behind her ears.

"He's coming back. I know it."

Teddy was curled in a circle, his dark paws nestled against the dark mask of his face. His whiskers twitched lightly beneath his forepaws. Hazel reached into the laundry basket and scratched behind his ears. "Once he comes back, he'll want to stay, won't he?" Teddy drew a long, deep breath, rolling onto his back and stretching his paws, exposing his long torso. He exhaled, purring loudly.

"He'll want to stay," she repeated to herself, trying to conjure a plan. She fanned her fingers over her lips, sliding them across her jaw till they came to rest on her neck. Her eyes rolled upward and she studied the ceiling. "He'll want to stay, but he can't."

On the floor of Mr. McCormick's closet, in the left corner, was a shoebox. There, beneath a soft, oil-stained cloth, Mr. McCormick kept his Colt 911 service pistol. As Mr. McCormick was neither a huntsman, nor a sportsman, it was the only gun he owned. Once, years ago, he had shown Hazel how to fire it, how to release the safety, slide the chamber, site her target, release her breath, and squeeze. But Hazel did not like guns. She didn't like the cold weight in her hands or the little flame that flashed when the hammer struck. So she left the shoebox in the back closet even after the Fox anchor who was not Brit Hume interrupted normal programming with breaking news on an apparently fast spreading epidemic. This just before Mr. McCormick returned from his quarterly trip to Costco with his hand wrapped in his tie, blood seeping into the diamond pattern.

At the foot of the stairs, Hazel looked up. The cherry stain of the hardwood darkened the stairwell, but the sun through the window above the entry door cast an octagon of light upon the sixth and seventh steps. The top of the stairs was in shadows. She could hear the rhythmic thumping of her husband against the reading room door. All these weeks and he had still not tried to turn the brass knob.

As it turned out, Mr. McCormick was among the first wave of plague victims. Later, the cable networks would dub this day "Ground Zero" for mass infection. When Mr. McCormick went upstairs to lie down without unloading the perishables from the trunk, Hazel followed, imploring him to go to Urgent Care. He waved her off, demanding she bring the phone number for their lawyer. When she returned, he was already asleep. She dressed the wound and covered him with the afghan.

She must have known Mr. McCormick's situation was grave, for she left his tie at the end of the bannister where the blood darkened the finish as if the stain had dripped and been carelessly left to dry. That evening, when Mr. McCormick did not come down for dinner, Hazel pulled a tray table to her recliner and watched the news as she ate. When the anchor stoically informed the audience about a European *pandemic* that may have made its way to the U.S., Hazel paused the television to quietly slink upstairs and turn the key to the reading room door. Later that night, she returned to gather some necessities; on impulse, she pushed the sideboard from the hallway before the door, removing the coasters from under each leg when she finished.

Now Hazel placed her hand on the rail just inside the banister, her eyes trained forward. She studied the grade of the steps momentarily, then began to climb. She felt a little as if returning to a dormant house after wintering somewhere warm and tried to remember how she had left things, the arrangement of the rooms, little luxuries of forgotten items, a book of crosswords, a reading light, extra throw pillows. Only once after that first night did Hazel venture near that locked door. She found some fly strips under the kitchen sink and crept upstairs to tape them to the trim of the doorframe. She could see them now as she approached, floating over the sideboard. As she drew nearer, she had to cup her mouth and nose at the smell.

Just before the landing, the stair Hazel stepped on groaned as she transferred her weight to it. The thumping against the door stopped. Hazel held her breath. From the reading room came a low, protracted moan. Like a sound that unwittingly escapes through a sigh. Hazel waited. Again he moaned. She knew the sound. The prolonged, dull ache of chronic pain. Then something new—a scratching. He was fumbling with the knob. Hazel hesitated. Her skin hummed.

As a child, Hazel had contracted tuberculosis. She was taken out of state to convalesce at a seaside sanatorium. There was no beach—the grounds ended abruptly at a cliff that presided over a bed of rock and waves. Even in the open air, Hazel learned to distinguish between the smell of death and that of dying. She learned to cope with pain and isolation and friends who disappeared during the night. She developed a sixth sense for being watched. With the other children, she was kept separate. She could feel from the playground the eyes of the sick upon her, the grownups watching with envy from long corridors lined with hospital beds. The children pretended not to notice. Their single slide faced the sea. But they played in an unnatural silence, saving their laughter till they were tucked in at night, whispering with sheets pulled over their heads.

It was this sense that pulled Hazel's attention now, down the steps, to the front door. The handle was motionless, the door locked, yet Hazel felt the man's presence outside. Her eyes narrowed. She drew a short breath and held it. Her body, bent in mid-step, tensed. Her pulse drummed at her temples. Then he knocked.

A few quick raps, as if he wasn't sure he wanted her to hear.

Hazel tried to stare through the curtains that were drawn over the picture window. The jiggle of the doorknob above her rattled her back to consciousness. She turned and mounted the remaining steps. A quick left at the landing and she shut the door to the master bedroom behind her.

A grainy light filtered in through the blinds; the dust caught in the light floated up to the ceiling. The room felt artificial to Hazel, like a museum display, staged. Mr. McCormick's blazer was folded over the back of the rocking chair, his shoes neatly aligned at the foot of the bed. On his bedside table, a book he had been reading lay open. Beside it, the tassel from a bookmark draped perilously over the edge. But in the center of the bed, a cat-shaped impression stretched across the duvet. Hazel's lips curled in a half smile.

She found the shoebox where she remembered it would be. She brought the box to the edge of the bed and sat, cradling it in her lap. In the adjoining room, she could hear her late husband's confusion. The scratching at the door stopped and he shuffled her direction. She heard the tiffany lamp crash against the floor and the puzzle table upended. Then the familiar measured rasping against the drywall.

Her hands shook slightly as she lifted the oiled cloth and studied the contents beneath: gun, clip, a straight, narrow brush, a toothbrush, and a plastic bottle of lubricant. Tucking the cloth into one corner, she ran her fingertips over the barrel. Then she felt the crisscross pattern of the grip. Next door, Mr. McCormick made a sound as if clearing his throat of a nasty frog. Hazel cut her eyes toward the adjacent room. She gripped the gun and thrust the clip into the handle with the heel of her hand, pulling the slide to load the chamber. Setting the shoebox on the bed, she stood and cocked the hammer.

At the door of the master bedroom, she paused, leaning against the frame. On an ordinary day she would be napping on the downstairs couch. She was tempted to linger upstairs in her own room, to open a window for the smell, but there was the other problem to deal with now.

Hazel leaned heavily on the railing as she descended the steps, feeling light-headed. She watched the door intently, though she was certain the man was no longer there. At the landing, she transferred the gun to her right hand. She tried to see through the bevel of the frosted glass window that aligned the front door. Then she crossed to where the curtains met at the middle of the picture window and pulled the hem back by an inch. Putting her right eye to the opening, she looked out.

## 136  Heather Henry

At first she saw nothing. Then, her gaze drifted, drawn to movement just above the fringe of boxwoods. They were across the street but drifting closer. She counted three. She pulled her head back and let the curtain close.

"Shit fire."

When she had checked the front yard that morning, the streets were predictably empty. Since the outbreak, she had seldom had any problems with her neighbors. On occasion one might drift onto her street, but by the next day it would be gone. Most of her neighbors, Hazel assumed, had turned in their homes and been stuck there, like her husband, too witless to open a door.

It was *his* fault, the intruder's.

Hazel tilted her palm up, feeling the weight of the Colt sink into her hand. Then, with a start, she heard the jangle of bells outside. The wind chime from the backyard. She gazed across the living room to the kitchen, as if she expected to see the man walking through the entryway. Then she heard his knock, restrained as before.

Out of reflex and habit, Hazel looked around the room for Teddy. "Kitty, Kitty," she whispered, rubbing her thumb dryly over her fingers. No response.

She inched towards the kitchen with the gun extended away from her body as if the hand and arm that held it belonged to someone else. She stepped through the doorway, stopping before the screen of the sliding glass door. The man waited on the other side. Through the mesh she saw the outline of his curved body bend over the handle of the door. He gave the handle a tug. Then he turned his head—toward Hazel or the backyard, she couldn't tell. His body straightened. He took a step and his shadow against the mesh faded.

From the back yard, Hazel heard a hiss, like air slowly escaping. Over this rose a scattering of languid moans.

Hazel set the gun on the counter. She pulled the cords to the screen, but her hands trembled, and one side of the screen began to list. She separated the cords and tried to straighten the screen, but the side dipped deeper. Suddenly, the man appeared at the glass, his face eclipsed by the sagging screen.

"Please," he said. "There are too many of them. Please."

The moaning things drew closer.

"Please. Don't let them get me. Please. Just let me in. I'll leave through the front door. I won't stay."

He turned his body to face his pursuers, his back against the glass door. Then Hazel heard a sound that made her skin tighten. A high pitched whine that plummeted to a snarl.

"The dogs," he whispered, "the dogs are here."

Her hands were on the door handle without her knowing. She pulled the trigger of the lock and fell back. In an instant, the door slid open. The man tumbled in. From his knees, he heaved the door closed, flipping the lock. The dogs didn't stop, they smashed into the door, snarling and grinding their muzzles against the glass, smearing it with froth and blood.

The man pushed himself away from the glass, landing on his back. Kicking his heels, he slid across the tile until his head struck the opposite wall. Wide-eyed, he stared at the door, chest heaving, as if he expected the dogs to break through the tempered glass. Then the dead arrived, clawing at the door, moaning, hissing. When he had steadied himself, the man turned his face toward Hazel.

The gun was on the counter beside the sink, next to the glass door. He saw Hazel look to the gun and then back at him. Something shifted in his eyes, but he made no move except to sit up and position his back against the wall.

"Maybe we shouldn't stay here," he said. "I mean, in this room." He slicked his temples, wet with sweat, with his palms. He was still young enough that his dark hair toppled over his forehead. "They are not going to leave anytime soon," he said. "At least, not until something else distracts them."

Through the sink window, Hazel saw the dead advancing, limbs bitten or torn away, entrails spilling and tangling around their legs, open festering wounds. Some were in a state of advanced decay, brittle and emaciated, but others seemed almost pristine, like somnambulists trapped in a nightmare. They joined the throng that was already crushed against the glass door. The dogs snapped at them with rabid jaws, their thin lips drawn back, their jagged teeth set unevenly, their gums bulging.

She could feel the man's eyes upon her.

"If it weren't for you, I'd be out there," he said.

Just what she was thinking.

"We should go into the next room," he said, his voice calmer. "If they can't see us, they might settle down."

It was a lie. The dead were single-minded and relentless. He had said as much himself.

With every passing second, he grew more comfortable. Hazel eyed the gun. In the corner of her eye, she could see him straighten himself. He could be on his feet and to the gun in an instant. "Go on, take it," he said, reading her thoughts, reclining. "I'm not here to hurt you. You helped me."

Something in his tone was all too familiar to Hazel. It reminded Hazel of doctors. The casual promise, the unsolicited assurance, the practiced sincerity. With a sidelong glance, Hazel moved methodically toward the gun. The sounds of the hungry dead outside drew at her, but she kept her eyes on the man. When she felt the gun, she closed her hand around it and pulled it slowly to her belly. She squared her shoulders toward her visitor.

"You first," Hazel said, motioning toward the living room.

He pushed himself to his feet without hurrying, bending as he passed through the door to the living room. He was not tall but he was thick, as if he had once been an athlete and a layer of fat had settled over the muscle. He wore loose khakis and a white T-shirt, it could have been a man's undershirt. When he turned to ask her a question, she saw that he was clean-shaven.

"Do you mind if we open the curtain, let in some light?"

Hazel didn't feel that she could refuse. As the man went to open the curtains, she scanned the room for Teddy and was relieved when she didn't find him. The man turned toward the stairs as the drapes settled into place, his head gradually tilting to follow the incline of the steps to where Mr. McCormick scraped at the reading room door. When the man faced Hazel again, he seemed to see her for the first time.

"Shall I sit on the couch?" he asked.

"How long are you going to stay?"

He sat down in the middle of the couch, crossing his legs casually, relaxing one ankle on the opposite knee, folding his hands in a steeple on his lap. Hazel took her seat in the recliner by the picture window.

The afternoon sun stretched along the north wall, the willowy arms of the weeping elm from the front yard reached across the mantel and painted the fireplace.

"Is that your husband?"

"How long are you going to stay?" Hazel repeated.

He leaned forward. "That depends." He paused.

He wanted her to ask, "On what?" But she knew the answer. It depended upon her, on whether she could make him leave.

"They're more... *animated* at night, I've found. But I guess you'd know that." He sat back, extending his arms across the back of the couch. "It'll be dark soon."

As if to prove his point, something thumped against the picture window behind her. Hazel jolted forward. The man sat up, planting his heels on the floor, his widened eyes looking over her shoulder. Hazel didn't turn to see. She knew the things were filling her front yard just as surely as they had filled the back. He had brought them. He had taken her neighborhood house by house, freeing the dead from their internment as he went.

"They're swarming," he stated, matter-of-factly, as if settling a wager. "We won't make it till morning."

Something on the stairs caught Hazel's eye. Two steps down from where the ceiling cut off her view, she saw two pointed ears silhouetted between the banisters. Her eyes darted toward the man's. He hadn't noticed, his attention fixed on what was happening outside. By now the stairwell was encased in shadow. She wondered how long Teddy had been watching them.

"The Town Car in the garage," he said, pulling her focus. "How much gas does it have?"

She started to ask how he knew about the car but stifled the question. His smile was her answer. The windows on the garage door. "It's full," she said. "Mr. McCormick kept the car filled."

"We can't stay here."

"I'm not going anywhere with you."

He arched his back and took and exaggerated breath. "Fine," he sighed. "But I need that car." Their eyes locked. "Where are the keys?"

Hazel's eyes wandered slowly to the staircase and up to the steps her Siamese had recently vacated. "They're upstairs. In my husband's pants' pocket."

He settled back into the cushions. In a casual voice, he said, "I'm going to need that gun."

Hazel didn't move.

"Don't make me take it from you."

She pointed the gun at his chest. He didn't flinch. In the darkening room, his dark features became more dramatic. He grew handsome. "You take the gun," Hazel said, "and you put *him* down. Take the car and you take *them* with you."

"No guarantees," he answered. "About *them*, I mean."

Hazel rose stiffly and set the gun on the coffee table in front of him. He waited a moment, his eyes barely visible except for a faint glimmer of light reflected in his pupils. He leaned forward and placed his hand on the gun.

"You can't live forever, Mrs. McCormick," he said before rising.

She watched him cross and begin climbing the stairs, his gate measured and deliberate. Above, she heard her husband snarling and beating on the reading room door. As soon as the man's head disappeared from view, Hazel moved quickly.

She found her purse hanging from the shoulder of a dining room chair. She heard the man reach the landing. She struggled to grasp the tiny pull of the zipper. Overhead, the sideboard scraped against the hardwood. Her husband growled. Hazel pulled her right hand to her chest, squeezing it into a fist. She felt the blood flow back into her fingers. Above, the reading room door opened. Hazel ripped open the zipper and plunged her hand to the bottom of the purse, rooting for her keys. She heard an unholy scream—her husband's—and the explosion of the gun. Once. Twice. Finally, he was quiet. She felt the serrated edges of her keys and squeezed.

"Teddy," she called, scanning the room. "Kitty-kitty-kitty."

She crouched, circling the dining room to the living room, searching his favorite hiding places. She arrived at the foot of the stairs and froze. The top step creaked.

"Mrs. McCormick, the keys weren't in your husband's pockets."

His face was entirely in shadow. As he slowly descended, the eye of the gun emerged from the blackness, materializing in the moonlight. She was holding the keys between her breasts. A dull current ran through them and along the inside of her arm.

"Oh, you found them," he said, bringing himself to a halt about a third of the way from the top, his shoulders and face still shrouded in darkness. He leaned down, peeking under the line of shadow. "Your husband's dead."

In the rising moonlight, his face had a pale blue cast. Behind Hazel, outside the door and picture window, swelled a cacophony of moans and growls. The man smiled and Hazel felt a hollowing in her bones. She tried to draw a breath, but her lungs felt flat.

"They seem agitated, don't you think?" He straightened, his face disappearing in the blackness. "I'll need a distraction."

A figure flicked behind him, a tail whisking in and out of the moonlight. The blood rushed back into Hazel's frame. She took a step back. The man stepped forward. The Siamese sprang.

The cat's body caught the man's foot in midstride. The momentum swept the man's leg out from under him. He fell back, striking his head on a step. The dead weight of his body pulled him down the stairs. His foot strayed and caught between two uprights, but his body continued down. His leg snapped below the knee, jerking his body sideways, wrenching him parallel with the steps.

The gun had flown out of his hand and ricocheted off the front door, landing at Hazel's feet. Teddy was beside her, leaning into her leg, his long tail curled around her calf. She reached down and picked up the gun.

The man groaned. His neck crooked unnaturally as his head propped against the wall above the third step. One arm reached the floor, the other angled against the wall, over his head. One leg was folded under him. The other was broken, the foot still trapped. The bone had ripped through his khakis and a dark stain spread from the opening.

"Chhhrrrrip?" Teddy asked, looking up at Hazel.

"Almost, Teddy," Hazel answered.

The man groaned again, coming to consciousness.

Hazel watched the hand that rested on the floor. The palm was open with the fingers slightly curved as if to receive something. The tips of his thumb and fingers flexed.

Hazel stepped around the hand, reaching for the tie that still rested atop the newel post. She crossed to where his foot was jammed between banisters. Setting the gun on the next highest step, she looped the tie around his ankle, pulling it taut. The man groaned. She looped it again before cinching it to the lower rail with a jerk. The man screamed in pain. He reached for his fractured leg with one arm, his broken arm still contorted over his head. Hazel knotted the tie once more, pulling the ends with all her strength.

The man convulsed in an effort to untangle his body. His screams excited the dead outside. The Siamese, crouching on the arm of the couch, flicked his tail, his ears flattening. Hazel collected the gun and backed away from the steps to the couch, gathering her cat in her arms. The man's screams became a mad, frantic laughter. Slowly Hazel withdrew.

At the kitchen, she paused. The hall to the garage was pitch black. She placed the back of the hand that held the gun against the wall to guide her. In her other arm, Teddy squirmed, trying to pry free. She clamped her elbow above his haunches. Behind her, she heard the man calling for her, pleading, until she could not distinguish his voice from the sounds coming from outside. At the door to the garage, she stuck the gun barrel in the elastic of her slacks. She left the door open behind her.

Moonlight streamed through the windows of the garage door, casting slanted squares of blue-gray light on the floor and on the hood of the Town Car. Outside the windows, dull figures massed. Hazel ignored this and the screams coming from inside the house as she felt among the keys for the car key. She placed Teddy on the driver's seat, shooing him to the passenger side and being careful not to allow his escape as she got in. She set the gun on the dash. Pumping the gas twice, she turned the key. The engine rattled before roaring to life. Locking the car doors, Hazel pulled Teddy to her lap, scratching just behind his ears until she could feel the rumble in his chest. Reaching for the visor, she felt the remote and pushed the button. The garage door raised before her like a long screen. She watched the dead file in.

For a moment, the car was engulfed. But the dead surged past, flooding the house. Only a few figures remained in the drive as the Town Car prowled toward the street, the bodies glancing off or folding under its slowly churning tires.

# The Sitting Dead

Patrick MacAdoo

"I'll walk ya up there," Sebastian said.

Cindy blinked. Sebastian didn't seem like the heroic type. A little under six feet tall and on the pudgier side of two hundred pounds. His thin brown beard and mustache, and his round-rimmed glasses, his heavy green sweater curving out bellywise under his unbuttoned flannel shirt, and his faded jeans and brown hiking boots made him appear more like the sensitive type, maybe even a sympathizer. But it was cold as hell outside, and the library was closing in half an hour, and all the other dudes had already blown her off, and she had to get up the street like *right now*.

She smiled at him, without parting her lips. "I gotta check on my mother. She's been up there by herself for days."

"No doubt." The corners of his eyes dipped. She couldn't tell if his concern was sincere, or if he was trying to trick her out into the dark. God knew other guys tried it constantly. "The apartments over the Safeway. That's only three blocks from here. You just need me to walk you."

She nodded. "But past the Sitting Dead."

He scoffed. "They're just old people."

"*Zombies.*" She looked around the room, but apparently nobody heard her utter the Z word.

He shook his head. He kept his voice library-hushed while saying, "*Smart* zombies. They know better than to try anything. The cops would clear 'em out if they did. Anyways, after dark, on foot," he shook his head, "going around? Too many nooks and crannies. Way too dangerous."

She glanced sideways. The other homeless were packing up their things, preparing to migrate to the shelters, the MAX lines, and the Portland streets. By morning time, another two or three would be digested and gone forever, or worse, zombies themselves. But there were new homeless popping up all the time, so there was no danger of running out. "You must think I'm stupid."

"No, no." Sebastian sat back. His eyes darted back and forth. "Cautious. It's smart to be cautious these days."

Cindy pitched her voice into a girlish soprano while saying, "So you'll really walk me?" She hated the girly-girl routine, but she couldn't take any chances.

Sebastian stood up. "Let's go."

On the stone benches outside the library, the homeless dallied before dragging their shit out from the tree cover and into the rain to… wherever. Their ravenous eyes sized her up. *Whore*, they probably thought. Or worse.

She and Sebastian crossed the first street in silence. She studied the boarded up storefronts. The liquor store, with its black iron grating protecting its windows and door, was the only business on this block to survive the zombie crash.

A slight wheeze snuck into his breathing as the sidewalk began to steepen. He coughed. "Pretty genius, when you think about it."

She let his words hang for a moment. "Think about what?"

He whispered, "Them. The Sitting Dead." He sucked in a slow, quiet breath. She wondered how he'd managed to escape them so far, as out of shape as he was. "I mean," he said, "letting themselves get infected."

She tuned him out. She knew what he meant, knew where his lecture was going. The state took care of the undead. Special housing, medical care, hell, even food. A lot of states didn't bother. Hell, a few southern states actually legalized zombie hunting.

"Everybody thought the Apocalypse would be sheer chaos," Sebastian said. "like *Road Warrior*, ya know? They thought society was fragile, that it would just crumble. They didn't realize that institutions are stubborn entities."

She raised an eyebrow. "You go to college?"

They stopped at the corner and waited for the red light to change. She pulled her threadbare olive jacket tighter around her thin torso and hunched her head against the near-constant wintertime drizzle. Across the street, the scaffolding was still up on the block-long building, the renovation limping along, the plywood-and-piping tunnel narrowing the sidewalk to a healthy man's shoulder-width. Sitting Dead territory awaited on the tunnel's other side.

He sighed. "Yeah, I did. I dual majored in the Humanities and Sociology. I was gonna go to law school."

She snickered.

"Yeah," he said. "I know. But the point is, the Apocalypse was more financially apocalyptic than anything else. Used to be a bicycle shop across the street."

She knew, but she didn't bother saying so.

"Kind of like the Great Depression," he said, "but a million times worse. And the zombies, of course."

"Of course."

"People wouldn't even think to call it the Apocalypse if not for the zombies. I mean, if it was only the housing market, or Wall Street, that caused another financial collapse…"

The light changed. The cars halted. Most of the drivers were besuited and, she figured, commuting home to the much, much safer suburbs. Judging from the modest traffic, she supposed that the 'stubborn institutions' still rooted in downtown were slowly rotting on the vine.

Halfway across the street, Sebastian, talking faster, breathing harder, said, "I don't blame them."

"Blame who?"

"The Sitting Dead. They're either too old, or too sick, or too fat, or some combination thereof, to escape the zombie gangs for long. So why not undergo the process? You know there's underground clinics that do that sort of thing."

She didn't bother saying that everybody knew that. She didn't bother saying that he was a bit hefty too, that maybe he shouldn't be ripping on them, but she knew what he was driving at, the folks that got so fat that their legs couldn't carry them anymore, and they joined the powerchair set.

"Either meat," he said, "or, they can go on smoking and eating corn-syrup crap, kept alive by the virus. I mean, you know what I mean."

She did. Everybody knew that smart zombies craved living human flesh, but they could eat other stuff too, as long as it was rich, or salty, and fatty. No bland vegan diets for the 'smartzies.'

When they reached the sidewalk he stopped, and held out a hand for her to stop. "Just stay behind me. If they try anything, run back towards the library."

She nodded. They entered the tunnel. She could smell the cigarette smoke already. The building's upper floors used to be cheap housing for the aged and the disabled. Now it was zombie housing, but because the building was still government housing, it was still non-smoking, so the smokers had to go outside. The Sitting Dead congregated there, in wheelchairs, powerchairs, some with oxygen tanks and tracheotomy holes, puffing away, reeking, the stink of decaying flesh even worse than before.

His stride shortened, his steps slowed. The drizzle pattered against the tunnel's plywood roof. She let a little space open up between them, in case he spooked and ran her over. The low-wattage street lamps, installed when being green was the big deal, barely made a dent in the darkness. The tired mumbles of the Sitting Dead slowed his feet even more.

She whispered, "Maybe we should go back."

He pitched his voice lower, saying, "What about your mother?"

She shivered. She tried to master her shuddering body, but malnutrition and sleep deprivation weakened her will. He settled a thick palm on her shoulder. For a moment, she thought he might draw her into a hug. Part of her craved his well-fed warmth. Her shivers coalesced into a painful cramp. She bit her lip, and descended into stillness, except for the familiar dull throb that pulsed behind her left eye.

He withdrew his hand. His white teeth reflected the weak streetlight. "Don't worry. I'm sure she's fine. We need to get you out of the cold."

She gave a hitching nod.

He led her out of the tunnel. The mumbling ceased, but the glowing coals of the tips of their cigarettes marked their positions. Six of them, five sitting, one leaning on a cane. She couldn't see their eyes, but she could feel their hungry gazes crawling over her skin.

She clamped her mouth shut and exhaled through her nose in the effort to evade a mouthful of charred-tobacco fumes, and the stench of creeping putrefaction that swirled underneath. Back before the Apocalypse, when they were just the old and the infirm, she used to cross the street rather than walk into their ever-present cloud of secondhand smoke. Her lungs began to ache, the lack of oxygen began to dizzy her. She would've averted her head to take a breath, but she didn't dare take her eyes off of them. That's how they got you.

During a lull in traffic, dentures scraped louder than the splash of raindrops against the pavement. Her knees shook, her gate stiffened. There were no guarantees. Just because they were out in the open didn't mean one of them wouldn't lose it. If one of them lost control, it'd start a feeding frenzy, they wouldn't be able to help themselves. She reached the point where she had to take her eye off them, had to turn her back on them.

Sebastian had outdistanced her by a sidewalk square and a half. She bitched at herself for not taking his hand. She scrambled to catch up, her heavy footfalls instigating pins and needles that numbed her soles. She felt the last radical upward slope of the sidewalk in her shaky calves. She reached out a hand and brushed the back of his flannel shirt. She knew if she looked back they'd have shifted, instinct causing them to reorient themselves in her direction. She couldn't stop her head from rotating.

She smacked ear-first into hard bone, then arms grabbed her and she screamed. Her fists beat rapidfire against the dark figure. Big hands seized her wrists and shook her.

"Cindy!" Sebastian's voice cut through her panic. Streetlight shine winked off the lenses of his glasses. "It's all right. We made it."

She gasped. She twisted. Their cigarettes' tips glowed orange down the block. She uncoiled. A couple steps would take them into the next street. She exhaled and collapsed against his chest. He wrapped her in a bearhug. She let her sobs wrack her body until she was cried out.

She eased away from his obvious hard-on and out of his arms. Head down, she said, "I'm sorry."

"Shush. It's all right now. I told you they weren't gonna try anything. Now lets get going. Never good to stand around too long at night."

They crossed the street and passed the YWCA building. "I hear they have a six-month waiting list," he said.

She shoved her fists deeper into her jacket pockets. She knew. She gave up trying to get a bed there a long time ago. The Y took up half the block, a glass-walled building—formerly housing a tea shop and an art studio—now a boarded-up husk, took up the rest.

"Yo yo yo! What we got heyah?"

Boards clopped to the sidewalk, polystyrene wheels rumbled over the gritty, wet concrete. Half a dozen skaters cruised out of the deeper shadows of the glass building's recesses. The hems of their loose dark nylon hoodies flapped around their knees as they traced a lazy circle around Cindy and Sebastian, who pulled Cindy close to his backside. Their hoods hung below their eyebrows, almost to the bridges of their noses. Four of them clutched cans of high-octane energy drinks. The other two aimed sleek videocameras at their quarry. Cindy knew what that was all about. Skaters with videocameras did two things: either they taped each other performing tricks, or, they filmed death matches, capturing homeless folks and making them fight full-on, brainless zombies. She'd seen the clips on the Net. But everybody knew they went after loners. They were just showing off, killing time. They wouldn't do shit.

"She looks tougher than shoe leather."

"Back off chubs."

"Got no beef witchoo. We want the skank."

Cindy trembled. The latest thing. Girls versus zombie girls. She grabbed the back of Sebastian's flannel and bunched its fabric in her fists. Six of them, young, strong, and vicious, not old people or fat people too weak to stand up. Maybe, beneath their billowy dark raingear, knives, maybe even guns. Sebastian didn't stand a chance.

"You can't just kidnap somebody off the street," Sebastian said.

One of the skaters swerved close, reached out and took a swipe at Cindy. His sleeve snapped beside her ear. She yipped. He snickered and rolled away.

"Can do any motherfuckin' thing we wanna do, chubbsy."

Mean titters spun all around her and Sebastian.

"Hand her over chubbsy, and be on your way."

"We gonna take her no matter what."

"Save yourself a beatdown, chubs."

No cops in sight. Cindy pressed her face into Sebastian. She felt the tension in his back. The skaters rolled around them. Any city people out and about at this hour would be savvy enough to cross the street, to not get involved. She shifted her head, saw with one eye one of the camera-wielders sneak a close-up of her. Even if Sebastian fought for her, they were gonna get her. If she got lucky and managed to beat the zombie without getting bit, they'd just make her do it again. Sooner or later, she'd get bit. Her teeth chattered. She leaned back and swept her gaze back and forth. She had to make a break for it.

Sebastian, his voice descending to a growl, said, "You morons are ridiculous."

The skaters' mean chuckles died. Their eyes and mouths flattened to slits.

Sebastian snorted. "Look at you suburban assholes, in your Sporto gear, posing, pretending to be badasses. Lemme give you a tip. You wanna look street, don't wear your brand-new purty kicks on your little field trips to the city."

Cindy studied their shoes. Sebastian was right, all brand-new sneakers, nice and clean. Wannabes.

"Wannabes," Sebastian said.

Cindy blinked. The tiniest of smiles twitched her lips.

"You ain't shit."

Sebastian faked a lunge at the speaker, who jerked and spoiled his smooth coast. His board lurched and bucked him off. He went down to a knee and his palms on the wet pavement, before leaping back up and darting for his errant board.

"You middle-school punks are lucky some real city skaters haven't caught you trespassing. They'll take your fancy shoes and boards, leave you naked and shivering in the rain. Probably already been spotted, probably they're already on the way."

Cindy winced. Sebastian was bluffing. A pair of the skaters kicked off their boards and flipped them up to their hands. She'd heard of skater punks bashing dudes to death with their rides.

"I bet you virgins never filmed anything but your shitty little kid moves," Sebastian said. "Closest any of you ever got to a deathmatch was on your computer."

The other skaters pulled up to the pair that had dismounted and hopped off their boards. Cindy swallowed. The rain pattered off their nylon hoods. She couldn't see their eyes, but she could see them baring their teeth. One of them, the throes of puberty cracking his voice, said, "We're in high school."

Laughter shook Sebastian's frame. "I think I hear wheels."

The splatters of fat raindrops, the whine of tires on the highway, maybe, Cindy thought, far off, the approaching roll, heavy wheels of true roughriders.

"Y'all better get going," Sebastian said. He feinted at them again, spitting, "Scat!"

Two of them broke back towards the Y, no doubt, towards their vehicle. Their hasty retreat impelled two more to peel away from the pack, then another. The last one snarled at Sebastian, then trotted after his buds.

Cindy exhaled a hot breath. She whispered, "If I'd been alone."

Sebastian scoffed. "I'm sure you could've handled them."

Cindy wasn't so sure. She'd heard about the rich people in their gated communities, how they snubbed the law, didn't register infected family members, instead hid them away, waiting for them to get better, or at least to get smart. Probably at least one of the skater-posers had a sister, or a niece, or whatever, that raged in full-on flesh-eating mode. They would've dragged her to their van. They might've gang-raped her before they threw her into some dank basement with their zombie kin.

Sebastian held out a hand. "C'mon. We're almost there."

She took his hand. She fell in beside him. Safeway's lights lit up the whole next block. They hit the green light right when they reached the end of the sidewalk. "You wanna take some food up to your mother?"

"Uh, I don't have any money."

"Don't worry about it. I got some credit on my card."

He led her inside, past the black-armored stormtroopers at the door. If she was alone, they would've checked her ID. He led her along the aisle that ran perpendicular to the end of the checkstands. They passed the store's main aisles and the mostly ragamuffin shoppers. The upstanding folk did their shopping in the daytime. He slowed his pace in the produce department.

Perusing the mealy bananas, he said, "The fruit's bad."

She smiled. Now who was the poser?

"Ever since the honeybees went extinct," he said. He turned to her, his eyes twinkling, and said, "I guess you can tell I'm more a Ding-Dong and Doritos kind of guy. Corn doesn't need bees."

"You don't have to do this."

"Let's get her some bread and milk, at least. Just the basics."

She felt the tears condensing on her eyelids. She swivelled her face from his earnestness and raked her sleeve across her eyes. "She doesn't need anything."

"Just in case." He patted his belly. "I can stand to miss a meal or two. Anyways, you said you haven't seen her in days. She might've used up her card, and I got extra."

He flashed his foodstamp card. She stared at the blue card. She'd sold hers for nine cents on the dollar. *Stupid.* She nodded. "Okay."

She trudged up the stairs. Behind her, the paper bag crinkled as he shifted it from one arm to the other. He'd bought too much. Milk and bread, like he said, but eggs, and meat and cheese too.

She stopped at the upper landing. The low-watt bulb above her cast dim light down the hall, concealing the grime and graffiti. No light crept out from underneath the doors down the hallway.

"I didn't know anybody still lived in these apartments."

She took a step. "She got a rent-control deal... I-I don't think she's home."

"Where else would she be?"

She took another step. "It's too late. She must be asleep already."

"You have a key, right? We'll just tiptoe in, you can check on her while I put away the groceries."

She took a shorter step. "Maybe she was evicted."

He settled his free hand on her shoulder blade. "You don't have to be embarrassed. I live in a place a million times worse than this. Hell, my building's slated to be condemned. Would be already, if the city government wasn't so severely understaffed. We all do what we gotta do to get by. My sister and me do the best we can."

In the darkness, she turned to face him. "You live with your sister?"

"My parents... the Apocalypse was too much for them..."

She knew what he meant. People lost everything, prompting a tidal wave of suicides.

"Gotta keep her in school," he said. "School costs money, so we gotta cut corners somewhere."

"You take care of your sister."

"Speaking of which, I gotta pick her up from piano lessons pretty soon, so... we should get going."

She bit her lip. She figured he intended to hang around, and hang around, and hang around, try to wear her down, while working up the nerve to make a play to get down her pants. She could hardly believe he meant to drop off the groceries and split. She was standing in front of the door before she knew it. She fished her key out of her pocket, and wiggled it into the door. The lock clicked. She opened the door and felt her way into the darkness. Her soles made the thick plastic rumple. He closed the door behind them and flicked the switch on the wall. The apartment remained dark.

"Probably forgot to pay the bill," she said. Her voice sounded too loud.

He scratched along the wall, then set the bags down on a counter. "I got a penlight."

A thin beam swept through the empty apartment. "She doesn't have any furniture—"

A smack of skin against skin preceded the penlight's tumbling flight through the air. The penlight whapped to the plastic-covered floor and spun to a stop. Its beam aimed back towards the front door. She ducked against the nearest wall.

Their shadows loomed monstrous as they fell on him, those that could still stand. They wheezed and gasped. He was young and healthy. But the others, astride their humming power chairs, zoomed in from the other rooms and threw themselves on him, bulldogged him to the ground.

She slid down the wall, clamping her palms over her ears, scrunching her eyelids shut. She curled up as small as she could. She hated this part. It seemed like forever before the bony hand clutched her wrist.

She shuddered. The zombie crone slapped a baggy in her palm. Cindy squeezed the hard crystal. Enough to keep her for a few days. The sloppy chewing and gulping made bile rise to the back of her throat. She had to get out of there now, get somewhere she could light up.

The zombie crone maintained her grip. Her mushy voice made Cindy flinch as she said, "What a nice butterball you brought us." Cindy looked up. The penlight's glow revealed the crone's toothless grin. The crone popped in a set of false teeth, worked her gums until they fell into place, then said, "Now if you'll excuse me, it's dinnertime."

Cindy pocketed the baggie. She wept as she circumvented the feeding frenzy in the middle of the living room. She snatched the groceries on her way out. She could sell them, maybe get enough for a day's bump, an extra day before she had to do this again. *Fucking zombies.*

# Isthmus

She said disparate
slowly, the word wisping
off her tongue as if it held
affection, held
sentiment, as if the world
was watching her
mouth keenly, waiting
for a command to love,
or worse.  I tipped

my grey pin stripe
fedora and said apocalypse
powerfully, the plosive
leaping from my lips
as if it held smoke,
held plague,
held shuffling zombies that break
into dance as the bass line of
*Thriller* pounds itself
starry against the sky.

—Gerardo Mena

# Guesswork

## Richard Farren Barber

I'd be the first to say it hasn't been easy since the virus hit town. In fact I'd probably say it's been hell on earth. But the last three days haven't been completely devoid of chuckles.

Take this morning. I was sitting on the back lawn, shotgun laid across my lap, and listening to the birdsong, when Robbie comes over the grass towards me. Robbie's the tabby from next door who tracks a path down my back lawn and shits amongst my rose bushes. There's no love lost between me and Robbie.

Halfway down my lawn Robbie stopped and got down on his haunches.

There was a starling and Robbie was almost licking his lips at the promise of fresh meat. He crouched down and shuffled forward and that dumb bird didn't know what was coming. Robbie was almost close enough to flick the fella's wing with his paw.

As much as I hate cats I have to respect them, they're killing machines, pure and simple. Robbie pounced. There was a flurry of feathers and a squalk, but it was over before it had even started. I heard the bird's neck break and then Robbie trotted past me just as proud as you like, with that bird hanging from his mouth.

He gave me the look. You know—the one cats give when they're telling you who's *really* in charge. He was still giving me the look when that bird pecked Robbie's eye clean out of his head. Laugh? I almost pissed myself.

Of course, I had to blow Robbie's head off. I couldn't take the chance he'd been infected. He might go for me. The rotten old thing was riddled with fleas. I watched them jumping off Robbie's body and for a moment the air was black with them.

When the echoes from the gunshot faded I heard the low chatter of the DeadHeads. The wind carried their voices across town. It made it hard to be certain where they were. I have to tell you that when I heard that murmur coming over the fence it turned my stomach. I *knew* they weren't coming for me. I *knew* they couldn't get in. But it's one thing to know it and another entirely to believe it.

They were over the other side of town where there's more meat. Occasionally I heard a scream or a volley of gunfire, enough to confirm that I wasn't the only one who made it through the first seventy-six hours with my brain intact.

To calm my nerves I went back inside the house. From my bedroom I could see out onto the street. I could see the barrier I made just after this started; a rough barricade of cars crashed together and then set alight. Jimmy Benson's brand new Lexus was in the heart of the twisted structure of metal. I took great pleasure in putting that in there, I just wished Jimmy Benson had still been inside when the petrol tank went up. Instead, I had to hope Jimmy was out there somewhere, drooling from a slack mouth and murmuring for brains, blood and guts.

That barrier saved my life, I've no doubt about that. The close isn't big—only 15 houses—and most people were in town when the virus struck. Kelly from number 8 knocked on my door and warned me—and even as she did her husband bit a chunk of flesh out of her thigh. I locked the door and then, when I was ready, I went out to hunt them both down. Once I'd emptied the close I built the barrier and set it alight, and over the next few hours I watched as DeadHeads walked past the fire to find their dinner elsewhere.

From my bedroom I looked at the burned-out husk of the barrier. It was still doing its job. I watched a couple of DeadHeads shuffle past the end of the road. It gave me the creeps to watch them, the way their heads lolled to one side as they walked, as if the muscles in their neck were gone. The two DeadHeads tried to climb through the barrier but after just a couple of seconds they gave up their half-hearted attempts and moved on.

I looked back down the close. Jackie's Saxo was still parked at the end, rocking gently. Looking at the street, if you didn't know better you'd think it was a normal workday scene on the backstage of England. It was easy to expect that at any moment the postman would come whistling around the corner on his bike. Just life going on as normal.

The door to number five was open.

"Shit."

I hadn't left it like that. I knew I hadn't left it like that.

I stared across the street. The door was definitely open. Maybe I hadn't closed it properly when I'd finished checking. Maybe it was off the latch and the wind had blown it open. Maybe... except I knew I'd shut it properly and there was no wind. Which meant...

"They've got in," I told myself.

Part of me wanted to ignore it, but how would I be safe if they were inside the barrier? I watched the house for five minutes, looking for movement, but there was nothing. I could almost convince myself there was nothing wrong, except for that open door. That fucking open door.

"Let's go, Terry." But still I didn't move. I'd lost the heart for the fight.

"Come on, Terry. Go! Go! Go!"

I trudged downstairs, with all the vigour of a condemned man. I shuffled out of my house and dragged my feet across the road until I was standing outside number five. Even then I couldn't muster up any enthusiasm. I checked the shotgun mechanically and pushed the door open with the barrel.

The Camerons lived at number five. Bill Cameron worked in the NHS—Porter, Head of IT, Consultant Surgeon—something like that. He was always out front fixing something, the guts of a motorbike or a washing machine strewn over his perfectly tended lawn. He was probably in town picking up spare parts when the virus struck. Betsy Cameron stayed at home and seemed to spend her time trying to look glamorous—someone should have told her she was one hundred miles from London, even further from LA, and no-one around here gave a fuck how she looked. What the hell sort of a name was Betsy anyway? That's a name for a pet, not a woman.

They had a daughter; Betsy II, a clone of her mother. Hannah? Heather? Helen! That was it—Helen. Ten years old going on twenty one.

## 158 Richard Farren Barber

"Quit it," I whispered to myself. I knew what I was doing—waiting on the doorstep until I found my backbone. I leaned forward, head over the threshold, listening out for the low, murmuring sound that said that there was one of them in the house.

Nothing doing at first, just the sound of my own heart thumping away. I took a step over the threshold. My mouth was dry.

The hallway was filled with shelves and cabinets and bookcases filled with twee nick-nacks; the sort of nasty tourist tat you pick up in gift shops in Toremelinos and the Algarve. On another day I would have brought the lot crashing to the floor, but for now I was more concerned with the idea that Helen might be inside, blood and brains drooling from the side of her mouth, and waiting to munch down on a Terry-burger.

I put my ear to the door of their front room before I opened it. I couldn't hear anything, although that left me with the awful image of Helen standing on the other side, eyes rolled up inside her head, waiting with a hungry grin for me to open the door.

I punched the door open and swept the barrel of the shotgun through the room—just like they do on all the best cop shows. Nothing. The room was empty, although there were enough Laura Ashley soft furnishings to keep the taste police busy for years.

The echoes from the door ricocheted through the house. No chance of being able to sneak up on Helen now. I moved back into the hallway and considered a tactical retreat to my house, but that wouldn't get this sorted. If there was a DeadHead in the close I had to clean it out.

I paused in the corridor and listened again. This time I could hear something coming from the back of the house. No murmuring. No groaning. It sounded wet.

I pushed on through the hallway to the kitchen. It was easy to remember the layout of the house because it was a mirror image of mine.

I saw her through the picture window over the kitchen sink: Helen Cameron. Although I couldn't see her face as it was buried in the belly of her pet rabbit. The poor thing was still alive, I could hear it mewling, even through the glass. I raised the shotgun and took aim, it was a risk firing through the window, I knew that, but less of a risk than going out there and facing down one of those things.

The sound of the shot exploded within the kitchen. The glass shattered and, in slow motion, I watched Helen Cameron thrown backwards. The shot shredded her head and her poor bunny.

"Thought you were a vegetarian, anyway," I whispered.

I unlocked the back door and went outside to check. There was nothing left of Helen's head, and most of her torso was stained red and black. Her feet pattered against the ground, as if she was trying to walk, but after a couple of seconds they fell still.

For a moment I stood over her body, staring at the blood and guts, the flecks of white and grey brain splattered against the garden wall. I licked my lips.

"Shit."

I rushed to the kitchen and threw up in the sink.

I walked back across the road to my house, not even pausing by the Saxo to check on Jackie; I didn't have the stomach for it. Not now.

I sat down on the chair in my back garden, the shotgun within arm's reach.

"What was that? What the fuck was that?" I asked, but there was no-one around to answer. I could still taste that strange mixture of vomit and... hunger? Was that what it had been? Staring down at the bloody remains of that girl, had I really been hungry?

"No," I whispered to myself. "I was careful. They never even got near me." And that was true. I hadn't even been within arm's reach of a DeadHead and all the reports, *all* the reports before the TV and radio had gone off air, had said the virus was transmitted when they bit or scratched you.

I checked my arms and legs. No bloody scratches, no bite marks, no broken skin. There was a slight red patch just above my right ankle where I'd been itching from one of Robbie's fleas, but apart from that I was fine. I went into the kitchen and checked my face in the mirror. It was pale, I looked more like a ghost than a fucking zombie, but there was no sign that I'd even got a drop of the girl's blood on me.

I pushed the memory of that hunger out of my mind. It was just... It was just... I couldn't think of a valid explanation so I just pushed it away.

The radio crackled beside me—a burst of black static. The noise frightened the life out of me, I'd forgotten I'd left it turned on. Since the virus struck there's been nothing but static across the radio and TV. On Sunday night I watched the channels fail one by one; the last one to go had been the shopping channel. There was something wrong about that—watching some braindead moron trying to flog me cheap make-up and sports clothing while the world was rotting around them seemed obscene.

The radio lasted a little longer; until late last night. I listened to some poor soul running through his end-of-the-world track list before a single gunshot sounded.

Just static… nothing more than that, no point getting my hopes up. But still I turned up the volume and I sat there watching the speaker, staring into the dimpled circle as if I could pull words out through wishing alone.

"…Hear me?…"

A burst of static obliterated the words, but there were words. This wasn't just my imagination. I reached over, turned up the radio again, and leaned in close. Part of me worried that I might be drawing more DeadHeads to me, but a greater part of me heard that voice and wanted to hear it again, to connect with someone else who didn't think chewing on your pet rabbit was acceptable.

"…If you can hear me… West Park…"

And then I heard his voice—not through the radio this time, but carried on the wind. Slight, almost lost in the distance, but it was there.

"West Park…"

Over on the other side of town. The stupid bastard must have set himself up in the park. What was he doing, trying to get himself killed? Part of me wanted to run over there and tell him to shut up, to hunker down like the rest of us and wait until… until…

But another part of me wanted to cheer. Go on! You show them who's in charge.

Despite the fractured words I got the idea what he was trying to do. "Come together and we're stronger," he said. There was an almost religious zealotry to his voice, a desperation. There was some sense to what he was saying. I have to confess I was tempted. After seeing Helen Cameron standing in her back yard, rabbit blood dribbling down her chin, I wanted to see someone normal.

As I sat in my chair and listened to the cracks and pops on the radio I started to plan a route in my head—from here to West Park. A route I thought might be safe.

When the first gunshot sounded I almost pissed myself. It came over the radio, clear as a BBC broadcast. I heard the echo on the wind. The silence that followed slowly filled with the low hum of voices. I could almost understand what they were saying.

Blood. Meat. Brains.

Blood.

Meat.

Brains.

There was a second shot. I waited, forgetting to breathe. Waited for a scream that never came. Instead the radio crackled and then the voices came: Blood. Eat. Meat. Flesh. Blood. Brains. The same words mumbled over and over and over. I reached across and snapped off the radio, but I could still hear their low voices carried to me on the wind.

I picked up the shotgun and turned it round. For a long moment I stared down the twin bores of the gun. I thought about Helen Cameron. I thought about Jackie. I thought about Kurt Cobain and that photograph—the blurred image of a room and his naked foot. I thought a lot about Kurt Cobain, I wondered how it would feel to taste the oily hardness of the barrel in my mouth, to breath in old gun smoke. To stretch down with my foot because my arms wouldn't reach... to...

I pulled back my arm to throw the gun away. Cast it onto the grass as if it was alive, as if it was poison. No. I wasn't ready to give in yet.

Instead I stood up and pointed the business end safely down at the ground. I checked that there were rounds inside the chamber and then I hurried out of the house. The speed helped. It meant I didn't have to think about what I was going to do.

The windscreen of the Saxo was shattered. The car shuddered slightly and I thought I could hear Jackie inside, grunting and moaning as she tried to find a way out.

I was ashamed. At some point I seemed to have forgotten my humanity. Jackie was an experiment. At the time I had seen nothing wrong with it—I had even patted myself on the back for being so wise, so thoughtful, so fucking calculated.

Jackie was infected. You only had to glance at her to know. She'd come roaring into the close and parked slantwise across the street, black veins already racing down her neck. I had hurried across to her and saw her through the side window of the car, her hands pawing at the glass. I left her in there. I figured she would show me how the disease progressed. She would indicate when it had burned out.

How sick could I be? How fucking sick? I remembered watching Jackie coming out of her house for her run at 7:00 in the mornings. I used to see her coming back an hour later, her skin slick with sweat. She used to wave when she saw me, wave and sometimes even say hello.

And this was how I treated her?

I levelled the shotgun at the windscreen and fired both barrels. Reloaded and fired again. And again. And again.

Fuck the noise. Fuck the DeadHeads.

I fired and fired until the inside of the car was black. Jackie's hand lay across the bonnet of the car. Black lines traced the veins up to her frosted pink fingernails.

"I'm sorry," I said to her.

I walked back across the close. Back to my own house.

Here's my plan: Wait it out. No-one knows anything about the DeadHeads so this is all guesswork, but I figure if I can hang on for the next week or so then the worst of it will be over. The DeadHeads will either burn out or run out of live flesh to feed on.

I got home and sat out on the back lawn again, rifle over my lap, a can of warm coke sitting on the ground beside me. I leaned down, took a sip of the Coke and then spat it out. It tasted like blood, warm blood; sweet and hot and thick as sugar syrup.

I picked up the gun. Put it down. Picked it up again. And I tried not to think about Jackie or Helen Cameron or Robbie. I tried not to think about the itch on my calf. I tried not to look at the black lines, drawn across my skin like a map of the railway network. The last time I checked, the lines were past my knee and creeping up my thigh.

And when I close my eyes I can see blood. Blood and guts and brains. I can even hear my ragged voice moaning and murmuring.

"Blood. Meat. Brains."

# Southern Hospitality

Ryan Dennison

*You know, for a crazy Bible-thumper—*
James slammed the butt of his shotgun against the side of a limper's head and watched the gash in the once-man's neck split wide open. He turned just in time to see Rev give an authentic Southern Baptist howl of salvation and drop a former bus driver with a .44 round between the eyes.

*—he makes for a darn good shot!*
Vaulting over the burnt, rusted hood of a Ford F-150, James raised the twelve-gage to his shoulder and blew a softball-sized hole in the knee of the last approaching zombie.

"For wherever the carcass is," Rev shouted, bounding up onto the husk of the pickup to gaze around. He raised his pistol and finished off the clip with a trio of shots into the head, chest, and asphalt surrounding James' crippled target. "There the vultures will be gathered together." He slid fresh rounds into the pistol and returned it to the holster he wore on his left shoulder. "Matthew 28, you know," he said, giving James a smirk. "Wonderful chapter!"

"What'r you say, Rev," James said, resting his shotgun against his shoulder. "You reckon these things everywhere?"

Rev shrugged and thumbed the Bible he kept strapped to his hip as if it were a gun—his two-edged sword he'd called it. "Lord only knows, brother. But he who endures to the end shall be saved!" He paced about the hood of the car as if it were a pulpit and added loudly,

"That's in the Word, too!"

James scowled and looked around, waiting for more of the undead to burst from wherever they came, but none did. "Keep it down, would yah, preacher? I've had my share of fightin' for today."

Frowning, Rev hopped down from the vehicle and warned, "The battle for your soul never stops, son. The devil ain't gonna let you catch your breath." When it was obvious no chorus of Amens or Hallelujahs was coming, he pointed toward the north. "I saw some buildings up ahead. I figure we can hole up for the night. Maybe find some food and ammo 'fore it get dark."

"Sounds like a plan."

Careful to keep his partner slightly behind him, James rolled his eyes. As they made their way along the suburban street, picking their way among the corpses, the sickly sweet tune of a hymn, sung under the reverend's voice gave the already hellish scene an aura of extra indecency. Approaching the final intersection before the series of large, steel buildings where they would camp for the night, James' ears detected a chorus of low growls coming from the right, close. Flinging himself behind a large, white van, he peeked out in the direction of the sound.

It was an army; there was no other word for it. At least thirty of the once-human creatures were prowling about. Some were rooting through trash or mindlessly uprooting the quintessential white, picket fences. But a solid dozen had encircled a large tree in the front of some middle-class home. For a moment, James thought there was someone trapped in the upper branches, but no, there was a dog, some sort of retriever leashed to the trunk. It snarled and whimpered, snapping at any of the beasts that happened to amble too close. Whenever it lunged, all of the undead would retreat, and give off a round of dry, sniffling noises that could only have been makeshift laughter.

One zombie, substantially shorter than the others, held out something for the dog. From a distance, it looked suspiciously like a human femur.

A chill ran down James' spine then raced back up. He turned to whisper a cautionary warning, but the man of God had no mind for the things of this world. Like prudence, apparently. Or survival.

With a grunt, Rev hauled himself onto the hood of an SUV. He drew his pistol with dramatic flare and dropped the child-sized shuffler with a single round. The noise of the shot drew the eyes of every other.

"Oh, hell, no," James muttered.

"And He will send His angels with a great sound of a trumpet!" roared Rev, firing round after round into the charging mass of decaying humanity. "And they will gather together His elect from the four winds!"

With a growl, James scrambled up the back of the only stable-looking vehicle he could find: a small Toyota. The rear windshield cracked as he dropped into a firing position and raised the shotgun.

"From one end of heaven to another!" Rev was raving.

"You're insane!" James accused, dropping a pair with a lucky shot.

Rev shot a quick glance his way, eyes full of ecstasy. "The Lord protects His servants!" he bellowed, and fumbled around in his pocket for a fresh clip.

With a frustrated growl, James threw himself down the hood of the car, landing heavily in the street. If the madman wanted to risk his life for some convoluted, holy crusade, he'd have no part of it.

He was so fixated on the reverend and his approaching congregation that he never even saw the diseased corpse that tackled him at a near-sprint. They both fell, and James yelped out an instinctive curse. He scrambled, and tried to aim, but no sooner had his finger found the trigger than he felt split and broken fingernails dig into the flesh of his neck and heard the rasping growl of his attacker in his ear. Panicking, he thrashed and pulled the trigger blindly.

By some miracle, the grip lessened. He scrambled to his feet. His ears didn't seem to be working properly. A second body struck his, and he stumbled wildly, but collided with a vehicle and managed to stay upright. He started to point the shotgun, but an attacker, whether the same or new, took him to the ground. The shotgun tore from his hands and slid out of reach. He yelled and lunged, but hands—so many hands—grabbed him. The growling was louder and louder. He felt hot breath on his face and a smell so foul he vomited into his mouth.

In the distance he could hear Rev preaching, punctuated by gunfire. The dog was barking now.

## 166 Ryan Dennison

He thrashed. Teeth bit him and he screamed. His eyes were rolling, surrounded by hellish faces and gaping, bloody mouths. The bodies parted slightly, and he could see Rev sprinting toward the steel buildings. At his feet, the retriever dashed, barking. Both were grinning, wildly.

The gap closed and James saw nothing but the dark joy in the eyes of those around him.

# Seven Eight One Five Four

Alyn Day

7.8.1.5.4. BEEP! Click.

She wrenched the door open with a strength she wasn't aware she possessed and slammed it behind her with a resounding BANG! Leaning all her weight against it, she allowed herself a moment to catch her breath before surveying her surroundings, a dangerous way to approach things, but she really didn't care at that point. Besides, she hadn't even seen any of those... *things*... on this level. Sure, she had run like a bat out of hell when the words "Containment Breach" had come over the PA system, spoken by an eerily calm sounding robot. What she and her coworkers had liked to call "The Doom Voice." They often made jokes about the voice going rogue and one day announcing "I'm going to kill you all" in that same bland, even monotone. Now that felt like something of a reality, and it was certainly no laughing matter.

She stood in the ladies' room on the fourth level of the life sciences and bioengineering wing of Heartfelt Research, Incorporated. It was locked by way of a secure coded keypad, like everything else in the building, only this one didn't require a badge swipe to engage the mechanism, just a few key presses and the little light on the module would switch from red to green, allowing anyone who knew the proper set of numbers entry. Sighing, she straightened and pressed her ear to the door, listening for any sounds from the hallway, anything that might indicate that one of those *things* had gotten a whiff of her. She was thankful that she had chosen flats instead of heels that morning, otherwise she might not have been able to make it through the long corridor as quickly or as quietly. She didn't know for sure whether or not any of them had gotten loose on this level, but she had run as if she felt them nipping at her heels, clutching at her calves with their drying, decayed fingers bent into claws. Her eager ears were met with only silence. She sighed once more, this time a bit more resolutely, before squaring her shoulders and investigating her surroundings.

The restroom itself was the same banal, sterile, functional design as restrooms all over the country, perhaps the world. Three pink stalls with swinging doors, one larger, handicapped accessible stall at the end, and a small bank of three touch-free sinks complete with soap dispensers filled with pink goop that looked like the stuff that leaked out of chocolate covered cherries when you bit them. On the wall hung a paper towel dispenser filled with rough, brown paper that tore into uneven hanks when pulled over a set of jagged metal teeth next to an automatic hand dryer. On the opposite wall hung a framed print of a peaceful meadow and below the picture sat a little wicker wastebasket lined with a black plastic bag, all collected between beige walls, over a pinkish tile floor, and under a small bank of fluorescent lights.

While not the best place to ride out however long it was until the infection was contained, it was hardly the worst spot in the world. She had water, after all, and light, as well as a large assortment of magazines to help her pass the time. She wished she had something in the way of food, as she had only managed to eat a candy bar prior to the containment alarm going off, but she supposed she could stand to skip a meal or two, anyway. If she got really hungry, she recalled reading somewhere that you could survive for a while on paper products, though she couldn't imagine actually getting that desperate. She picked up a magazine, the summer edition of some trendy publication aimed at teens, and sat down in a stall, wondering for the first time why the toilets in public restrooms didn't ever seem to have lids. She had just gotten comfortable, propping her ankles up on a handrail in the handicapped stall, when there came a droning whine and the lights flickered out. Her breath caught in her throat and she temporarily knocked herself off balance, nearly causing herself to fall. She remained silent, listening for any clue as to what was going on outside her little safe haven, but she could hear only silence, silence which seemed to be magnified by the lack of the sort of mechanical white noise that comprised the sound track of the Lab. After a moment, the generator kicked in, illuminating a single, tiny panel over the sink. "Well," she said, grimacing, "I guess the designers of this building thought it was OK for us gals to piss in the dark!" She fumbled for her purse, digging through old tissues, candy wrappers, and grocery store circulars until she found her father's old silver lighter. She had never smoked, but she carried the lighter around with her for luck, and because it reminded her of her dad. Now she hoped that it contained enough butane to work up some kind of spark.

Click, click, click.

"Damn! Come on, please?"

Click, click, fwsh.

A circle of wavering light illuminated the restroom stall. She looked around warily, holding the lighter aloft like an explorer in an ancient tomb. The restroom remained the same as it was moments before, only darker. She slowly made her way to the counter by the sink, painfully aware of the sounds of her footsteps on the tile, and glad once more that she hadn't worn heels that day. She lit the wick on a large pink, flowery smelling jar candle before extinguishing the lighter. In the dim glow of the candle's flickering flame, her reflection in the mirror looked haunted, ghostly. She leaned forward, placing her hands on either side of one of the sink bowls, peering closely at the girl in the mirror.

Thump.

The noise made her jump. She dropped the lighter, which clattered to the ground with a sound like a hand grenade exploding, at least to her fear heightened senses.

Thump.

There was definitely someone—or some*thing*—outside, in the hallway. She held her breath, afraid to move, staring at the doorway as if by sheer force of will she'd be able to see through it to whatever was making the thumping noise on the other side. It was far off, but not too far, and the second thump had sounded closer than the first, although she couldn't be sure if that was fact or her nerves playing tricks on her. She listened eagerly for the sound to return.

Thump... scrape... thump.

★ 170 Alyn Day

It was definitely getting closer. Could the light from the candle filter under the door? Could it be seen from outside? Should she chance making noise by blowing it out? Her eyes played a dizzying dance between the flickering flame before her and the door mere feet away. Beads of sweat stood out on her forehead. They didn't prepare you for this in infection containment training. Nothing those classes or lectures did could prepare you for the reality of your friends, your family, your coworkers joining the ranks of the living dead, coming back to life after they had succumbed to the infection or died at the hands of another victim, and coming after you. She tried to think back to the last instruction session. They had become so much of a chore that she'd begun to tune them out months before. It had been years since there had been an actual outbreak, after all, and wasn't society as a whole so much smarter now than it had been back then? So much better prepared to combat the infection?

Thud... thud... KaTHUNK..

She recalled the news reports on the last outbreak, and how they hadn't really seemed real. How her mother had objected to her taking a job with the company responsible for so much devastation and how she had shrugged it off as something done by accident in a now forgotten and irrelevant past. Now she wished she had listened. Her throat went dry but she didn't dare turn on the faucet for a drink of water. Instead she licked her lips and swallowed, trying to generate saliva, cringing at the sounds which were near deafening so close to her own sensitive ears. What would she do? What could she do?

"Remain quiet, remain calm." She drilled herself. OK, that was the first part. "Assess the situation." Well, she had locked herself in a fucking bathroom for starters, brilliant plan that had been. Everyone else had headed up the south stairway to the designated meeting place, Doctors Whitlock and Corby were joking as they walked down the hall, she remembered. But not her! Oh no, panic had gotten the better of her. Head towards a large, unsecured gathering of people when the containment units had been breached? March up 3 flights of stairs with a grouping of other, possibly infected human beings? No, thank you. And so she fled, all on her own, as far in the opposite direction as her feet would carry her, down through the corridor linking the hard sciences wing to the rest of her department, through the specimen rooms and the autopsy chamber, down a flight of stairs… to this, her pretty pink tomb. No, she couldn't think that way! She had isolated herself from other survivors for precisely this reason, heading away from the rest of the building to reduce the risk of running across someone who could be potentially carrying the infection; it was the safest, smartest thing to do. Or so she had thought at the time. But it hadn't worked. There was something outside the door. Some *thing* with lifeless, glassy eyes and a hungry black hole for a mouth, reaching, grasping hands and desperate fingers, maybe even someone she knew once upon a time.

Thud… thud… WHACK!

Something struck the door! In a frenzied blur of adrenaline, she took a step backwards, foot landing squarely on the fallen lighter and causing her to lose her balance, catching herself on the wall before she fell. There was something out there, and it had found her.

Maybe it was another survivor, she reasoned. Perhaps someone else had had the same idea, coming to a secluded area of the building alone rather than combating all those stairs, all those possible victims of the contaminant strain. Maybe whoever was out there was just disoriented by the lack of light in the hallway. She very briefly considered calling out, but decided against it. Better safe than sorry, as her mother had always said. Besides, even if it was one of those *things*, it was only one of them. She doubted one acting on its own possessed enough strength to break down a door no matter how ravenous its hunger. After all, it wasn't as if any sort of intelligence or memory remained after brain death, right? She wished she had paid more attention to Doctor Whitlock's research. She was supposed to be his assistant, so why didn't she recall any of his findings? It didn't matter. She was safe, so long as she remained where she was, and silent. As long as she didn't manage to attract more of them, the one outside could pound on the door until its face turned blue for all she cared. Then she realized its face most likely WAS something of a bluish shade and she had to stifle a laugh. Nerves, just nerves, she told herself, allowing her foot to slide off of the lighter and onto the tile floor beside it.

Thud.

Over time, her reactions to the sound were becoming less severe, less traumatic. It was a wonder what you could get used to, given the circumstances, she mused. Okay. She collected herself, trying to plot a timeline for her eventual rescue. Assuming the threat had been isolated and the building was secure, sweeper crews should be through the area within hours. She could handle that, easy peasy, piece of cake. Just a few short hours and she'd be home free. The sweepers would clear out the infected, including the one currently pounding on her door, and once that was done, they'd call for survivors. She would be among them. She'd need to be cleared, she knew, and quarantined, but that was alright, heck, that was even welcome. In fact, she was looking forward to it. She just had to keep from going mad in the meantime.

Thud.

"Little pig, little pig, let me come in!" She whispered, emboldened by the security her tentative game plan had afforded her. "Not by the hair of my chiny-chin-chin!" A fractured, giggling falsetto.

Thud thud THUD.

It had heard her, whoever it was. Whatever it was. The snotty little girl in her was glad. Let it hear her, let it sniff her even, catch her smell! Let it drool over what it was missing while she remained safe and sound, impervious to attack by one weak little dead thing that didn't even know enough to stay dead!

Then came a noise that chilled her to the bone, snapping across her nerves like a taught guitar string.

Beep!

The sound of one of the buttons on the keypad locking the door being pressed. Surely that had been an accident, right? A fluke? There was no way one of those *things* still possessed enough mental faculties to actually understand what it was it was doing. Brain death equaled brain dead. Right? She tried frantically to recall Doctor Whitlock's research on this very subject, but found she was unable. Panic clouded her mind like a thunderstorm, bright red flashes of hysteria like lightning bolts. Oh god, what had he said? Something about retained cognitive abilities, habit driving the dead from somewhere deep within their mostly useless brains. Surely they couldn't remember something as advanced as actually opening a door with a keypad, could they?

Thud.

WHAT HAD DOCTOR WHITLOCK SAID?! She tried frantically to recall something, anything, some scrap of information that could spell her life or death, but nothing at all came to mind when she tried to think of the long hours she had spent in Whitlock's office, recording his results so that she could type them out later and…

Recording! She still had yet to log some of his recordings! If she remembered correctly, her microcassette recorder was still in her purse, still with at least three days' worth of results and experimentation still on it! Her eyes flicked quickly to the door. If she played the tape, that thing would most certainly hear it and redouble its efforts to get inside, but if she didn't she risked possibly neglecting valuable, lifesaving information. She was torn for a moment, but only a moment. She dashed across the floor to the restroom stall and located her purse by the dim glow of the candle flickering on the counter.

THUD! THUD! THUD!

She fell to her knees, half in gratitude, half in desperation, as she dug through her purse, fingers at last catching upon the smooth, rectangular lines of her recorder. VICTORY! She cast her purse aside, the contents spilling out everywhere in a noisy clatter, but that didn't matter. She no longer cared about trying to be quiet. She held the small electronic device aloft, as if it were a torch and she the Statue of Liberty, before thumbing the button marked with the two little white arrows indicating rewind.

THUD! THUD! THUD! THUD!

Beep.

Her heart caught in her throat. She tried to recall the musical tones that differentiated the buttons in numerical order and found herself again at a loss. That couldn't have been the number seven, could it? Surely not. She was just being paranoid. And even if it had been, it was absolutely some sort of mad coincidence, right?

The tape recorder clicked to a stop, signaling that it had finished rewinding to the beginning of the tape.

A hiss of static.

"Doctor Melvin Whitlock, Bacterial Sciences Division. Project Lazarus, Day 38. It appears as though the test subject has suffered no ill effects as a result of the neurotoxin administered once again, leading me to the conclusion that the nervous system of the infected is no longer viable as a means of survival, or of attack. More research is necessary."

# 174 Alyn Day

THUD! THUD!

Beep.

She was sure it was a seven this time. She swallowed back tears of fright, her hands shaking so hard she could hear the vibrato in the recording of Doctor Whitlock's voice.

Static crackles.

"...Possessed of any sort of... reasoning ability..." bursts of white noise interrupt the flow of information, "... otherwise remain dead..." "... does seem to be... link between... memory..." "...it would appear that certain memories remain embedded somewhere in the brain, accessible by the subjects in their post infected state. Repetitive actions mostly, answering the phone, sometimes even dialing a frequently used number, like that of a loved one..."

Her face went slack. Oh god, no! That *thing* out there might actually be able to get in and get her. But most of the people on this floor were men, and the codes for the mens' and womens' room doors were different. She might be safe. She was probably safe.

Beep, beep, beep.

That was the first part of the womens' door code, she was sure of it. 781. She played it over and over in her head, it was like some sort of childrens' nursery rhyme in its familiarity, the way it had been drilled into her head with repeated use, just like it had been drilled into...

Beep, beep, beep, beep.

She screamed and threw her recorder at the door, shattering it. A rain of broken plastic and metal pieces clattered in front of the little gap between the floor and the bottom of the door, a gap through which she could just barely make out a slowly shifting shadow.

She dashed into the handicapped stall, nearly losing a shoe in the process, and slammed the door behind her, sliding the lock home for all the protection it would afford her. Restroom stalls were built to give the illusion of privacy, not of safety, and she had no delusions that the thin metal walls would provide much of either for very long, once that *thing* made its way inside. She cowered down between the wall and the toilet, clapping her hands over her ears and sobbing, no longer caring who or what might be listening.

7.8.1.5.4. BEEP! Click.

# Zombie Psychology

### Sarina Dorie

I'd been expecting my ex-boyfriend to show up sooner or later, and when he did, I knew he'd probably want to eat my brain.

When the moaning and thumping started, I ignored it, thinking it was my upstairs neighbor having sex with his girlfriend again. As the moaning grew louder and drowned out the sitcom I was only half watching, I realized the noise was coming from zombies.

I threw down my Psych 501 textbook and stumbled toward the drafty window, still wrapped in my leopard print Snuggie. I told myself I was ready for this moment. Still, it didn't make my heart pound any less as I yanked open the blinds and peered out into the moonlit night.

Kevin stared at me from the other side of the windowpane. Dirt caked his face, his once-shaggy, hipster haircut matted to his head. The red of his lips stood out against his ashen face. They were either covered with blood or lipstick—you never could tell with Kevin. Now that he was living-impaired, I didn't expect death to put a damper on his womanizing.

The dark suit he'd worn at his funeral last month was pretty much intact, and his skin hadn't fallen off yet. I couldn't say as much for his two friends standing on the lawn behind him. One was missing chunks of face and autumn leaves were stuck to his sweater. The other had an eyeball dangling down his cheek, his jaw slack and exposing a rotting black tongue. I'd seen worse-looking zombies back home in Louisiana, but the sight still made the spicy chicken wings I'd made for dinner rise up in my throat.

I covered my nose and mouth with my Snuggie, trying to block out the stench of formaldehyde and decomposing flesh that seeped through the cracks of the closed window. My voice was muffled. "What is it this time?"

"Leticia baaaaby, you know I'd only rise from the grave if it was important," Kevin said, his voice garbled in a slushy moan.

Considering the first time he'd risen had been to crash a football game at the University of Oregon, and the second time had been to crash a kegger, I knew 'important' was subjective.

I picked up the bottle of pumpkin spice fresh air spray from the bookcase and spritzed the window so I could breathe. "What do you want?"

"I missed yoooou. I needed yoooou."

I rolled my eyes, more annoyed than afraid now. "Yeah, you needed me so much you had sex with Sara Palmer in the parking lot of Dairy Queen."

"Baaaaby, you're the only ooooone for me."

"I'm not your baby," I said. "We broke up two months ago. Why don't you go to Sara's dorm?"

"Saraaaa doesn't haaaaave caaaable," Dangly-Eye said.

Kevin frowned and elbowed his friend which caused a few of the dude's ribs to tear through his shirt.

"He waaaaaants you for your braaaaaain, too," Missing-Flesh-Face said and then snickered.

"Guuuuys, you aren't helping." Kevin's raspy voice rose.

I crossed my arms, almost too indignant to speak. "Let me get this straight—you came here to watch some stupid TV show?"

"It's the big gaaaame."

"But you didn't come to me first, did you? You went to Sara's. And I assume from the bits of gore on your face you ate her brains?"

"Um...."

"Fine. We can do this the hard way," I muttered, turning back to the TV.

I wasn't a witch doctor or voodoo queen, but I had gotten my undergraduate degree in psychology at the University of Louisiana, and I had picked up a few things about magic—and men—along the way.

When I pulled the TV over to the window, they gave each other high fives with the best coordination one might expect from zombies—which meant falling all over each other. One of them lost an arm in the process. I headed for the fridge, retrieved the little yogurt cup of blood that I'd been draining from packages of chicken wings for the last two weeks, and set it on the bookcase.

All three of them had their faces pressed up against the window, peering at the TV, shouting and groaning what channel the game was on. I ignored them as I scanned the TV listings. I flipped through the channels, their shrieking reaching a crescendo as I passed the game and left the screen on some sickly sweet Hallmark movie.

I yanked the window open and poured the chicken blood on them. Before the placebo of black magic wore off, I said, "With this blood I command you: get your sorry asses back to your graves this instant, or your bones will be rooted to this spot forever and you'll be forced to endure chick-flicks for eternity."

They clutched at their eyes in agony, either because of the pregnant farm girl scene they'd just witnessed or the Tabasco sauce I'd mixed with the blood. They lurched away, stumbling into each other, wailing into the night.

Thankfully, there were some constants on this earth: one being that most men, dead or alive, would do anything to avoid watching girly movies on Lifetime.

## The Zombie Orchestra

atonal dissonance
no muscle memory
just hunger.

   —dan smith

        at the zombie dance club—
        everyone has two left feet or arms or eyes
        it's all up for grabs

            —dan smith

zombies can't text
but they do so want to
reach out and touch

   —dan smith

## Parade

Neighbors and strangers pass by
directionless, but still moving
much like him
Slowing down risks Death
Stopping welcomes it.

      —Brian Rosenberger

# Love Bites

Robert Neilson

## Part One—Happy

It started out as one of those typical boy meets girl scenarios. You know the one: boy meets girl, boy introduces girl to best friend, boy loses girl, girl discovers best friend is an asshole, girl cries on boy's shoulder, girl discovers boy was love of her life all along, boy gets girl back, boy marries girl pronto, girl gets pregnant, twice, boy and girl as happy as pigs in shit, boy becomes zombie. Hold on there, back up a minute. What's this zombie shit, you ask?

Well, I did say it started out typical. But, yeah, you're right, lets back up a bit.

Daniel worked in his dad's hardware store until the recession blew the business out of the water. For eighteen months he made ends meet by doing odd jobs: fixing roofs, painting fences, digging ditches. Mary ran a tight ship. Their apartment was always neat as a pin, the kids shone like they'd just been polished, dinner hit the table at six thirty every night. Despite the struggle they stayed happy as pigs etc. But there's only so long you can hang on by your fingernails. And that time was almost up when Daniel's uncle died and left him a farm. It wasn't much: a couple of hundred acres of mountain and a couple of hundred half-starved sheep. If he'd had a job he'd have let the government take it in lieu of taxes. But it looked like an answer; Daniel just wasn't sure what the question was.

Both Daniel and Mary were surprised when they discovered that Daniel had a talent for animal husbandry. He checked out sheep farming on the internet. He changed the way the farm was run. The sheep began to thrive. For a time it looked as though they were going to make it. Then the zombie plague hit.

They were out in the sticks. They never really found out how it started. All they knew was that there were flesh eating zombies roaming the countryside like canvassers before an election. Except when they came knocking on your door the zombies weren't looking for your vote. They wanted to take a bite out of you that would have embarrassed even the tax man.

It was a time to dig in and worry about survival. So, no change there, Daniel thought. He rounded up his sheep; zombies are less particular about the flesh they eat than you would think from the movies and stories. Sheep are okay if there are no humans handy. Anything with warm blood pumping through its veins will do in a pinch. Sure, they prefer long pig but they're not exactly gourmands. He sat his kids down: Stephen and Stephanie—if they had a sister it would be Stella and a brother would be Sean, the children had decided. He explained to Stephen about the zombies and made him promise to stay within sight of the farmhouse at all times and to keep an eye on his little sister. At seven Stephen was a pretty responsible kid. Before the zombie plague shut down the school he had been top of his class. Stephanie was not quite as trustworthy. At five she was a scatterbrain. It was possible that by the time she graduated college she would be summa cum laude, but no-one was betting on it.

She was a sweet child and that made all the difference. Her parents would not have changed an atom of her make-up had they been given the option. They loved her exactly the way she was, as they did Stephen. Despite their early relationship difficulties Daniel and Mary loved one another deeply. To be honest, they were the type of couple that kind of makes their friends throw up—or at least make retching noises to one another when they think no-one else is looking. They would sit holding hands and staring into one another's eyes for hours at a time. In company they talked incessantly about how great their kids were. When Daniel was out of work nobody could ever recall either of them complaining. When he began to make a go of the sheep farm nobody could think of a time when either of them sounded smug.

They were a difficult couple to dislike, though a little too sweet for some tastes. They went to church on Sunday, what little they had they were prepared to share, they never had a bad word for anyone and greeted friends and strangers alike with a cheerful smile. So it was inevitable that in an unjust world, tragedy would strike where least deserved.

**Part Two—Sad**

At the height of the zombie plague Stephen caught a virus of some kind. His mother rang the doctor and described the symptoms. "Bring him in to my surgery," the doctor told her.

"He's very sick, Doctor. I don't think I should move him. Can you come out?"

"No house calls."

"But, Doctor, he's burning up," Mary said, her voice filled with naked pleading.

"I'm sorry. I can't. It's too dangerous to leave the town limits."

"The zombies can't get you if you stay in your car."

"They're getting smarter from what I've heard. I can't take a chance. Too many people rely on me."

"We're relying on you."

"Get Daniel to come to my surgery. I'm pretty sure it's just a viral flu. I'll give him something that will sort little Stephen out in double quick time."

There was no point in arguing and she trusted the doctor. So Daniel was dispatched to the doctor's office to pick up the drugs. He drove fast because he was worried his little boy's strength was draining from him by the minute. He also felt it was less likely the zombies would bother him if he kept his foot down. The trip to town was just under ten miles on twisty back roads and Daniel made it in less than ten minutes.

The doctor's surgery was empty of patients. Neither his nurse nor his secretary had braved the deserted streets of the town to go to work.

The doctor sat alone. He dispensed the drugs personally from a press in his examining room. Daniel noticed that both packs he was given were marked Sample Not For Sale. The doctor scribbled instructions on a prescription pad and tore the sheet off. "Give him two of each of the pills when you get home, then one of each every four hours. If his temperature doesn't come down in eight hours, call me."

"Will you come out?" Daniel asked pointedly.

The Doctor's cheeks reddened slightly. He shook his head. "I'm sorry, Daniel. The entire community depends on me. I can't put myself at risk. I told Mary."

Daniel left it at that. The doctor was a good man if not a brave one. He would do his best and that would have to be good enough. "Thanks, Doc," he said, closing the door behind him a little firmer than necessary. It was the closest Daniel would let himself get to a statement of disappointment.

Evening was turning to night as he left the doctor's office. His headlights filled the narrow country road before him. Trees crowded close to the winding blacktop. Tiny red lights blinked through the gaps in the trees. A wave of them seemed to flank his progress. A mile from home two shambling zombies tottered onto the road in front of him. He slammed on the brakes and swerved around them, barely avoiding an ancient chestnut that bowed under the weight of its age, its lowest branches squared off by generations of trucks passing beneath. The zombies turned with all the speed of cruise liners. Daniel slammed the stick shift into first and accelerated away throwing a shower of dirt at his potential attackers.

Mary stood on the porch watching for him. As he pulled up, she ran to the car. "Did you have any trouble?"

"No," he lied, though only a little and white. He passed her the pills and repeated the doctor's instructions. Medicating family members was a mother's work. He pulled the car to the back of the house and slid it into the garage, carefully edging past the jumble of tools and light farm equipment strewn across the dirt floor. Normally the car sat outside in the driveway. But these were anything but normal times. The farm had not been attacked by zombies directly, but that did not mean that it was not a possibility. From the news reports on the local TV station it seemed that the zombies really only attacked people on foot and out of doors. But as the police spokesman warned, this situation could change at any time and it was everybody's duty to be vigilant, take no risks and stay home except in emergencies.

Little Stephen's temperature failed to reduce after he took the pills his father had brought. In fact it continued to rise alarmingly. Mary rang the doctor who advised her to wait until the child had taken the second dose of pills. If Stephen's temperature continued to rise they would have to bring him into town. Daniel took the phone off his wife. "Shouldn't we just come now?"

"No. He needs rest and quiet. The fever will break in the next couple of hours. Trust me."

Mary and Daniel had always trusted authority and they continued to do so. They trusted the doctor right up until the moment, two hours later, when their son died. One minute he was struggling to breathe, the next he simply stopped. Daniel had learned CPR in the boy scouts but it did no good. The child was gone.

The next morning Stephanie began to exhibit similar symptoms to those of her brother. Daniel put on his coat, took his car keys and walked to the door, his face dark as the heart of a Kansas twister. "The doctor will be making a house call," he said between clenched teeth, "whether he wants to or not."

"Be careful," Mary called to the slamming door.

On his second journey into town within twenty-four hours Daniel was not so lucky. The doctor had been right about the zombies learning. As he sped down the centre of the narrow winding road he swept around a bend to be confronted by half a dozen zombies grouped in two bunches of three with much less than a car's width separating them from each other and the border of trees. Daniel knew instantly that he would never brake sufficiently to miss the slowly plodding obstacles. A snap decision kept the nose of the car pointed straight down the crown of the road. He neatly bisected the two groups, taking out the centremost zombie from each group.

Hitting a human body at close to sixty miles per hour creates a terrible mess. Hitting two wrenched the wheel from Daniel's hands. Road and sky swapped places in extreme slow motion, then the roof of the car hit tarmac, flipped onto the driver's door then back to the wheels. For a millisecond Daniel thought it was going to stay upright but gravity and momentum would not be denied. The car rolled again and again. Only the resolute trees stopped it. Daniel was held in place by his seat belt. His chest felt as though it had been kicked by a horse or possibly stood on by an elephant. His brain had certainly rattled off the inside of his skull sufficient to scramble his senses totally. He registered that he was the right way up. He moved his legs and flexed his hands. But he could not have estimated how long these actions took. The light was going out of the day when he finally dragged himself clear of the wreck. He brushed himself down gingerly, with a splash of extra ginger for good measure, but could find no evidence of wounds that might become fatal.

Every bone and sinew in Daniel's body complained as he walked back up the road toward the farm. He was hungry and thirsty. He needed to take care of that. He had another priority but no matter how hard he concentrated, he failed to remember what it was. Mary would tell him when he got home. He tried to smile when he thought of her. His facial muscles were in no condition to obey. He was hurt worse than he had initially thought. Even walking was a problem. But he knew he had to get home. He had things to do. Promises to keep. A mission. He pushed each foot painfully forward, one after the other. Mary, he thought. He spoke her name. His throat felt paralysed. All that came out was an elongated, Mary-shaped moan.

As he approached the farmhouse the front door was flung open and his wife ran to greet him. She had been crying most of the day. He had been gone more than ten hours. She had been convinced the zombies had got him. Stephanie's fever was rising despite regular doses of the pills meant for her brother. Mary crashed into her husband's chest, expecting his arms to enfold her. He groaned and staggered backwards. His arms hung straight by his sides. With a supreme effort he held himself upright. "Oh, Daniel, what happened to you? You look awful. Are you hurt? Where's the car? Oh my God! Did you crash it? Oh, Daniel, I was so worried about you." She grabbed his arm and began to drag him inside. "Let's get you cleaned up. Tell me what happened?"

Daniel's head spun. He tried to keep up with the babble from his wife. He tried to make sense of what she was saying. He recognised the words but not their meanings. He attempted to connect them and their meanings but they were avoiding his neural pathways. He wanted food and he wanted comfort, both of which would be supplied by his wife. He attempted to clasp her warmth to him. His hands came up to shoulder level in a series of barely controlled jerks. His brow furrowed. One of the arms cuffed her shoulder, knocking her momentarily off balance. He attempted to form an apology but his throat and tongue refused to comply. "Maaarrryyy!" was all he could manage. He spread his lips wide and clacked his teeth.

Mary retreated until she was outside the circle of his arms. She beckoned for him to follow her into the kitchen where the light was bright and she could examine him properly. Tears sprang to her eyes. There was a large gash at the side of his neck. It could have been an injury from the car crash, but she instinctively knew it was not. The edges of the gash were ragged but not ragged enough to disguise the fact that there was lump of flesh missing. He moved across the kitchen in a jerky, shuffling, motion, his legs barely bending at the knees. He groaned again, incoherently. Even in the few minutes he had been inside the house he had become visibly less human. There was no denying the fact that he was in the last stages of turning into a flesh-eating zombie.

"Come on, Daniel, I'll get you cleaned up." She pulled out a sturdy, wooden Captain's chair and pointed him toward it. "Sit down. I'll get you... Are you thirsty?"

He clacked his teeth again and made a gurgling noise in his throat that might have been a recognition of her words. A shudder of revulsion ran along her spine despite her best efforts to think of him as Daniel, to remember him as he had been rather that see him as he was now.

Daniel flopped onto the chair. She poured water into a tin mug that had been in the cupboard unused since their last family picnic, the previous summer. The tears began to flow more freely. She bit down on a whimper and went into the back yard. By the door, a coil of clothesline hung on a nail. It had been forgotten since Daniel bought an electric dryer when Stephanie was born. He had sold three sheep to pay for it. She remembered the sacrifice and began to sob uncontrollably. The sound of the chair legs scraping on the tiled floor snapped her out of it. Daniel was attempting to stand.

"Stay there, love," she said.

He moaned assent, turning his head slightly in her direction. His neck no longer seemed limber enough for him to turn his head fully. It could be whiplash, she thought, though more likely it was zombiehood. She dismissed un-Christian thoughts of an insurance claim and quickly wrapped the clothesline around his wrists, binding them to the arms of the chair. He pulled tentatively at the bonds. She pulled the line tight and wrapped a length around each of his legs. He stared at her without comprehension. She could see the confusion in his eyes, the blankness that had replaced the humour and intelligence she always could find there previously. She hauled on the line, tightening it about his shins. There were yards of it still left. She circled the chair and encased his chest with the sturdy line. She was no expert at knots but she doubled and trebled them before stepping back to appraise her work.

Daniel struggled weakly. She stepped close to check one of his arms. He snapped at her, his teeth missing her cheek by a layer of skin. His lips brushed her flesh. She raised a hand to touch the spot. In her mind it became a kiss goodbye, though Daniel was already gone. The body strapped to the chair in her kitchen was a flesh-eating zombie, she needed to keep that straight in her mind, no matter how much it might resemble her husband.

A weak cry from upstairs jerked her into action. She whirled and mounted the steps to check on her daughter. Stephanie was in obvious distress. Her pyjamas were soaked in sweat. Her face was a fiery red with streaks of damp hair sticking to her face like damp leaves in Fall. Mary mopped at her daughter's cheeks with a damp cloth and laid it across her forehead. She placed a thermometer beneath the child's tongue. The mercury rose inevitably to one hundred degrees and beyond, topping out at one-oh-three. Mary was unsure how high a temperature a child could survive but she was sure it was no more than a couple of degrees more.

She thought about how quickly every aspect of her life had changed, how rapidly she had lost everything she held dear. Her head sagged into her hands and the tears she had been fighting back coursed freely along her palms and down her wrists to soak her cuffs. She thought about her son lying cold in his bed. She thought about her husband, trying with all her kindness and humanity to avoid the word monster.

But that was what he was. An undead monster. Her head lifted from her hands. Her eyes fell reluctantly on Stephanie. For a long time she watched as the life began to ebb from the beautiful little girl who was now her only child. She would soon be dead.

Dead, she thought. Undead. It was almost too awful to contemplate. But she wouldn't be dead. And she would be with her father. Did zombies have families? Or feelings? She knew that they tended to hunt in packs. What kept them together? What drove them forward?

Dead, she thought. Not dead.

Mary stood quickly, not wanting to think too much about what was running through her head. It wasn't quite a plan; she couldn't let it be. Considering the consequences of her actions was too much for her. She lifted the burning child from the damp bed and hurried down to the kitchen. She stood just beyond the reach of her zombie husband. He sniffed at the air as though attempting to identify the newcomer. His chin jutted toward them and he made tiny biting motions, but almost gently.

With infinite tenderness Mary held her child toward the zombie. He nipped her arm with what Mary could only imagine was reluctance. The flesh broke and blood welled into the wound. The zombie licked tentatively at it. Before Daniel could change his approach, Mary whipped the child out of his reach. Whatever infection he carried had been passed to his daughter. Mary wondered how long it would take to affect Stephanie. She was small and weakened by her fever. Did that mean it would be faster or slower? Her zombie husband leaned towards her and moaned. The sound was, for her, heart-wrenching. Stephanie pushed herself out of her mother's arms. She slipped to the floor and stepped close to her father. He sniffed at her. She grasped the front of his shirt and pulled herself up onto his knee.

Mary stood and watched: horrified, frozen. Zombie Daniel clicked his teeth and emitted a short grunt. Little Stephanie moved close into the crook of his arm. She plucked helplessly at his bonds with her tiny fingers. Mary could not decide what to do. Leaving her darling daughter with a flesh eating zombie seemed totally wrong on so many levels, no matter how strange the circumstances she had herself created. The flush in her daughter's cheeks was ebbing. The child was going to live. Mary reached out to pluck Stephanie from her father's knee. The child hissed and snarled like a cornered cat. Her pudgy little-girl hands batted at her mother.

Mary stepped back in surprise. The zombie-virus had taken hold almost immediately. Mary's legs felt as though the bones had turned to melted rubber. She grabbed the door frame to stop from falling. But staying upright was beyond her strength. She slid down the frame and sat in the doorway. Her head leant against the wood. The sharp angles were uncomfortable but that was unimportant. Her husband and daughter sat unmoving in the chair. Apart from Daniel's terrible pallor they looked almost natural. Mary loosed the tears that had built for most of the day. There was no longer a need for her to stay strong. She had nothing left to fight for.

Her zombie daughter slid from Daniel's knee and knelt at her side. Stephanie laid a doll's hand on Mary's arm. The fever was gone. The child's touch was cold. Her mouth made a curious mewling sound. Mary looked into the face of her daughter. The child's head was cocked to one side as though posing a question. Mary wondered if they would be a family or if all zombies were alone within their own skulls. She felt her daughter's milk teeth on her arm and knew that the question would be answered soon.

If it wasn't she would never know. Or care.

# Zombies at Casino Buffet

William Van Wurm

"One day God will see me for who I truly am," thought Big Ed as he considered the many choices on the buffet. "He will give me a crown when he sees all the stuff I have been up against," he thought as he turned his nose up at the frontal lobe slices, obviously overcooked, under the glaring heat lamp. Big Ed considered himself a purist. "These zombies act like this garbage is a delicacy. It's soul killing is what it is! One's formative years are his permanent sense of things. The formative years set the boundaries, they chart the course of one's existence forever!" he continued his internal invective as if from a podium to a faceless audience in his mind.

No sooner had he formed this thought than evidence to the contrary came into view. His father, or "Grandpa J" as the kids called him, brushed against him as he helped himself to the overcooked lobes. "I highly recommend you get some of these, Eddie," his father said. When his son responded with a look of bewilderment and a deep sigh, Grandpa J added "Oh, I forgot. You think you're too good for the buffet."

Big Ed was in fact always agitated at the buffet, though he could never tell his family exactly why. Indeed he did not fully understand himself. One might think he could just relax the one or two times a year they came to the casino buffet. But from the moment he walked though the doors and gazed up at the towering cathedral ceiling with the flying buttress supports and heard the clanging bells of the slot machines and breathed in the vaguely familiar aromas meant to mask the scent of cigarettes, his blood pressure skyrocketed, often to the point that he bled from his eyes.

Today was Zoe's ninth birthday and she had chosen to come here. Now Big Ed looked across the medulla bar at her, his only daughter, as she transferred mini-oblongata after mini-oblongata from a giant pile to her plate. "Don't take anymore than you can eat!" he warned her. The very abundance of the delicacy disgusted him. How had such a large amount been amassed? Some unnatural process to raise, sustain, and harvest the beasts, no doubt. Now they ended up here, in piles, beneath the bright lights and sneeze guards. He had no doubt that Zoe would eat every single thing she placed on her plate, and he was secretly disgusted by her corpulence. Big Ed had moral issues with the harvesting of creatures young enough to have such small oblongatas, but what really troubled him, he thought, was that his daughter took it all for granted.

The whole spectacle was in stark contrast with the mealtimes of his youth, before everyone had moved to the cities and the whole world had been corrupted by excess. In his childhood, often the whole family went out together in the late evenings to raid isolated farm houses in search of marooned travelers. They had always hoped for a feast of young lovers, but this never happened. The shacks were usually abandoned. At best they found an old man with Alzhiemer's who had run away from a nursing home or a survivalist holed up in what he suspected a safe place. Now that was fellowship—when they helped one another tear their prey limb from limb—unlike this when they were never even seated together for very long because someone was always leaving the table and returning to the buffet and its illusion of infinite choices.

He remembered sometimes going to bed hungry as a child, but "hunger is the best sauce," he had once heard somewhere. "Scarcity makes one appreciate things. It builds character," he thought. Even in this country, there was a time when the zombies went hungry. It could happen again. Times of scarcity could return. A part of him hoped that they would.

Big Ed always returned from the buffet to his seat with some approximation of the down-home, simple cooking he grew up with.

He eschewed the exotic items from the buffet altogether. Little Ed sat down next to him with a plate of eyeballs in a demi-glace sauce. "You better eat every one of them! Every damn one of them!" Big Ed threatened, who was suspicious of many of the buffet offerings. Little Ed and the other foodies in the family had assured him that eyeballs were an extension of the brain.

"Not as good as Mom used to make," Big Ed commented as he dug into his plate of deep fried sciatic nerves. His wife Jennifer rolled her eyes. "If you would get some of the good stuff you might actually stand a chance to enjoy this," she replied. But what really roiled her was the reference to his mother. Though she had passed away when he was nine years old, in some ways her specter was ever present and Jennifer could never live up to his distant memories of her. Jennifer sometimes wanted to suggest, in her own defense, that nobody could possibly be as angelic as his recollection of her; that surely the very fact that she passed away at such a tender age had contributed to her sainthood in his mind. But that was sacred ground that she could never trample.

"It's hard for me to enjoy anything when it's $30 per plate," replied Big Ed, though he knew full well that he would not be the one to pick up the bill. Grandpa J would pay, as he always had since Big Ed had lost his job with a large accounting firm and was now reduced to stints of CPA work with a temp agency. "My taxes go to pay his government pension!" Big Ed had once exploded to Jennifer.

"Does no one else have moral issues with the buffet?" Big Ed wondered. It seemed to be against everything he believed in or thought was good. That was it. It was dehumanizing. The good things had been replaced by nothing but appetite, and consumption itself was held up as a virtue. As he contemplated this, something tickled his nostrils and he sneezed. His nose came off in the CSF soup. He defiantly scooped it out with his sallow hand as it floated atop the salty broth. The kids fought to hold in their laughter, as if fate had suddenly judged their father and admonished him to lighten up a little.

"Everything bad in the world is here, concentrated in one place," Big Ed thought. "Us zombies included."

# Anglo Saxon Zombie Conquest

Where, in your high science
and singular ownership of the day,
and now even the night,
will I find the trueness of blue?

You have gobbled the world
in continental bites, kept your blood
small, your lines pure like acid.
When, my grandfathers,
did you begin believing only in yourselves?
I am a Barbarian.

I have the papers to prove it, and papers
prove everything. You taught me that.

My blood is a sword;
my blood is a broken word;
my blood crawls
from sea to shining sea.
I am helpless in my armor.
I cannot touch you from here.

—Stewart S. Warren

# A Mind is a Terrible Thing to Taste

### Nick Kimbro

There was this girl once who claimed to know what I'd eaten for dinner based on the flavor of my spunk. If I'd had hot wings, for example, she would claim that it was hot. If I'd had coffee, she would claim that it was bitter. Salad, either light or gritty, depending on what lettuce I'd used. Sometimes I would test her by consuming strange combinations: peanut butter on Tostitos, for example, with a raspberry vinaigrette. Her palette was not that discerning.

I have not tasted spunk, before or since, but a mind is very much the same way. I cannot tell what the person has eaten—in most cases he or she will not have eaten for a long time—but every once in a while when I sink my ruined teeth into their brains, rather than a shock of flavor, I experience another shock: like remembrance without any detail—a burning, a brief crackling of synapses.

I cannot verify these findings. Though the Infected surprise me sometimes with their intelligence, they do not speak, and so I mustn't speak.

'Infected' is the word I have for them. It was also the word I had before, so I am in need of a new word, I think. We did not want to call them the other thing because we had seen those movies. We knew that those movies were movies, and that those words were words used in movies. Also, we had learned already that a lot of what happened in the movies was wrong. People in movies tend to be very cruel following a disaster or outbreak. They decivilize. Their animal instincts take over and they become ruthless. The truth is that we usually find them in their homes having been dead for some time, gnawed upon by their pets. Fortunately, we are not shy about leftovers.

In the beginning, I lived alone in my studio beneath a shitty tin complex in East Austin. A number of artists had taken refuge there following the outbreak, surrounded by their work, as if it possessed some keen ability to help keep them invisible. For most, it was sound reasoning.

At that point we still were waiting for the military to fix everything. We knew they had started it—we knew without knowing it, possibly because of the movies—and we listened to the airwaves, waiting for their promises to come through. All we heard was static, then nothing. This we referred to as The Quiet.

We remained in our studios, the more romantic among us continuing to work in spite of what had happened, crossing paths only when we ventured out for food. Then we were not friends, but competitors. We resented each others' successes.

For a long time, the wind was all that we heard. Then their distant baying began, quietly, growing in volume as they worked their way through Barton Springs, down West 6th, and into the lower-class neighborhoods where we were.

I'd known that I was going to kill someone for a while before they arrived. It had occurred to me even before the outbreak, when all we had were the movies. My victim's name was Brian Celio. He was a painter who worked in the top level of the building next to mine. When the East Austin Studio Tours came around, his was the studio all the rich bitches from West Austin mingled at, murmuring to one another about his daring technique of cutting up prints and gluing the scraps onto canvases, then painting big black stick figures over them engaged in different prurient acts, the imagining of which, as far as I could tell, was his one creative talent.

When the moaning finally arrived one evening, I listened to them banging against the corrugated tin. Everyone in their studios remained silent, hoping we could fool them into going away. Soon, the banging gave way to the sound of wood columns cracking, tin walls caving in, and then the screaming began.

That was my cue.

I burst from my studio splattered in red paint, my face bone-white, black bags slung beneath my eyes, and stumbled across the dirt courtyard toward Brian Celio's studio. It was dusk, and there was still an orange glow in the air even though the sun had disappeared from sight. A number of Infected glanced at me as I passed, and I will admit that I was nervous. They hobbled on legs that looked as though they had been broken multiple times, their clothes hanging off of them in tatters, their skin decomposing. They did not seem to mind me, though. Instead, stumbled past in pursuit of other, less-composed prey.

I rapped on the door to his studio: "Brian, it's me," I told him. "Open up. They're coming this way."

"Find your own hideout!" he cried from within. I could imagine him cowering in the back corner of his studio, armed with a palette knife he'd never, ever learned to use. I yanked against the twin doors, but they were chained.

"The doors aren't holding them, Brian. They've gotten to everyone and they're going to get to you too if you don't open this fucking door and follow me."

He was silent for a moment. "But," he whimpered, "what about my work, my canvasses. You want me to leave them?"

I sighed. "I don't care what you do with your goddamn paintings. Bring them with you. Hang them around your neck for all I care—maybe it'll frighten them away. But if you don't come with me now you're going to be eaten alive. Hear me? Eat-en a-liiive."

I could hear him swallowing spit, trying to decide whether or not to trust me. A group of Infected wandered a short distance behind me and paused to see what had caught my attention. I marched in place so that they would see, swung my arms against the door and moaned, "UHHHHNNN."

"What's that?" whispered Brian. He was beside the door now.

"Nothing. Just open up and come on before it's too late."

The three behind me stopped and were facing in my direction now: two deadmen and a deadwoman began to stumble toward me. I could hear Brian inside fumbling with the key in the padlock, and when he finally did open the door, damned if he didn't have one of his god-awful paintings clutched firmly under one arm! I wanted to shout at him, but as soon as he saw the three Infected persons stumbling toward us he cried out and dropped the painting, tried to run back inside but I grabbed him by the shoulders and sank my teeth into the soft flesh of his neck.

I bit down hard, much harder than I needed to, and when I pulled back blood spurted out like he was in one of the movies and had a pump wired through his sleeve. His hand jerked up to cover his wound and he collapsed. The group of Infected reached us and paused for a moment. I tensed, waiting to see what would happen. They lunged forward, scrambling across the ground, and each began to chew on one of his limbs. I exhaled relief, and reminded myself to groan as I crouched over the top of him.

"Hector?" he whispered. He looked stunned, unable to feel any of the pain. I bent forward and pretended to eat his neck, meanwhile straining to hear. "You were always jealous," he said, very softly, and I could not believe it. I turned back to him and grinned—which was a mean thing to do, looking back—then grabbed a nearby rock and smashed his head with it. The skin opened immediately, revealing a smear of bright red fluid, and in two or three more tries his skull finally split open. The brains there were bruised like an abraded piece of fruit, more liquid than anything else, and I stared at them for a long moment, mesmerized. Those around me paused in their chewing, bits of flesh hanging from their lips, and glanced between me and it— encouragingly, I thought. I poked at it, hoping that I could remove a piece, although it did not pull apart like I'd hoped. I glanced at his face and his eyes were still open. His body twitched slightly. I bent forward and sank my teeth in, again biting much harder than I needed to, pulled a piece away and began to chew. This sent the other three into a frenzy. One at a time, they each lunged forward and buried their faces into the gaping wound on his head, came up chewing.

That's when it happened: the flash, the feeling. It felt like what I'd experienced sometimes late at night in my studio, when I was sure I was the only one working, when I could see the form in front of me, wet and shimmering, and I was exhausted, but too enthralled to tear myself away.

"Motherfucker," I breathed (the others were too preoccupied to notice). It was Brian Celio's inspiration I felt! Brian Celio's faux-rebel bullshit! I felt sick. I wanted to puke, but knowing the potential consequences of this I managed to swallow instead. I could feel it warm inside my stomach. And as crazy as it sounds, I felt then that I had lost something: an innocence, perhaps, that had zero to do with the fact that I had just murdered and eaten another man's brains.

When the others had finished they rose with blood smeared over their faces. The two men stumbled off, heads tilted sideways, listening for which direction the screams were coming from now. The woman, however, stayed a moment. She was very pale and had long hair. She reminded me of a woman I'd seen hosting the news at one point. A web of dead arteries stretched across the skin of her neck, and her cheeks, I could see, were beginning to wear thin. She stared at me for a moment with eyes that were not quite vacant before stumbling after the two men toward the other side of the complex where all of the mayhem seemed to be taking place.

I watched her depart, and cast one more glance at Brian, who's gnawed-upon corpse laid soaking into the ground, before stumbling after her, leaning first one way, then another, moaning at the darkening sky, hoping that there would be no one left to judge me when all was through.

The problem I have found with Infected is that they do not stop. They stumble on, able to run when pursuit calls for it, but unable to sit. When there is nothing to pursue they keep moving, as if in a trance, as if sleepwalking, and I move with them, also in a trance. It is strange what happens to your mind when you walk for long enough, the way it empties, but also your body. In the beginning, I found I had to copy their way of walking; stumbling from side to side as though walking through a strong wind, although the sky was heavy and hot and still. My gait is more honest now. There is little left in my head besides need.

Despite everything though, I do sometimes require sleep. I am forced to slip away when nobody's looking, and when I do, I feel like a younger brother called in early for bedtime. I don't think that anyone notices exactly, except for maybe her, although I cannot tell whether her awareness of me is something real or something I imagined. I follow after her like a shadow. The skin on her heels is decomposing although I cling to them anyway. Her body is a little more ruined every day, the holes in her cheeks widening, although I am a part of her ruination and it does not bother me.

I have begun to call her Anna—in my head, of course.

If she does notice me leaving, she gives no sign. When exhaustion overcomes me I slip away as quietly as possible and find myself a place out of the way, where, to make matters worse, I often lay awake for long periods. In these moments my mind is active; they are the only times I ever feel truly alone.

Sometimes when I have gone to sleep but am not sleeping, I paint. I keep a palette knife tucked inside my pants, and though oil paints are hard to come by, some time ago I did manage to find a bottle of linseed oil. I have found that if I mix it with blood I can make a pretty convincing cherry color. Bone powder too can be used to pull off a chalky off-white. Not an artist's dream palette, but the two of them are often enough to suggest some vague semblance of form, and to provide texture.

I paint on walls, I paint on boards. Usually portraits of those from whom I gather the blood and the bone. There is a problem, though. That first experience with Brian, the sensation I felt eating his…you know…has stayed with me. When I paint, I can feel it—an electric heat like inspiration—and I cannot distinguish his inspiration from my own. This distresses me. In the mornings I am happy to leave, to be out in the open again, the sound of my own feet against the pavement filling the dead air. If the others have not come across any survivors, they are usually easy to catch up with. I find them moving in the same direction, at the same pace they were however many hours ago.

I locate Anna.

I move beside her.

We are partners together in stumbling.

I sometimes wish that Infected did sleep, then I could paint her at night: record her features, map her deterioration, leave record of her in the places we stumble, like snake skins. I watch her flesh falling away from her and I am ashamed of my own complexion, which, covered by grime and gore, is nevertheless whole and unblemished.

I am ashamed of my pretenses.

One night, after I have broken off from the rest, I stand over a broken body in front of a blank wall, trying to will myself to begin, to transform that image into form and color. I am careful not to get inspired, because that would remind me of Brian, and also what I have given up. The memories I have do not feel like my own. I feel the knowledge inside of me all coming together, the invisible lines that once held it apart now disappearing. I am confused. Without realizing it, I grasp the palette knife in my hand and hold it against my forearm, press down hard. Blood seeps from the wound and forms a shell over my skin. I do it again, cutting different parts of me until I am hardly recognizable. I do feel pain, but the pain inspires me. It feels new and significant, like a butterfly transforming into a caterpillar. My body is the canvas, and as I am cutting myself, not once do I think of Brian Celio.

When I rejoin with the others I am giddy. My flesh is in tatters. I locate Anna and keep glancing at her as though waiting for her to notice. She does not, and I guess I'm fine with that. We stumble upon a group of survivors and now they appear different to me: they are like deer in headlights, emaciated and searching for food. The violence we commit against them does not even feel like violence.

We stumble onward. Propelled by need, sustained by inertia... the word sounds foreign in my brain. Inertia. I look toward Anna, certain that it's a much better name for her, but Anna is her name already and she would not appreciate me changing it on a whim.

I realize I can no longer remember my own name, but I forget the fact immediately. Forget about my forgetting. I am devolving, but I am too tired to think to think about it. Too hungry.

We eat what we find. We waste nothing. We do crave some parts more than others.

The mind.

The source.

That mysterious burning.

I move closer to Anna—or was it Inertia?—and our proximity feels more and more natural. There are probably nine of us drifting down the highway somewhere. The land is flat and barren, scattered with rusted oil pumps that double themselves with shadow. And as the sun slips down the western sky, I turn and see it shining through the woman's wrecked cheeks, glinting on the enamel as though she is carrying the sun in her mouth, as though she is swallowing the daylight.

I move closer and brush her hand with my own, wait for a reaction.

I brush her hand again, and repeat the action several times more before finally taking hold. It is not cold like I imagined it would be, but hot; hotter, in fact, than any living thing could be. I feel seared by the heat although I hold on, waiting for a reciprocation, waiting for her hand to take hold of my hand also, or a sign perhaps, from her eyes that are not quite vacant, her body that is not quite ruined.

The last of the sunlight disappears behind some distant hills, leaving a trail of colors in the sky, and as it does I notice the tops of buildings coming into view on the horizon. I know this city, I know. I know its name somewhere, but right now it escapes me. With each step the buildings grow larger, looming there, dark and still, empty by all appearances, although we know it is not. Somewhere there are people still hiding. Somewhere there are meals to be had, and these meals call to us, scream to us, make our stomachs grumble. I groan to let the others know what I see, what it means, but the woman—my Anna—knows, I know, because her grasp tightens suddenly on my hand. I turn to look at her face, but it is fixed on the horizon, on the building tops, the corners of her mouth slightly upturned.

I follow her gaze and smile at the shadows gathering there on the horizon, and in a flash of lucidity I think this feels like the beginning of something. It feels like the beginning of something good.

# Zombie A Go-Go

## Brian Behr Valentine

"Reporter or cop?" The bartender demanded of Marley while cleaning a glass.

"Neither."

"You're looking around all bug-eyed like a reporter but you dress like a cop."

"I said, neither."

"Look pal, you're not pale enough to be undead."

Marley growled, wolf-like and the bartender brightened. "Hey, you're a lycanthrope!"

"Yes, and a corporate banker."

"Me too… a lycanthrope, I mean. I'm not blood thirsty enough for corporate America," he chuckled, then stuck his hand out. Marley sniffed, then held his own out in return.

"Sorry about the third degree. The owner don't like the straights snooping around, ya know?"

"I can imagine."

"And… Dude, look: No marking. I'm also the janitor."

"Do I look like some kind of cur," asked Marley with derision.

"Sorry. It's happened before. People get excited. Say, how about a beer?" asked the bartender

"Sure."

"On the house."

"Cool."

"In this place, it's almost always Bloody Mary's. Fucking vampires," he added with distaste. "So what brings you down to the underground?" the bartender asked placing a foaming mug in front of him.

"A girl," Marley said sipping. He turned on the stool to lean against the bar.

The place had three poles on small platforms around the darker edges of the room, and one central platform with a lot of lights. Marley watched the strippers and drank deeply. When the beer was done the bartender had a fresh one ready.

"Thanks," said Marley.

"Gotta charge you for this one."

Marley pulled some cash from a pocket and tossed it on the bar.

"If you're looking for a girl, you'll need to see *Count Dracula* down there." The bartender nodded in the direction of a table where three undead girls sat with a vamp in full Halloween get up.

"What's with the outfit?" Marley asked. He didn't know a lot of vampires, but the ones he did know despised the gaudy cape and bowtie get up.

"You know pimps; love dressing up, no tact, no couth. But if you want a girl, he's the 'king of undead head,' or so he claims. Get it bit right off if you want. Course, a vampire can stick it right back on and you couldn't, so I guess you'll probably want to forego that particular option," he chuckled.

"I'm not looking for a hooker," Marley said absently, not enjoining the bartender's attempt at mirth.

"A lap dance then? Girls are over there on the couches waiting. All zombies in this place, though. Thus the name." He shuddered.

"I'm looking for a particular girl."

"Ah."

"Ah, what?" asked Marley with a low growl.

"I see it once in awhile."

Marley nodded then looked down into the beer.

"She a fresh one," the bartender coaxed.

"Couple of weeks."

"She'll be on the center stage. The fresh ones start there. Then after a while…" He indicated the farthest stripper poles. Marley glanced at the girls. Even in the subdued lighting he could see the death on them.

Their movements were rhythmic but stiff. Bone showed in places. Being alive, it sickened him to watch these decomposing corpses do a sexy bump and grind. When one of the worst girls did a stripper-squat showing only a few shreds of grisly meat hanging from her pelvic bone, Marley turned back to the bar.

"Embalming only lasts so long," the bartender commented. "The vamps get high on the formaldehyde; the girls get ugly quick once it's sucked out. Too bad: a dive like this is the only way they can support themselves. Not that they need much, but broke is broke, you know?"

"Yeah," said Marley distractedly.

"So… you wantin' to tear her up all over again," asked the bartender. "Had a lot of fun the first time and wanting another go?"

Marley didn't answer and the bartender looked him over. "Somebody important?"

Marley nodded as he gazed down into his glass.

"Ah… she didn't turn?" the bartender guessed.

"No," said Marley with morose, lip-trembling emotional pain.

"Just… died?"

Marley nodded.

"Your wife?"

"Fiancée," Marley choked out.

"Thought you'd run across the moors together under the moonlight for eternity."

Marley nodded, sobbed once, then leaned back and howled mournfully.

## Cloud Gazing

Floating clouds look like chunks
of flesh to a starving zombie,
who moves like a shark under the surface
of zenith he wishes would fall,
so he could rage closer to the sun
that burns his jaundice, half-decayed skin,
the keeps him chasing his own gluttony,
stuck in a figure eight inferno of inhabited
apocalypse, devouring the soon to be extinct
living of which he wishes he was made.

—John McCarthy

# Dead Song

## Jay Wilburn

The man walked into the dark room and closed the door behind him. He put on the headphones and sat down on the stool. Images of zombies flashed on the screen in front of him. He ignored them and opened the binder on the stand. He pulled the microphone a little closer and waited.

In the darkness, a voice came over the headphones and said, "Go ahead and read the title card again for us slowly so we can set levels."

The man read with particular slowness and articulation, "Dead Doc. Productions presents *The Legend of Tiny "Mud Music" Jones* in association with After World Broadcasters and Reaniment America, a subsidiary of the Reclaiment Broadcasters Company, with permission of the Reformed United States Federal Government Broadcasters Rights Commission."

He waited silently after he finished.

The voice finally came back on, "Sounds good. We're going to get coverage on the main text for alternate takes. We're also going to have you read the quotes as placeholders until we get character actors to replace them. Read them normally without any affected voice. If we need another tone or tempo, we'll let you know and we'll take another pass at that section. There is also some new material we are adding into the documentary."

"Okay," the man answered.

The voice ordered, "When you're ready, go ahead with section one, then stop."

The man took a drink of water, swallowed, and then waited for a couple beats. He began, "Dead World Records was one of the first music companies to come online after order was restored. They were recording and signing artists during the height of the zombie plague. Tobias Baker and Hollister Z are credited with founding the company.

"They operated from a trailer and storage building on Tobias's family farm, surviving off the land, and clearing zombies from the property between recording and editing."

A black and white image of zombie pits scrolled across the screen as the guys in the booth ran the images to check timing. The man ignored it.

He continued, "They do deserve credit for recognizing the continued value of musical culture and history while everyone else was focused purely on survival. They had the vision to gather and record the unique musical evolution of the Dead Era which shaped all music that came after it."

A grainy video of the men working in their studio rolled on the screen. The man stopped and watched as he waited.

The video froze and the voice said, "Skip to section four. The text is edited from the last time you read it. Read it over once and tell us when you are ready."

The man obliged them by scanning it over. He said, "Ready."

The voice said, "We're rolling on section four."

The man took another drink before he began, "The real unsung heroes of the rise of Dead World Records Inc. are clearly the collectors that agreed to bring the recordings back to the studio. Many of them were musicians themselves and trekked hundreds of miles through zombie infested territory to find musical gatherings of the various unique pockets of survivors."

A picture of Tiny flashed on the screen with his name under it. He was wearing shorts, hiking boots, and holding a walking stick. A picture of another man wearing a helmet and carrying a bat replaced it. The name below it was Satchel Mouth Murderman.

The man continued, "Music from this period is clearly defined by both isolation and strange mixtures of people and cultures. The gatherings of these musical laboratories (many of which were destroyed and lost long before the zombies were) is the legacy of men like Tiny "Mud Music" Jones."

Stills of Tiny with arrows pointing him out passed over the screen.

The man read on, "Tiny traveled farther and gathered more than any other collector. His introverted style and musical talent won trust and entry into enclaves of people no one else could penetrate. Some historians believe much of what we know of Dead Era culture is built off the exploration of Tiny Jones."

The man stopped.

The voice ordered, "Go with section six when ready."

The man began as soon as he had the page, "Tiny was so named due to his four foot eleven inch stature. Even Tobias Baker and Hollister Z didn't know him by any other name besides Tiny. He carried a pack which looked heavier than him with more instruments and recording equipment than food and clothes. He usually played for his supper and in turn got others to play for him with tape rolling."

After a short pause, the voice said, "Section seven needs to have a foreboding tone. It's going to be over some heavy music. Articulate it well. Go when ready."

The man read, "He is also the source of the Mud Music legend making three infamous trips into Dead Era Appalachia in search of it."

The voice said, "Let's do that again. Try a little more flow, but a darker tone."

The man read it again. The voice acknowledged, "That was good. Go with section ten now when you're ready."

The man began, "Tiny discovered Donna Cash, whereabouts unknown. Donna Cash is the most quoted artist on the Tribute Wall on Survivor Book. Bootleg recordings of her work are still in the top one hundred downloads each year. Donna Cash was best known for mash-ups of Madonna and Johnny Cash on the drag queen circuit. She was touring when doing so was deadly even for individuals not in drag.

"Tiny is responsible for the only known original recordings of 'True Folsom Blues,' 'Vogue the Line,' 'When the Ray of Light Comes Around,' 'Like a Ring of Fire' and many other songs that have been covered thousands of times by both straight and drag acts in the Recovery Era. Donna Cash has also been documented more times on the missing person Sighting Wall on Survivor Book than any other person. Mr. S. Parker, the current CEO of Survivor Book, has put a permanent block on Donna Cash sightings.

"Other popular artists on the Dead Era drag circuit that were first recorded by Tiny included Pink Orbosin, Ms. Britt Britt Rotten, and Jerri Leigh Lopper."

The man stopped again and took a drink of water. The voice said, "Let's go with section fourteen."

The man scanned the first few lines before he started, "Tiny Jones recorded examples of New Swing from Pittsburg, Philadelphia, and Cincinnati. The music was originally used as a distraction for zombies while scavengers went out into the cities for supplies. Traditionally, it is played on rooftops. New Swing is a blend of Big Band, modern Jazz, 50's Rock, and R & B. It is defined by a reverb off of buildings. Most modern New Swing musicians create the sound electronically. Tiny recorded P. City Warriors, The Big Bloods led by the late Cap Kat Krunch, and the New Philly Phunk which still plays in Las Vegas with a new lineup.

"'*We let Tiny record after he fought his way to the building and knocked on the door holding two zombie heads in his hands. Would you say no to a cat that showed up like that?*'—Miles Diddy, P. City Warriors original line-up"

The man paused again.

The voice asked, "Do you need a break?"

"No, I'm fine," the man answered.

The voice said, "Turn to section twenty-one and start from the third line on to the end of that section."

The man recited, "Glam Grass was discovered outside of Nashville. A tour group of old eighties metal stars ended up in a militia compound with a religious cult. After the fire, Tiny's recordings were the only record of the founders of this musical form. It was defined by electric guitars accompanied by traditional blue grass instruments. The Glam Grass artists usually sang about religious subject matter, often out of the book of Revelation. The style is described as typically heavy, but surprisingly upbeat."

The voice said, "Now section twenty-seven."

The man read, "Across the South, a style known as Death Gospel emerged from places where churches became the refuge of nonbelievers. It was a movement where metal influence came against traditional hymns. Unlike Glam Grass, Death Gospel was darker, slower, featuring minor chords, and was usually played acoustically. This style was documented by several collectors and is still a staple of churches in the Deep South."

The voice directed, "Section twenty-nine."

The man turned one page and found his place, "Tiny was involved in spreading the music and not just recording it. This is noticed most in the style known as Cherokee R&B or Red Blues. Tiny is credited with moving the music from North Carolina all the way to Oklahoma.

"'*The day he came to the fences, the zombies parted and allowed him through. He was the first white man admitted to the Cherokee Nation Compounds.*'—Chief Blue Wolf Pine, rhythm guitar and vocals, The Silent Dead Players.

"With variations across the South and West, Red Blues included Native American chants combined with tradition blues instrumentation and riffs. Later, Red Blues diverged more from this original formula. The later style was sometimes referred to as Blue Sioux."

After a longer pause, the voice came back and said, "Section thirty-five has been rewritten. Start that from the beginning."

The man read it silently, then began, "Shock-A-Billy was one of Tiny Jones's favorite collections. It featured shock rocker make-up, dark subjects, and Punk/Country combinations. It was mostly advanced by touring acts. Tiny expressed that he felt a kinship with the traveling musicians. Shock-A-Billy artists that stayed in one place were looked on as cowards within the community, posers. The tour busses were often dragsters pulled by animals.

"'*There were competitions between the Shockers to see who could get the most elaborate dragster. At one point, my band had the three-story 'Tarmansion.' It was built on the chasse of a tractor trailer and was pulled by 26 horses. It's a wonder we didn't get eaten by zombies trying to put on a show just traveling from point A to point B.*'—Big Bubba Tarmancula, Big Bubba Tarmancula and the Tarmen, Rock and Roll Hall of Fame.

"Shock-A-Billy tee shirts, tour posters, and images are infused in pop culture throughout the Recovery Era."

The voice said, "Read section forty now."

The man drank the rest of his water and then read, "Several

styles of urban infusion developed during the Dead Era and were all connected by and counter-influenced by one another through Tiny's travels.

"Gangster and Western was defined by rivalry as opposed to isolation. Vocals are considered more melodic than traditional B.Z. Era rap. There were often references to local blood feuds between ranches that don't make much sense to modern listeners.

"The ranchers herded animals for food and herded zombies between ranches to foil rustlers and to threaten rival ranches. The results were often quite bloody and costly to human life. Tiny was the only collector to ever go to certain sections of Texas, Arizona, and New Mexico.

"The most infamously violent ranch war was between Big Daddy Bronco and His Boys vs. the Lincoln County O.G.'s. Tiny was the only one that succeeded in recording music from both camps.

"Hip Bach is the tag given to another style of music Tiny documented where inner city orchestras and concert halls became the shelters for local populations.

"*In all the history of time, you have never heard a style as close to God and as close to the street as this. This music allowed people to transcend the situation and see the secrets of life while being surrounded by the walking dead.*'—Mr. Butter Hands, Low Town Symphony.

"Tiny Jones often traced music back to its source as he did with Slam Jo. Tiny traveled all the way to the Lud Mine Camp in the Sierra-Nevada Mountains. Slam Jo featured spoken word over banjo. New Wave Slam Jo documented by Tiny and other collectors began to incorporate other instruments.

"Tiny Jones was a legend in the Zed Head community. He was deeply involved in documenting the evolution of this daring style of music which mixed techno and house music over recordings of zombies.

"The most famous story of Tiny's involvement was the two weeks he accompanied DJ RomZom out in the open in a gathering expedition through Los Angeles.

"Many fans question modern Zed Head since most D.J.'s don't gather their own moan tracks anymore.

"The recent release of the alleged 'final recording' of Tiny 'Mud

Music' Jones has resulted in a rebirth of the Zed Head movement. Border Patrol forces and security have been increased to discourage Zed Head gatherers from attempting to perform unauthorized expeditions into the uncleared, gray zones."

The voice clicked back into the headphones, "You're doing a great job. Turn to section sixty-four. This is all new material."

The man turned to the page.

"Go when ready," the voice requested.

The man read, "'*Tiny and the Mud Music Legend is the modern Area 51, Brown Mountain Lights, and Kennedy Assassination rolled into one. How do you tell a ghost story to a generation of people that either witnessed Z-Day and survived all the way to the Recovery or that were born in the world after the Dead Era began? What are you going to say that can scare a generation that treats the zombie drills in school like a tornado drill? You tell them about Tiny and the Mud Music. I hadn't stopped being scared since that day.*'—Kidd Banjo, former Dead Music Records collector and solo artist."

A map of the B.Z. Era United States with red lines drawing themselves across it appeared on the screen and distracted the man for a split second, but he found his place in the script and continued like a professional, "The first expedition Tiny Jones made into the Appalachian territory took him into the area that today roughly constitutes the border of Gray Zone 3. This collection exposed him to traditional mountain music not unlike recordings from the early 1920's B.Z.E. from the same area. Tiny described trailers with wooden add-ons and trinket trash, folk art he saw on the expedition that expressed the same style, character, and sentiment of the music that had managed to stay unchanged through a century and a zombie invasion."

The map now had blue lines appearing and drawing deeper into the mountains. The man read, "The second expedition into the infamous region known as Gray Zone 4 came back with a corrupted recording that could not be found later.

"'*Something was different about Tiny after that second trip. He was devastated by the recording being garbled. He had me and Hollis drop what we were doing and immediately sit down in a closed, locked room to play it for us. He had whispered the words 'Mud Music' like it was something akin to voodoo. When it started out, it gave me chills because the sound was all fucked up and unearthly. I thought it was the music at first because of course this was Tiny and there was no telling what he might bring back. Then, I saw him crying like he had just watched his new born child get torn apart by the zombies. He was shaking and beating his fists against his head. Hollis had to hold his hands down to stop him. Believe it or not, that's the last time I ever saw Tiny.'*—Tobias Baker, co-founder Dead World Records Inc.; former CEO D.W. Farms; deceased.

"'*Tiny was changed. He was the most enthusiastic lover of music I had ever known. He was tough as a block of oak. I believe every story I ever heard of him parting seas of zombies, cutting off their heads and carrying them in to impress musicians, and walking right through them to find the music. He was fearless because he loved the music so much. After that trip, he was obsessed. He sat and listened to that recording over and over and over and over and over. After he left, we never found that recording again, but I still hear that shit in my nightmares because of him repeating it and repeating it those last few nights. He sat with his ear to the speaker swearing that it was under the interference. That it was under that ruined recording. Then, he said he heard the voices of the singers speaking to him. He tried to describe the instruments they built. I can't remember now, but I wish I had recorded him talking. I didn't know that when he left that last time that that was it. I would have tried to stop him, if I had known, but he was Tiny Jones. I don't think I could have stopped him if I had tried.'*—Hollister Z, co-founder Dead World Records Inc."

The man stopped and looked up to see a blown-out, color photo of Tiny Jones leaning over with his ear to a speaker.

When his headphones crackled, it made the man jump a little. The voice just said, "Section sixty-five."

The man collected himself and began, "He did not return from his third expedition. There were no other confirmed sightings either. Only Donna Cash has more unconfirmed sightings on Internet America.

"As witnessed by Tobias Baker and Hollister Z, Kidd Banjo returned to the farm with a cassette he claimed was given to him by Tiny Jones. Kidd Banjo was a collector for Dead World and in the Recovery Era he rose to prominence as a Shock-A-Billy Revival artist. Cassettes were not in common use at the time and there are no other Tiny Jones recordings on a cassette tape. Kidd claimed he was in the Fort Guilford Colony in western Virginia near the North Carolina border. Somehow Tiny had entered his room in the fort, had awakened him without disturbing the other men in the bunks, and had given him the tape without being detected by the guards either entering or leaving the heavily secure fort.

"Kidd Banjo insisted it was Tiny and that he was covered in cuts and bruises. He told Kidd to take it directly to D.W. Farms. He said it was the only way he could record it and get out. He said he had to go back or they would know what he had done and they would come looking for him. Kidd asked who 'they' were, but Tiny shushed him and left without answering.

"The following is an excerpt of the recording that was recently released by Dead World Records and has been heavily sampled in recent Zed Head tracts. Please, be warned that the sounds are disturbing including apparent zombie attacks and human screams.

"There is only one section that has distinguishable words near the end of the 38 minute 20 second recording. The voice has not been definitively identified to be Tiny Jones. The two most common interpretations of the section you are about to hear is either 'The horror of it. They obey the mud music. Death is beautiful.' Or 'The whores they obey. The mud music death is beautiful.'"

The man stared at the words he had just read for a long moment. When he looked up, there was a black and white photo of the side of a trailer. There were painted words on the side which read, 'Don't come looking for us again or we'll come back for you.' There was an arrow superimposed over the photo pointing at something under the words.

The voice came back on and said, "Section sixty-six."

The man turned the page and read on, "The following vandalism was found on the trailer on the D.W. Farms property about a week after Kidd Banjo delivered the cassette he claimed was from Tiny Jones. Hollister Z claims the medicine bag hanging from the nail at the bottom of the photograph contained a pair of human testicles among other items such as teeth and fingernails. This was never confirmed and there was no indication of whether or not Tiny died as a result of foul play or from any other cause.

"Other collectors did go into the Appalachian region in search of the secret of the 'last recording' of Tiny Jones and the legendary Mud Music despite the sinister warning. Those that claimed to know of the Mud Music told the collectors stories of mystical powers including the power to tame or command zombies with it, of deals with the devil-god of the walking corpses, and of the fact that the source was always to be found somewhere deeper in the hills. No other collectors were able to bring back any recordings of this legendary music either."

The man stopped and saw a shot of a newspaper with a file picture of Tobias Baker under the headline: **Dead World Records Exec Found butchered in Gray Zone.**

The voice said, "Section sixty-seven."

The man actually said, "When did this happen?"

The voice came back on, "Stop there. I think you're in the wrong section. Sixty-seven starts with 'recently.' See if you can find the spot again."

The man turned the page, "I have it."

The voice said, "Begin when ready."

The man reached for his glass, but realized it was empty. He went ahead and started, "Recently, Tobias Baker, co-founder of Dead World Records Inc., was granted an unprecedented clearance for a manned expedition into Grey Zone 4, one of two uncleared areas deep in the Appalachian Mountains. Contact with radio and GPS were lost on the second day of the expedition. Aerial searches did not reveal the location of the expedition nor evidence to their whereabouts. Three days after the expedition was scheduled to end, Border Patrol claims seven men began approaching the gates from inside Zone 4. It wasn't until they were within ten feet and had not identified themselves that they were identified as zombies. The guards opened fire. The Border Patrol claims the zombies placed one severed head each on the ground by the gate. The seven zombies then returned to the woods despite taking heavy fire. Cameras at the gate malfunctioned before this alleged event and sources asked to remain unnamed.

"Upon inspection, the seven heads proved to be zombified and active. Officials were called in. The heads were deactivated using surgical lasers. They were then placed in secure cases using robots.

"It has been confirmed that six of the heads belonged to the members of the ill-fated D.W.R. expedition including Tobias Baker. The seventh head, which was considerably more decayed and was missing all its teeth, has not.

"An unconfirmed rumor on Internet America claims the head is that of Tiny Jones. DNA samples are unavailable and the R.U.S. agency involved has not commented.

"Hollister Z, co-founder of Dead World Records Inc., has been unavailable for comment.

"The following is an unconfirmed voice mail recording that surfaced on Internet America two days before the heads were found. Be warned that this recording contains graphic details of decapitation and dismemberment. It is quite disturbing."

The man stopped and looked up at a picture of a decayed, severed head in a thick plastic case.

The voice said, "Begin with section sixty-eight, when you are ready."

"I think I need a break. I'm out of water," the man said as he stared at the screen.

There was a long pause. He was about to repeat his request when there was a click in his headphones and the drawn out hiss of an open mic. He waited a little longer and then thought he heard distant whispers in the background. He listened as he looked at the severed head on the screen in front of him. Then a voice came on and said, "When it is time, we will get you."

The screen went blank and the room was completely dark.

"What?" the man asked with a rush of fear.

The voice repeated, "We will break for about ten minutes. When it is time, we will come get you."

After another couple seconds, his eyes adjusted to the darkness in the room.

The man removed his headphones and walked toward the door in the dark.

# Skin Eulogy
*for Rick Genest - "Zombie Boy"*

praise the skull that becomes a bowl of soup
praise two black eyes and a gored out nose
praise the quiet piano keys of the mouth
the mandible and empty moan
praise the spine that refuses to curl
praise the body, too brittle to hold
praise the mottled skin, ragged and draped from ribs
praise the quilt that hides beneath skin
praise tendons; praise muscle fiber
    human roots that nourish seeds
praise dark insects sheltered by soil
centipedes and sow bugs
worms willing to eat doubt and grief
praise quarantine and her safe distance
death's silent screaming intimacy
inside the chest
praise the cemetery within each person
    the Reaper that will not be outrun
    watching through a canopy of bats
praise the grave's open hand
praise the spider's web; praise holding in
praise embalming's infinite hangover
praise bone; praise marrow
praise the spinneret's chrome shield
praise the Reaper who does not look away
praise the Reaper who completes every hunt
praise legs homeless and stumbling
praise the dead willing to stand

    —Colin Gilbert

# Wings

## Megan Dorei

There is a building on the corner of 3rd and Mass. It used to be a Borders for as long as I can remember, a brick-and-mortar closet full of books and music and coffee. But when the economy went to hell and the government began the inoculation process, the bookstore simply became one of many to nail boards to their windows.

That building and I are the same. Hollow. Empty. Rotting slowly from the inside. We used to hold so much color and life and vibrancy. Now we're in a shambles and no one bothers trying to see past the boarded windows. There is nothing there for them, nothing to salvage.

Say all but one.

Jo and I got inoculated at the same time but only I got sick. I think it must be because I don't eat Mexican food, but Jo doesn't like me to joke about it. Truthfully, no one knows why the injections poisoned some and not others. Medical tests are still being run, although I'm starting to suspect the government already knows and they're just not telling us because it's their fault. Jo says I'm being paranoid. I think she just wants me to shut up.

"Is this really supposed to take this long?" she asks the doctor impatiently. She is trying to chew on her fingernail—which she's already gnawed down to a nub—but her elbow is resting on her leg which, in classic Jo "Fidget" Evans fashion, is bouncing frantically up and down.

I smile at her, holding perfectly still on the exam table. "Why are you so concerned? *You've* got all the time in the world," I point out. I mean it as a joke, but Jo's never appreciated my sense of humor.

She levels me with a flat black glare. She doesn't say anything, but the "fuck you" is clear in her eyes. I wince at her guiltily.

It's been a month since my diagnosis. The virus is supposed to be a slow-acting infection that can sometimes lay dormant for years but I've already accelerated past the three-month marker. It has the doctors baffled. Usually one of the infected has about nine months to live after diagnosis. At the rate I'm going I'll have about three. Two, now.

"Miss Evans, you have to understand that exotic cases such as Danni are—"

"She is not a *case*," Jo interrupts. Her knee has stopped bouncing but she can't stop her hands from trembling. "She's a human being."

I can't see Dr. Weitz's face but I've always had a pretty good imagination, and the thought of his reaction makes me giggle.

"*What?*"

I hold up my hands hastily. Weitz grunts in disapproval but straightens me without a word.

"Well, Jo, I'm just not sure that term really applies to me anymore," I reply.

When the first reported case of what they call "autoimmune cytocide" came to light, the tabloids immediately nicknamed the virus "zombie-cide" because the first of the infected lost control of all bodily functions and ate his entire family.

It's been a little over a year and all total there have been one hundred and sixty thousand reported cases of "zombie-cide" in the United States.

I smile to myself, ignoring the quick prick as Weitz jams the needle into my spine. *And they used to joke about the zombie apocalypse*, I think.

Once Weitz has finished he sends Jo and I on our way. Plenty of other patients for him to see, I'm sure. It's no wonder he's become so impersonal when the whole world is depending on his professionalism.

On the way out, I creep closer to Jo until our arms brush. The walk to and from Dr. Weitz's room is always my least favorite part. The walls are lined with families, women sobbing into the arms of their spouses, children clutching at their parents' arms or wailing at the ceiling. And their eyes. Their eyes, which stare with fear or anger or blame. I will never get used to their resentment.

In the beginning, the virus was scoffed at. Some crazed man with a disease that the newspapers had staked as the living dead to feed the zombie craze. But people got sick. They slowly deteriorated, losing their senses—their sight, hearing, sense of smell, sense of taste, and eventually their mind. When they regained their senses, it was in the most lethal and primal sense of the word. In the end, the victims fed on any living being that they happened to be close to.

People began to panic. No one knew where the infection had come from, no one knew what it was, and no one knew of a cure. Even when evidence came out claiming that it was the government's fault—that something in the recent West Nile flu shots initially *caused* the zombie infections instead of preventing the flu—no one would be calm. Some people, myself included, lost all faith in the government. Others blindly turned to anyone offering a cure.

Stores—including pharmacies—began closing their doors, afraid to let the sickness spread. Our already-wounded economy dipped frighteningly close to a second depression. Hospitals were overrun—with zombies, with people who only *thought* they were zombies, and with people whose pharmacies no longer tailored their treatments.

A scapegoat was needed. Some blamed the government. Most blamed the zombies. And sometimes, looking at those faces in the hallway, I couldn't help feeling the same.

Without a word, Jo slips her fingers through mine and squeezes my hand. My body flushes with heat and I smile at her gratefully. She clutches my hand tightly until we step out into the semi-warm March air. Off to the right, the protestors shout and shake their picket signs at each other.

After the country fell into chaos and the blame fell on the zombies, two opposing groups of protestors formed. The zombie rights activists belong to OBSB—"Our Blood Still Beats." Nearly all of them are already zombies, but there are still some uninfected who have chosen to fight for us. Then there's the AEO—the "Abomination Eradication Organization." They fight with the same shameless tenacity as Fred

Phelps' gang, but whenever I think of their ridiculous name I just laugh.

I breathe deeply, ignoring the screaming protestors. "Beautiful day," I comment, stretching the kinks out of my arms. As the virus progresses, muscles deteriorate, leaving them perpetually sore. Kind of like the body aches I get when I have the flu.

Jo is silent beside me. I can't tell if her eyes are narrowed because of the blinding sun or if she's glaring at the sky. I purse my lips anxiously.

"Jo? Do you want to come over to my house? I just got some Smirnoff. The green apple kind you like," I add temptingly.

Jo shrugs and doesn't look at me. "Might as well. Feels like a drowning sorrows kind of day," she replies. I wince.

I didn't tell Jo about my diagnosis until last week. She'd been in Manhattan since the fall—a dancer at Juilliard—and I didn't want to be the cause of missed opportunities. She'd finally gotten away from me—the monster, the troublemaker, the poison pill. I didn't want to fuck that up.

But I had been drunk that night—my liver was going to fail anyway, so what was the point of preserving it? I called her, and even though I don't remember much of what I said I can remember clearly that I had to dial her number four times before she would actually pick up.

In the morning, amid the stupor of my hangover, I awoke to the frantic rapping of her knuckles on my front door. She had to sit down and tell me the conversation word for word just to remind me.

She's come to all of my doctor's appointments—taking an instant disliking to Dr. Weitz and "all his needles"—and staked a claim on a room at the Day's Inn just off the interstate. I keep telling her to go back to school, that there's nothing she can do for me now, but she refuses to listen.

"Jo…" I say now, but she won't let me get farther than that.

"C'mon, I'll drive you home," she sweeps over me. Her hand crushes mine as she steers me toward the parking lot.

Something comes over me then. I can't explain the steely resolve but I let it ground me anyway. I dig my heels into the concrete with surprising strength, jarring us both to a halt.

Jo whips around, glaring. "What are you doing?" she demands.

I shake my head. "No. We're not going home," I declare.

"*What?*"

I grin at her meaningfully. "We're going to Wal-Mart."

Her eyes grow wide with disbelief. She catches the double meaning in my words immediately. "*What?*" she repeats, completely blindsided.

I bob my head once decisively. "Yep. C'mon," I say and start to drag her into the parking lot.

"Danni, what the hell are you thinking? You need to go home and rest, you can't be—"

"Jo," I interrupt, turning to her. My tone is sharp and stern, and she flinches back as though I've slapped her. "I have two months left and then I am going to die. I'm thinking that I need to get in as much chaos as I can before that."

I see the tears welling up like little diamonds along the rims of her eyes. I stare at her without blinking, feeling her hand grow sweaty in mine. The spring sun blazes on my gray, sallow skin, and I can almost feel the cells crackling in the heat.

Finally, Jo nods. "Alright. Let's go," she murmurs, catching the one tear that falls on her finger.

On the ride across town, I roll down my window and lean out to feel the breeze rake its fingers through my hair. Jo glances at me, and for the first time since she arrived I see her smile.

"Music?" she asks, pulling a CD from the glove compartment.

My throat chokes up unexpectedly. It's one of the old mix tapes I made for her back in middle school. I nod, knowing my constricted throat will not let me speak.

We sing at the top of our lungs, windows rolled down, soaked in the breeze and the sunlight. Nostalgia sinks through me, a heavy and inspiring perfume drenching my bones. For a few precious moments, I can forget that I am dying.

Wal-Mart is as busy as it's always been, despite fear of the zombie epidemic. I grab Jo's hand and skip inside, both of us laughing over nothing.

"Where should we start, Butter Bagel?" Jo murmurs in a low, mock professional tone. The sound of my nickname in her voice makes my heart flutter.

"I don't know, Lily Flower," I reply, scanning the air-conditioned plane of discount clothes and groceries. I stop when I see the pharmaceutical aisles, jammed with customers.

"Mission: Magnum," I mutter. Jo screws up her face to keep from laughing and nods as seriously as she can.

We sneak into one of the aisles, one that's less densely populated, and head straight for the condoms. Trojan, Durex, Crown—all fly into our hands until our arms are full of them. Then we sneak into another aisle, wandering next to a middle-aged man with a cart full of hamburger meat and potato chips. Once we're sure he's not looking, we drop three boxes of condoms into his cart and scuttle away.

We continue this way, leaving little latex surprises in people's carts and baskets, pausing occasionally to sample their reaction before moving on to the next victim. By the time our arms are empty our bellies are stinging from holding in the giggles, and we finally collapse against a shelf of dog food, braying loud, obnoxious laughs.

"Oh, holy shit," Jo finally says, wiping a tear from her eye and grinning at me. "That was good."

I nod. "It was pretty awesome," I agree. Then I grow serious. "But our mission is not yet over."

"What's next, Butter Bagel?"

"Mission: Marco Polo."

We stroll casually out of the pet food aisle, staying quiet until we reach the clothing section. Then, with a look from Jo, I cup my hands to my mouth and holler, "Marco!"

Almost immediately, someone hollers, "Polo!"

Grinning, I call "Marco" again and a few more people respond. And so the game continues until someone in a navy blue shirt starts to follow us.

Jo nudges me. "Dude. Check the guy scoping us," she hisses.

I nod. "I noticed. C'mon. It's time for Mission: Cart Race anyway."

My blood pumps heatedly through my veins. I'm almost bouncing as we head back to the cart corral, pulling out a cart for each of us.

"Where should we hold this drag race?" Jo asks me.

"Probably one of the back aisles. In between the pet food and the tires."

As we make our way down there, my eyes keep flickering to Jo's face. There is color in her cheeks and a glimmer in her eyes. Since she'd gotten here, she had started to resemble a zombie herself—dead eyes, pale as a ghost, thin-lipped glares. Even her blonde hair seemed to sag. But now, she is how I remember her before everything got complicated.

We line up side by side, and several shoppers glance at us curiously as we exchange taunting glances.

"Ready?" I ask.

Jo leans over her cart aggressively. "Ready, bitch," she retorts.

"Three...two...one. Go!"

We take off, sprinting to gain speed and then hopping up on the bottom bar to ride the momentum. Our laughter echoes down aisles as we skate across the scuffed tile, rushing through customers who part like the Red Sea before us. I imagine I'm a bird, bulleting through the air at breakneck speed, gliding on freedom. The world below me is so small, the people below only little dots. I cannot see their pain. I cannot see their suffering. From far away, everything is beautiful.

Jo and I crash against the wall at nearly the same time. It's a photo finish and we turn to each other, mouths open to argue, but a security guard jogs into the aisle, scowling at both of us.

"Hey! You two need to leave," he says, pointing toward the exit.

"Why?" I ask innocently.

"You're causing a disturbance. You could hurt someone."

"But, sir. These carts are out of control. Technically *we* could've gotten hurt. Don't you think you should give us the benefit of the doubt?" I reply. Jo tries unsuccessfully to stifle her giggles.

But the security guard is having none of it. "*Out*," he barks.

The guard tails us until we're safely out the door. Jo turns to me, laughing, and leans her head on my shoulder.

"Oh, man!" she exclaims. "Just like old times!"

"Yeah," I say, nodding in satisfaction. "Calls for a little celebration, wouldn't you say?"

Jo's brow furrows. "What do you mean?"

Smirking, I reach into my jacket and pull out the box I'd managed to hide there. "Just a little souvenir."

Her mouth pops open with a little gasp. "Danni, you clever bitch!" she cries delightedly. "What is it?"

"It's like a chocolate orange, but strawberry flavored."

Grinning, she grabs my arm. "C'mon, let's go celebrate."

She drives us to the park near our old middle school, and we sit out on one of the old wooden benches. Nobody else is there. The ground is still soggy from melted snow and the equipment still slippery. We sit there in comfortable silence, pulling the chocolate ball from its red tin wrapping and cracking it open. The sweet smell of strawberries floats lazily on the air around us.

"It's supposed to snow tonight," Jo finally comments, licking melted chocolate from her fingertips.

I turn to her mischievously. "Wanna go sledding?"

She shoves me. "No! You remember what happened last time," she replies.

"Yeah, you got snow burn on your ass."

"Not my fault."

I snort but let it go.

It takes a second for me to notice. I am peering out across the open field behind the playground, at the tree line in the distance, when my vision starts to blur. The trees become fuzzy, indistinct shapes and the sky pales. I don't realize that I'm crushing the slice of chocolate in my grip until Jo shakes me.

"Danni, what's wrong?" she asks anxiously.

The cloudiness passes, vanishing slowly, but a sudden rush of painful blood makes my head ache and my stomach feel sick.

"I... I don't... know," I mumble brokenly. The world spins and I clutch at Jo's shoulders for support.

Her voice comes from far away. "What should I do?" she frets. It echoes in my head for a minute before I'm able to respond.

"Hos-pital..." I croak and then the swirling world swirls out of sight.

When I wake up, the glaring lights are obvious. I'm in the hospital for the second time today.

I sit up but hands gently push me back down. "Keep still, Danni," a familiar voice murmurs. Jo looks down at me, her eyes bloodshot and her cheeks pale. All the good humor from earlier has vanished.

"What happened?" I ask.

Her lips tighten until they turn white. "Weitz says you're progressing faster than he predicted," she murmurs unwillingly.

My stomach tightens. A million questions whirl in my head but there's only one that matters.

"How long?"

Jo looks away. I need her to answer me. My fingers dig deep into her arm, forcing her to look at me.

"How long?" I repeat.

She shakes her head and tears spill down her face. "They... they said... less than a month."

A pit opens up beneath me. It feels like I've just been flung off a cliff and my stomach has been left up above my helplessly plummeting body.

Less than a month. It was a shock when they told me I had two. Now they're telling me I don't even have that.

Less than thirty days.

"They told me..." Jo tries to continue, but the sobs drown her words.

I hang from her arm like a drowning man. "What? They told you what?" I demand.

"They told me you could... go... any day now."

My vision is starting to fail again. The blood drains from my face, leaving me light-headed. After a few painful heartbeats spent like this, I scramble desperately to ground myself.

*Let's look at this logically,* I think to myself. The calmness seeping into my veins is like molasses—it can't move fast enough.

*You knew you were going to die anyway. This just means it'll be a little bit sooner. That's all. No big deal.*

But there's still enough room in my head to imagine everything I'll be missing. Everything I never got to do and all the things I'll never get to say. I look at Jo and this feeling grows infinitely stronger.

The determination from before explodes within me, so powerful it makes my legs feel weak. And yet at the same time I feel stronger, so strong. I turn to Jo.

"Is it snowing yet?" I demand.

She blinks at me. "What?"

"Is it snowing?" I repeat impatiently.

"Y-yes..."

I nod. "Help me out of here."

Her eyes flare wide with panic. "Danni, you can't—"

And for the second time that day, I cut her off. "Jo, you know what I said earlier? About causing chaos before I die? Well that deadline just got shortened. Now are you gonna help me or am I gonna have to do everything by myself?"

I glare at her for a long time. Her tears continue to fall and I wonder if they'll ever stop. Finally she sighs, hanging her head in defeat.

"They'll come when they hear you flatline."

"Doesn't matter. We'll be out the window in a heartbeat."

Jo pulls out the I.V.s and disconnects me from the heart monitor. The flatline is a long, piercing drone in my ears that I can't tune out.

"C'mon!" I hiss, heading for the window. Jo yanks it open and wintry air whistles through the room.

Scrambling over the ledge, I leap into the snow beneath and wait until Jo hops down next to me. We take off running immediately, skirting the main paths and ducking under windows like regular fugitives.

Once we reach the parking lot, however, we slow, breathing deeply against the sharp, biting air. The snow drifts down in lazy circles around us, but in the southern sky I can see where the clouds end. Beyond that hangs a patch of liquid navy, dotted with distant stars. Something opens in my chest at the sight and I smile.

"Danni, aren't you cold?" Jo asks, rubbing her arms with her hands.

I blink, jarred by her question. Looking down, I realize that my feet are bare and the only covering I have on is the thin, pale hospital gown.

Jo's mouth falls open. I stumble over answers but I can't seem to get the words out.

"I... I..."

The truth is I can't feel anything. I can feel that the ground is solid beneath me but I don't feel the snow crunch under my feet. I don't feel cold at all.

*Less than a month.* The words reverberate through my skull like a demonic mantra. I shake my head.

"C'mon," I declare, marching faster through the snow.

"Danni, are you sure you don't want to—"

"No, Jo. I'm not going back. If these are my last days I'm not gonna spend them in some hospital bed," I reply firmly. She doesn't say anything else.

Jo cranks the heat in her car, but I feel nothing. This makes my heart pound faster in my chest but I try to keep calm.

"Where are we going?" Jo asks as we pull out of the parking lot. The answer leaves my lips before my brain knows what I'm saying.

"Borders."

She peers at me as though I've lost my mind. "*Borders*, Danni? You do know it's closed, right?"

I stare straight ahead. "I know."

She shakes her head but says nothing else.

When we finally arrive at the brick building, Jo parks and looks at me. Her eyes are serious. "Danni, you'll tell me if you start to feel weird, right?" she asks.

I wonder if she's asking whether or not I'll warn her before I try to eat her.

I nod. "Of course," I reply.

She doesn't look convinced but she pulls the key from the ignition and steps out of the car without another word. I follow suit, noticing how huge the parking lot feels with no one else in it.

A snowflake lands on my nose. I only know this because I see it drift down. On a whim, I open my mouth and try to catch a snowflake on my tongue. Instead I just spin in careful circles, mouth hanging open like an idiot, because I can't feel anything.

I feel eyes on me, and when I look up the expression on Jo's face makes my stomach clench. Her eyes are narrowed, her expression scrunched into one of wariness. Like she's afraid of me.

I feel *that* all too clearly.

"Jo," I mumble. Tears prick at my eyes and feeling slowly simmers back into my veins. I don't care, though. All I care about is that look on Jo's face.

"Jo, please don't be afraid of me," I beg.

Pain flickers across her pale blue eyes. "I'm not afraid of you," she says. "I'm afraid *for* you. Don't you see how much it's *killing* me that I can't help you?"

She crosses the space between us and wraps her arms around me tightly. The warmth of her sizzles away the last of the numbness and I clutch desperately at her, breathing in the scent of her wild, tumbling hair.

We stand there in the snowy parking lot for an eternity of heartbeats. I don't want her ever to let go, but with my sense of feeling returning my feet start to burn from the cold.

Jo pulls away, glancing down at my fidgeting feet. "What's wrong?" she asks.

I smile at her sheepishly, teeth chattering. "I've got my feeling back," I reply.

She gapes at me for a few seconds, stunned, and then closes her mouth. "Here, let's get you inside," she says, gently guiding me back to the car.

"No," I protest, pointing to the brick skeleton. "We came here for a reason."

Jo follows me silently to one of the boarded-up windows, shaking her head as though she can't figure out why she's friends with someone so insane. I smile at the thought and reach out. Gripping the board tightly, I start to yank.

She gasps. "Danni, what are you doing?" she exclaims.

"Breaking and entering," I reply. "Now are you gonna help me or not?"

Jo dances from one foot to the other, biting her lip uncertainly. But finally, with a groan, she grabs hold of the board and yanks at it with me.

After a few strong tugs the board breaks with a creak, revealing the dark cavern behind. I step inside cautiously, feeling around with my foot to make sure I won't be walking into anything. Jo climbs in after me, grabbing for my hand.

"Should've brought a light," I whisper, shuffling carefully through the dark.

"Should've told me you were going to commit a felony," Jo mutters.

Then, as we clear a corner, a rectangle of pale light catches my eye. One of the boards across the room has fallen from its window, letting in the subtle glow from outside. I head for that, dragging Jo around the empty shelves that were left behind.

We lay down in the rectangle of light, stretching out beside each other. The whole place still smells of coffee and books and I breathe deeply, savoring the scent.

Jo raises her eyebrow at me. "So, why exactly did you break into an empty bookstore?" she inquires dryly.

I grin. "Don't you remember when we first met?"

A slow smile appears on her face. "Yes," she replies. "We were both trying to sneak peeks at the risqué books."

Laughter bubbles up in my throat. "Yeah, and I conned you into buying me a latte," I add.

Jo chuckles. "Clever little bitch."

She stares at me for a long moment. Her smile fades slowly, and the look in her eyes is indecipherable. Finally she reaches across the gap between us and holds both my hands in hers.

"I love you, you know."

Her words spread through me with unbelievable warmth, shivering in my bones, and a soft sigh escapes my lips.

"I love you, too."

Jo smiles, but not like before. The sadness tugs it down at the corners of her lips.

"Are you afraid?" Her voice is thinner than ever, so quiet that it melts effortlessly into the darkness around us.

Looking into her eyes, I know the answer without even thinking.

"Not anymore."

The silence stretches between us. Our eyes never blink. Jo licks her lips. Her fingers rustle against mine. Then, slowly, she leans toward me.

I close the distance and press my lips against hers. Her mouth is soft, softer than I ever imagined, and the feel of it turns my limbs to liquid. I forget everything in that moment. The deteriorating economy, our deteriorating society. Even my deteriorating cells. Nothing matters except her lips and the fact that I can feel them.

When eventually we pull away, we stare at each other like deer in the headlights. Jo's eyes are glassy, sparkling. Her mouth is parted in a little "o" of surprise.

"I don't think either of us were expecting that," I finally say.

We burst into laughter, breaking the silence with the light sound of it. My body feels extraordinary, lighter than a bird's feather. Once again I feel like I'm flying.

Jo smiles at me and reaches out to stroke my cheek. I tremble with the feel of her skin on mine. My eyes flutter shut.

"I'm sorry I don't look prettier for you," I hear myself sigh through liquid lips.

"You're beautiful," Jo responds.

I open my eyes and her gaze meets mine. I feel the lightness dissolve around us.

"I'm sorry, Danni. About the fight. I never should have started it," Jo starts but I cut her off.

"Don't talk about it. It's in the past now," I say.

Another beat of silence.

"They'll shoot me." From the wax and wane of my senses, it won't be long.

Jo shakes her head vehemently. "I won't let them."

"You have to. I'll kill people."

She continues to shake her head. I purse my lips, thinking, and when the idea comes to me it unfolds slowly, tentatively.

"Then... *you* do it."

Her eyes widen. Her hands grow rigid around mine.

"*What?*"

"*Please*," I beg. "I don't want some stranger to do it. Please."

She shakes her head again, slower this time. "Danni, I can't—"

"You *can*," I insist. "Please. It's all I'll have left. This one choice."

How I go, how I die. I've always felt it's out of my control. Now, suddenly, it doesn't have to be.

Jo is silent for a long time. I tremble, waiting for her answer. Her eyes water and tears overflow.

"Alright," she agrees. "Alright, alright, I'll do it."

I smile at her, feeling tears of my own wobble and break loose from my eyes. "Thank you," I breathe in a watery voice.

Jo nods, the smile broken on her face. "Anything for you, Butter Bagel," she replies.

The fever chokes me. Not just my throat, but my arms and my wrists and my legs and my ankles. It burns in my stomach and rages in my brain.

A month has passed. I lasted longer than the doctors predicted. I can no longer speak, not even Jo's name. I feel the moans rip through my throat but I don't hear them. I can't see or hear or feel Jo, but I know she's there with me. Wiping the sweat from my body with cool towels, tucking the blankets tighter around me after I'm done thrashing. She's stopped trying to give me food or water.

Suddenly the heat in my body flares to an all-time high. My weak muscles clench and my thoughts start to slip around the edges.

So this is the end. When I arise from this sickness, I will know nothing but the hunger for human flesh.

Jo will be there, waiting.

Eyes open. Scan the room.

Face of young woman looking down. Eyes like twin oceans. Hair like sunlight. Familiar.

Sniff. Scent of her is heat. Hunger. Food.

Snarl rips through throat. Lips curl back to reveal teeth. Scramble from bed.

Woman backs away. Gun in hand. She trembles.

Mouth waters. Scent of her is overpowering. Intoxicating. Stomach howls.

"Danni."

Sound breaks through woman's mouth like call from a bird.

Stop. Cock my head. Blink.

Woman stares at me.

"Danni. I love you."

Want to move forward. Stomach shouts a protest. Feet are rooted to floor.

Tears run down woman's face.

"Danni, I love you and you are more than just a case. You are more than this. You are more than anything."

Heart clenches. Fingers claw at my chest. Confused by this pain. Not quite physical. Not quite pain. Something in between. Unknown.

Look again into woman's eyes. For a moment, see birds. Feathers.

## 232  Megan Dorei

Flight.

Heart rushes. Eyes well with warm liquid.

But stomach howls louder. Fingers clench. Teeth gnash. Throat beckons hungry snarl.

Woman raises gun. Takes aim.

Our eyes meet. Birds. Soft lips. Wind through my hair.

Then, nothing.

# Contributors

**Jennifer Clark** lives in Kalamazoo, Michigan. her first book of poems, *Necessary Clearings*, will be published by Shabda Press in 2014. *Main Street Rag*, *Structo* (U.K.), *Paper Crow*, *Pear Noir*, and *failbetter* are a few of the places that have made a home for her writings. She has work forthcoming in *Thema Literary Journal*, *Storm Cellar Quarterly*, and *You are here: The Journal of Creative Geography* at the University of Arizona.

**Gerri Leen** lives in Northern Virginia and originally hails from Seattle. She has a collection of short stories, *Life Without Crows*, out from Hadley Rille Books, and over fifty stories and poems published in such places as: *She Nailed a Stake Through His Head*, *Sword and Sorceress XXIII*, *Dia de los Muertos*, *Return to Luna*, *Sniplits*, *Triangulation: Dark Glass*, *Sails & Sorcery*, and *Paper Crow*. She also is editing an anthology of speculative fiction and poetry from Hadley Rille Books that will benefit homeless animals. Visit http://www.gerrileen.com to see what else she's been up to.

**Mark Onspaugh** is a California native who was raised on a steady diet of horror, science fiction and DC Comics. He has published over forty short stories and his tale "The Broken Hand Mirror of Venus" was nominated for a Pushcart Prize in 2011. You can visit him at www.markonspaugh.com.

**Carolyn E. Bentley** lives in what is essentially a former penal colony with 2 children, a mother-in-law, a potted plant, and a dog who routinely channels an entire Chinese fire drill. **Daniel M. Pipe** is an artist and writer who watches entirely too many monster movies with his wife and three kids, often followed by unsupervised periods with paper and pencil. The two of them have been collaborating in one form or another since they met, years ago in that former penal colony, and have watched more than a few bad movies together themselves.

**James S. Dorr**'s all-poetry *Vamps (A Retrospective)* is a 2011 release by Sam's Dot Publishing, joining his mostly fiction collections *Strange*

*Mistresses: Tales of Wonder and Romance* and *Darker Loves: Tales of Mystery and Regret* from Dark Regions Press. More information on Dorr can be found at http://jamesdorrwriter.wordpress.com.

**Gregory L. Norris** grew up on a healthy diet of TV science fiction and creature double-features. He once worked as a screenwriter on two episodes of Paramount's modern classic, *Star Trek: Voyager* and is a former feature writer and columnist at *Sci Fi*, the official magazine of the Sci Fi Channel. His work appears regularly in national magazines and fiction anthologies. Norris is the author of numerous novels for Ravenous Romance (www.ravenousromance.com), *The Q Guide to Buffy the Vampire Slayer* (Alyson Books), the recent *The Fierce and Unforgiving Muse—Twenty-Six Tales From the Terrifying Mind of Gregory L. Norris* (EJP), and the forthcoming *13 Creature Features* (Reaser Brand Communications). Visit him on Facebook and online at www.gregorylnorris.blogspot.com.

**John McCarthy** is a writer and cross country coach living in Springfield, Illinois. His work has appeared in *The Conium Review, Popshot Magazine, Ghost Ocean Magazine* (Wave Series), and *The Buddhist Poetry Review,* among others. While mostly an academic writer, he loves zombies and altruism. He can be contacted at jjmccarthy90@gmail.com.

**Brian Rosenberger** lives in a cellar in Marietta, GA and writes by the light of captured fireflies. He is the author of *As the Worm Turns* and three poetry collections.

**Joshua Clark Orkin** is a tiny, cloven-hoofed demon who dwells in your childhood bedroom. His turn-ons include licking tears from your face, harvesting your nightmares, and hiding when your parents come to check on you. He promises to stop scaring you if you print this ragged account he has brought from the nether, but, then, he is not to be trusted. You know that. You've always known that.

**Jamie Brindle** has been writing short speculative fiction for around fifteen years now; occasionally it is even published. He works as a junior doctor in the UK, and finds writing horror a great way to ground himself after long shifts in the bizarre fantasy world of the NHS. You can find his e-books at https://www.smashwords.com/profile/view/JamieBrindle. Some of them are free.

**Marge Simon**'s works appear in publications such as *Strange Horizons, Niteblade, DailySF Magazine, Pedestal, Dreams & Nightmares*. She edits a column for the HWA Newsletter, "Blood & Spades: Poets of the Dark Side," and serves as Chair of the Board of Trustees. She won the Strange Horizons Readers Choice Award, 2010. In addition to her poetry, she has published two prose collections: *Christina's World*, Sam's Dot Publications, 2008 and *Like Birds in the Rain*, Sam's Dot, 2007. She won the Bram Stoker Award™ for Superior Work in Poetry with Charlee Jacob, *Vectors: A Week in the Death of a Planet*, Dark Regions Press, 2008. New poetry collections 2011: *Unearthly Delights* (self illustrated in color), Sam's Dot Publications, *The Mad Hattery* (art by Sandy DeLuca), Elektrik Milk Bath Press. Member HWA, SFWA, SFPA. www.margesimon.com.

**Sandy DeLuca** has been a painter since 1985, and she has been a writer since the late 80's, penning nonfiction articles and photography for magazines and newsletters throughout the 90's. One of her claims to fame is writing under the pen name Autumn Raindancer. Two of her poetic chants were published under that pen in the popular New Age book *To Ride a Silver Broomstick* (Silver Ravenwolf). She created GODDESS OF THE BAY publishing in the late 90's, producing several anthologies and a string of small press magazines. From 2001 to 2003 she edited and owned DECEMBER GIRL PRESS, producing novels and short story collections. She was a finalist for the BRAM STOKER for poetry award in 2001. At present she is a full time writer and painter. She's written and published five novels, two poetry collections, several novellas, and has collaborated with Marge Simon on several poetry/art collections; notably *The Mad Hattery* & *Vampires, Zombies & Wanton Souls*. She is assistant curator at NEW HOPE GALLERY, in Cranston, RI and continues to exhibit her art in local venues.

**Terrie Leigh Relf** is a lifetime member of the Science Fiction Poetry Association and an active member of the Horror Writer's Association where she serves as the Bram Stoker Poetry Committee Chair. In addition to teaching academic writing at both Woodbury University of Architecture and National University, she is on-staff at Sam's Dot Publishing where she wears a variety of skins. Recent publications include *The Waters of Nyr*, *The Ancient One*, coauthored with Henry Lewis Sanders, and *The Poet's Workshop—and Beyond*. Upcoming publications include *The Wolves of Tintangel* co-authored with Edward Cox, *Jupiter's Eye—Redux*, and *Origami Stars*.

**Vonnie Winslow Crist** is author of *The Enchanted Skean—Book I of the Chronicles of Lifthrasir* (YA fantasy), *Owl Light* (speculative stories), *The Greener Forest* (fantasy tales), *For the Good of the Settlement*, and *Blame it on the Trees* (sShorts). For more nfo: http://vonniewinslowcrist.com and http://wonniewinslowcrist.wordpress.com.

Zombies have always been a source of great amusement for **Kathleen Crow** and her son, Michael. But as she grows older she realizes that her bad knees would make surviving a zombie apocalypse problematic. Kathleen has been published in such magazines as *The First Line* and *The Drabbler*.

**Brian E. Langston** is a poet, fictionalist, and musician masquerading as a software developer. He currently lives in Seattle, Washington. His poetry has appeared in *Attic*, *Octopus Dreams*, *Gargoyle*, *Perpetuum Mobile*, and *Poems Against War*, among others, and he published the chapbook *The Ruined City* in 2008.

**Gene Stewart** says: I am a cancer survivor. A rare retinal cancer, the only known risk factor for which being a Scottish ancestry, took about half the vision in my right eye but innovative methods by the leading researcher of radioactive plaque treatment for that kind of cancer by Dr. Jerry Shields saved my eye and my life. I am grateful, and hope the charity anthology raises a lot of money and awareness in our many fights against the many forms of cancer. A shout out to Jay Lake, a writer friend who is publicly fighting his cancer, and to Marcy Jameson, my physiologist and friend, who is doing so more privately. And to my father, who got leukemia from exposure to the Three Mile Island venting of radioactivity; he was a truck driver delivering a load of furniture for Ward Trucking to a store in Mechanicsburg that morning, and had to pull off the side of the road to puke, having tasted metal in his mouth and having caught a wave of strange weakness come over him. We now know what it was. Further salutes to various other relatives, friends, colleagues, and acquaintances who have fought the C Monster, or are fighting it. We can beat this Medusa. Eyes on the shield, everyone. Information about me and my writing, including samples and surprises, can be found at my website: www.genestewart.com/wordpress.

**Colin James** has poems forthcoming in *Lalluresmute* and *The Prospective Journal*.

**M. Alan Ford** lives and works in the Valley, dude. He's 52 and spends his time working, reading, writing, and engaging in various other studious pursuits. His interests are category fiction of all kinds and academic subjects of all kinds. He has a B.A. in Psychology and stays in school as much as he can. It's a hobby. Some people build model planes, he attends school.

**Clifford Royal Johns**' stories have been published in science fiction, mystery, and mainstream magazines and anthologies. His first novel, a science fiction, noir mystery crime novel, *Walking Shadow*, has just been released by Grand Mal Press.

Only recently joining the ranks of parents everywhere, **Nancy Chenier** has been striving to function within her own sleep-deprived state of zombie-hood. She lives and writes in Vancouver with her husband and the new squid. Some of her fiction has appeared in *Abyss & Apex*, *OnSpec*, and *Bards & Sages*.

**Heather Henry** lives in southeastern Wisconsin with her partner, their two-year-old son, and three cats. She teaches composition, creative writing, and literature courses at Mount Mary College in Milwaukee. She is currently working on a series of zombie stories and on an urban ghost story.

**Patrick MacAdoo** is the author of *Weeyatches*, and the forthcoming *Bigass Squirrels*. Patrick is pretty sure that the whole headshot thing is zombie propaganda, and urges you all, when the Zombie Apocalypse comes, to go for the guts.

**Gerardo Mena** is a decorated Iraqi Freedom veteran. He spent six years in Spec Ops with the Reconnaissance Marines. He has won or placed in several national contests, was nominated for a Puschart, was selected for Best New Poets 2011, and has pieces published or forthcoming from *Ninth Letter*, *Cream City Review*, *Raleigh Review*, *Diagram*, and *Prairie Schooner's Online Digital Project*, among others. For more info go to www.gerardomena.com.

**Richard Farren Barber** was born in Nottingham in July 1970. After studying in London he returned to the East Midlands. He lives with his wife and son and works as a Development Services Manager for a local university. He has written over 200 short stories and has had short stories published in *Alt-Dead*, *Blood Oranges*, *Derby Scribes Anthology*, *Derby Telegraph*, *ePocalypse—Tales from the End*, *Gentle Reader*, *Murky Depths*, *Midnight Echo*, *Midnight Street*, *Morpheus Tales*, *MT Urban Horror Special*, *Night Terrors II*, *Scribble*, *The House of Horror*, *Trembles*, and broadcast on BBC Radio Derby. During 2010/11 Richard was sponsored by Writing East Midlands to undertake a mentoring scheme in which he was supported in the development of his novel *Bloodie Bones*. His website can be found here www.richardfarrenbarber.co.uk.

**Ryan Dennison** is a Senior at Taylor University, where he will be graduating next spring with a degree in Professional Writing. In addition to being a full-time student, he is also a freelance writer and a writer/copy editor for Taylor University's Marketing Department.

**Alyn Day** is an active member of the New England Horror Writers living outside of Boston, MA. She is an avid horror enthusiast with an inclination towards zombies. Publications include *So Long and Thanks for All the Brains*, *Daily Frights 2012*, *Women of the Living Dead*, *Zombie Tales*, *Here Be Clowns*, *Horror On The Installment Plan*, the upcoming *Thadd Presley Presents*, *Quick Bites of Flesh*, *Daily Frights 2013* and *Mirror, Mirror*.

**Sarina Dorie** is a speculative fiction writer, artist and belly dance teacher who currently lives in Eugene, Oregon. She has sold 20 stories in the last two years to a variety of magazines including *Daily Science Fiction, Flagship, Allasso, Roar, New Myths, Untied Shoelaces of the Mind, Penumbra*, and Crossed *Genres*. Sarina's fantasy novel, *Silent Moon*, won two second place and three third place awards from Romance Writers of America. This novel is now available on Amazon and Smashwords For more information, please visit: www.sarinadorie.com.

**dan smith** is the author of *Crooked River*, a poetry chapbook. He is a member of the Deep Cleveland Tribe of Poets and the Cleveland Speculators. He likes to do free jazz punk rock poetry with the Deep Cleveland Trio. dan smith and the Deep Cleveland Trio's CD *Matinee Motel* is available at CD Baby. NOTE:It is rated not suitable for under 17yrs due to language and some content.

**Robert Neilson** is married with children and lives in Dublin. In partnership with his wife he runs a successful retail business in Dublin city. His short fiction has appeared extensively in professional and small press markets and he has had two plays performed on RTE and one on Anna Livia FM. He also presented a radio show on Anna Livia for a year. He has had two short story collections published, *Without Honour* (1997, Aeon Press) and *That's Entertainment* (2007, Elastic Press) as well as several comics and a graphic novel. His non-fiction book on the properties of crystals is a best-seller in the UK and Ireland. He is a founding editor of *Albedo One* magazine. Visit his site at www.bobneilson.org for more information.

**William Van Wurm** says: I am a pediatrician on the Mississippi Gulf Coast. I have been writing as a hobby for over 20 years, but almost never about zombies. I have recently been published in *Harmony* (University of Arizona) and online at *Deadmule.com*. I have been married for 19 years. I have two children and a dog.

**Stewart S. Warren** is a writer, evocateur, and catalyst for positive community. He is the owner of Mercury HeartLink, a small press in northern New Mexico, and is the founder of the Albuquerque Poet

Laureate Program. Visit him at www.heartlink.com.

**Nick Kimbro** is an MFA candidate at the University of Colorado at Boulder. His work has appeared or is forthcoming in *The Yoke*, *Spring Gun Journal*, *Space Squid*, *Weird Tales*, *Heavy Feather Review*, *Fogged Clarity*, and his novella, *Surface Interval*, was published in August by Jersey Devil Press.

**Brian Behr Valentine** (52) formerly an engineer in the electronic Imaging and package printing field, is now a winemaker and winemaking consultant. He writes for the pleasure of it and is currently working on several novels.

**Jay Wilburn** is a teacher in Conway, South Carolina where he lives with his wife and two sons. His first novel, *Loose Ends: A Zombie Novel*, is available now. He is a columnist for *Dark Ecclipse* and *Perpetual Motion Machine Publishing*. Follow his many dark thoughts at JayWilburn.com and @AmongTheZombies on Twitter.

**Colin Gilbert** is a writer and freelance editor living in Texas. His poetry has been awarded the Hughes, Diop, Knight Literary Award and can be found in recent editions of *Matrix*, *Mobius*, *Inscape* and *Pedestal Magazine*. He is the author of one collection of poetry, *The Mattress Parlor* (Scribble Fire Press, 2011), and is most likely reading in a random library with a cold Dr. Pepper at his side.

**Megan Dorei** is a recent high school graduate. She does not attend college yet, choosing instead to take a year off from school to focus on her writing. She has another story that will be published in Less Than Three Press's *Kiss Me at Midnight* collection and a plethora of stories that have yet to be written. She lives in McLouth, KS.

**Frenchi** is a photographer, but she's not easy to find. Try looking for her wherever monsters buy their shoes.

# The Contributors would like to honor the following...

N.E. Chenier would like to honor Judy Adler.

Jennifer Clark would like to honor Mary Clark

Vonnie Winslow Crist would like to honor her mom, Alice Crosby Winslow, her godmother, Marguerite Brooks, her uncle, William D. Crosby, her mother-in-law, A. Katherine Crist, and her husband, Ernie Crist. She would like to remember three of her grandparents, Fred D. Crosby, Beth Dare Crosby and Oliver Parry Winslow, and her father-in-law, George K. Crist.

Kathleen Crow would like to honor Wilbur "Wayne" Meek and Mildred "Eloise" Link.

Sandy DeLuca would like to honor her mother and father, Anthony and Esther Giusti.

Megan Dorei would like to honor Mark Lawson.

Sarina Dorie would like to honor Florence Dunn and Caroline Gzyjewski.

James S. Dorr would like to honor Ruth, also known as Vashti.

Colin Gilbert would like to honor Darlene Hogue.

Heather Henry would like to honor Deborah Barnes, Johnita Starns, and Barbara Simpson.

Brian E. Langston would like to honor Jennifer Makowski and Irma Prieto.

Gerri Leen would like to honor her mom and her two cousins.

Patrick MacAdoo would like to honor Audrey Suzanne Morris.

Gerardo Mena would like to honor his father, Jay Mathiesen.

Robert Neilson would like to honor his sister, Joyce Brownell, and his uncle, Ron Heggie.

Gregory L. Norris would like to honor Diane Elaine Gauthier, "my beautiful mother."

Mark Onspaugh would like to honor Chan Adams Bell, Helen Onspaugh, and Judith Perkins.

Joshua Clark Orkin would like to honor Alice Clark.

Terrie Leigh Relf would like to honor her mom, her aunt, her cousin, her nephew, and several friends passed from various forms of cancer.

Marge Simon would like to honor her mother (poet/teacher—deceased), Sandy DeLuca (writer/poet/artist), Ree Young (writer/poet/artist/teacher), Stephen M. Wilson (poet/editor), John Irvine (poet/editor), and Sandra Lindow (poet/teacher).

Gene Stewart would like to honor Jay Lake, Marcy Jameson, and his father as well as various other relatives, friends, colleagues, and acquaintances who have fought the C Monster, or are fighting it.

Jay Wilburn would like to honor Charolette Durst and Chris O'Dell (deceased) and John Shriver (still fighting).

William Van Wurm would like to honor "my grandmother… a fighter and a survivor."

Elektrik Milk Bath Press would like to honor Noodles and Chrome, as well as all those we have worked with who have bravely shared their own cancer stories with us. We won't name names, but know we are always thinking of you.